'Lily Bard is one of the best-drawn and most compelling characters in contemporary mystery fiction – complex, smart, streetwise, tough'
Booklist

SHAKESPEARE'S LANDLORD

'Riveting . . . Lily's triumphant progress from scarred loner to fierce fighter is very rewarding. Bravo, Ms Harris!'
Pen & Dagger

SHAKESPEARE'S CHAMPION

'Full of surprises, this second fast-paced and gripping Lily Bard adventure showcases the amateur sleuth's strength, determination and martial arts prowess . . . An engaging puzzler that's propelled along by Lily's easy, no-frill narration'
Publishers Weekly

SHAKESPEARE'S CHRISTMAS

'Harris has reached a new high. Don't miss it'
Booklist

SHAKESPEARE'S TROLLOP

'An ending that will take everyone by surprise . . . An extremely compelling read'
Romantic Times

SHAKESPEARE'S COUNSELOR

'Lily Bard . . . is the equal of Kay Scarpetta, Kinsey Millhone, and V.I. Warshawski'
Library Journal

Also by Charlaine Harris from Gollancz:

SOOKIE STACKHOUSE

Dead Until Dark
Living Dead in Dallas
Club Dead
Dead to the World
Dead as a Doornail
Definitely Dead
All Together Dead
From Dead to Worse

Dead and Gone
A Touch of Dead
Dead in the Family
Dead Reckoning
True Blood Omnibus
True Blood Omnibus II
True Blood Omnibus III
The Sookie Stackhouse Companion

HARPER CONNELLY

Grave Sight
Grave Surprise
An Ice Cold Grave
Grave Secret

LILY BARD

Shakespeare's Landlord
Shakespeare's Champion
Shakespeare's Christmas
Shakespeare's Trollop
Shakespeare's Counselor

The Lily Bard Mysteries Omnibus

The First Aurora Teagarden Omnibus
The Second Aurora Teagarden Omnibus

Wolfsbane and Mistletoe (Co-edited with Toni L. P. Kelner)
Many Bloody Returns (Co-edited with Toni L. P. Kelner)
Crimes by Moonlight
Death's Excellent Vacation (Co-edited with Tony L. P. Kelner)

SHAKESPEARE'S CHAMPION

A LILY BARD MYSTERY

CHARLAINE HARRIS

The right of Charlaine Harris to be identified as the author
of this work has been asserted by her in accordance with
the Copyright, Designs and Patents Act 1988.

First published in Great Britain in 2011 by
Gollancz
An imprint of the Orion Publishing Group
Orion House, 5 Upper St Martin's Lane,
London WC2H 9EA
An Hachette UK Company

This edition published in Great Britain in 2011 by Gollancz

1 3 5 7 9 10 8 6 4 2

A CIP catalogue record for this book
is available from the British Library

ISBN 978 0 575 10527 0

Typeset at The Spartan Press Ltd,
Lymington, Hants

Printed in Great Britain by Clays Ltd,
St Ives plc

The Orion Publishing Group's policy is to use papers
that are natural, renewable and recyclable products and
made from wood grown in sustainable forests. The logging
and manufacturing processes are expected to conform to
the environmental regulations of the country of origin.

www.charlaineharris.com
www.orionbooks.co.uk

This book is dedicated to my newsletter group,
the Femmes Fatale
(http://members.aol.com/femmesweb),
who make me laugh
more than I have since I left college.

Prologue

The man lying on the padded bench had been working out for two hours and he was drenched with sweat. His short blond hair was matted at his forehead, and his sharply etched body glistened. His hacked-off sweatshirt and shorts, originally blue but now faded, showed dark rings under the arms. It was October, but he had a glowing tan. He was exactly five feet ten inches and he weighed one hundred seventy-four pounds, both facts being of crucial importance to his regimen.

The other members of the Body Time gym had gone home an hour ago when the gym officially closed, leaving this dedicated and privileged being, Del Packard, to his solitary calling. After the others had gone, Del's spotter arrived, wearing ancient black sweatpants and an old gray sweatshirt with the sleeves scooted up.

Del had let the spotter in with his own key, on loan from gym owner Marshall Sedaka. Del had talked Marshall into issuing him a key so Del could work out every free minute he could beg from his job. The competition was only a month away.

'I think I'm going to make it this time,' Del said. He was resting between sets. The weighted bar lay in its rack above his head. 'I was second last year, but I hadn't put in the hours I have this year. And I've practiced my posing every day. I've gotten rid of every hair on my body, and if you think Lindy has stood that without complaining, you can think again.'

His spotter laughed. 'Want another dime?'

'Yeah,' said Del. 'I want to do ten reps, okay? Only help me if I'm hurting.'

The spotter added a ten-pound disc to each end of the bar. It already held a total of two hundred and seventy pounds.

Del tightened the wrist straps of his lifting gloves, flexed his fingers. But he delayed for a moment longer, saying, 'You been to that Marvel's Gym? It's the biggest place I ever seen.'

'No.' Del's companion also adjusted his black leather gloves. Lifting gloves stop at the first knuckle and have padded palms. Del's spotter had forgotten to bring his, he'd explained, and had pulled a pair of regular gloves out of the lost-and-found box. Now, the spotter casually pulled down the sleeves of his sweatshirt.

'I don't mind telling you, last year I was pretty nervous. There was guys in that middleweight division pumped up like tanks, been in training since they could walk. And their outfits! And here was me, ole country boy. But I did all right.' Del smiled proudly. 'This year I'll do better. No one from Shakespeare but me is entered this year. Marshall tried to get Lily Bard – you know her? blond? don't talk much? – to enter in the women's novice division, or the open, but she said she wasn't about to spend eight months pumping up to stand in front of a bunch of people she didn't know, all greased up like a pig. Well, that's one point of view. I look on it as an honor to represent Shakespeare at the Marvel Gym competition. Lily's got great chest and arm development, but she's pretty weird.'

Del lay back on the bench and looked up at the face of his spotter, who was bent over him, gloved hands resting casually on the bar. His spotter lifted his eyebrows in query.

'You remember, I was kind of worried after we had that conversation last week?' Del asked.

'Yep,' the spotter said with a dash of impatience in his voice.

'Well, Mr Winthrop says everything is okay. Just not to talk about it to anyone.'

'That's a relief. You gonna lift this, or just look at it?'

Del nodded his blond head sharply. 'Okay, I'm ready. After this set, I'm quitting for the night. I'm dead beat.'

The spotter smiled down at him. With a grunt, the spotter lifted the bar, now weighted with two hundred ninety pounds. He moved the bar into position above Del's open hands and began lowering it.

Just as Del's fingers were about to close around the bar, the spotter pulled it toward himself a little, till it was right over Del's neck. With great control, the spotter positioned it exactly over Del's Adam's apple.

Just as Del opened his mouth to ask what the hell was going on, the spotter dropped the bar.

Del's hands scrabbled convulsively at the weight crushing his neck for a few seconds, hard enough to make his fingers bleed, but his companion squatted down and held either side of the bar, the gloves and sweatshirt protecting him from Del's fingers.

Very shortly, Del lay still.

The spotter carefully examined his gloves. In the overhead light, they looked fine. He threw them back in the lost-and-found bin. Del had left his gym key on the counter, and the spotter used it to unlock the front door. Halfway out the door, he paused. His knees were shaking. He hadn't any idea of what to do with the key, and no one had thought to tell him. If he put it back in Del's pocket, he'd have to leave the door unlocked. Would that look suspicious? But if he took it with him to relock the door from the outside, wouldn't that tell the police that Del had had someone with him? This whole assignment was more terrible and perplexing than he'd imagined. But he could handle it, he reassured himself. The boss had said so. He was loyal and he was strong.

Hesitantly, the spotter rethreaded his steps between the pieces of equipment. With his face compressed into an expression of disgust, he tucked the key in Del's shorts pocket and rubbed the enclosing material around the key. He backed away from the still figure on the bench, then walked out hastily, almost running. He automatically flicked the light switch down on his way out. Glancing from side to side, the spotter finally broke and ran to the dark corner of the parking lot where his pickup was waiting, fairly well concealed by a few wax myrtles.

On his way home, he suddenly wondered if he could now get a date with Lindy Ròland.

Chapter One

I grumbled to myself as I slid out of my Skylark, Marshall's keys clinking in my hand. Since I made my living doing favors for people, it hardly seemed fair to be doing a favor for free this early in the morning.

But this fall a flu epidemic was scything its way through Shakespeare. It had crept into the Body Time gym enclosed in the body of my friend Raphael Roundtree. Raphael had coughed and sneezed in karate class after working out in the weights room, neatly distributing the virus among almost all the Body Time clientele, with the exception of the aerobics class.

And me. Viruses don't seem to be able to abide in my body.

When I'd dropped by Marshall Sedaka's rented house even earlier that morning, Marshall had been at that stage of the flu where his greatest desire was to be left alone to his misery. So fit and healthy that he took sickness as an insult, Marshall was a terrible patient; and he was vain enough to hate my seeing him throw up. So he'd thrust the keys to Body Time into my hand, slammed the door, and yelled from behind it, 'Go open! Tanya's coming after her first class if I can't get anyone else!'

I'd been left with my mouth hanging open and a handful of keys.

It was my day to work at the Drinkwaters' house. I had

to be there between 8:00 and 8:15, when the Drinkwaters left for work. It was now 7:00. Tanya, a student at the nearby Montrose branch of the University of Arkansas, might get out of her first class at 9:00. That would put her arrival time at somewhere around 9:40.

But Marshall was sometimes my lover and also sometimes my workout partner; and he was always my sensei, my karate instructor.

I'd blown air out of my mouth to make the curls at my forehead fluff, and driven out to Body Time. I'd decided I'd just unlock the gym and leave. The same people came every morning, and they could be trusted to work out alone. Most days, I was one of them.

Marshall's almost incoherent appeal for help had come when I had been dressing to leave for the gym, as a matter of fact, and I was already in my sweats. I could go to work at the Drinkwaters' as I was, though I hated beginning my earning day without having showered and put on makeup.

I don't like breaks in my routine. My job depends on the clock. Two and a half hours at the Drinkwaters' house, a ten- or fifteen-minute gap, another house; that's my day and my income.

Body Time is in a somewhat isolated position on the bypass that swerves around Shakespeare, allowing speedier access from the south to the university at Montrose. Marshall's gym has a large graveled parking lot and big plate-glass windows at the front, which are covered by Venetian blinds lowered at six on winter afternoons, four in the summer. There was already a car in the parking lot, a battered Camaro. I expected to see some impatient enthusiast waiting in its front seat, but the car was empty. I walked over, cast a cursory look over the car's clean interior. It told me nothing. I shrugged, and crunched across the gravel in the chilly, pale early morning light, fumbling through Marshall's keys. As I sorted through them to find the one marked *FD* for front door, another vehicle pulled up beside mine. Bobo Winthrop, eighteen and chock-full of hormones, emerged from his fully equipped Jeep.

I clean for Bobo's mother Beanie. I have always liked Bobo despite the fact that he is beautiful, smart enough to scrape by, and has everything he has ever expressed a wish for. Somehow Bobo had charmed his way into Marshall's good graces, probably by working out on as demanding a schedule as Marshall himself. When Bobo had decided to start college in nearby Montrose, Marshall had finally agreed to hire the boy to work a few hours a week at Body Time.

Since Bobo isn't hurting for money, I can only figure his job motivation is getting to ogle many women of all ages in form-fitting outfits and getting to see all his friends, who naturally all have memberships in Body Time.

Bobo was running his fingers through his floppy fair hair by way of grooming. He said groggily, 'Whatcha doin', Lily?'

'Trying to find the right key,' I said, with a certain edge to my voice.

'This is it.' A long finger attached to a huge hand nudged one key out of the cluster. Bobo gave a jaw-cracking yawn.

'Thanks.' I put the key in the lock, but as I did I felt the door move a little.

'It's unlocked,' I said, hearing my voice come out sharp. I was now really uneasy. The back of my neck began to prickle.

'Del's already here. That's his car,' Bobo said calmly. 'But he's supposed to lock the front door when he's here by himself. Marshall's gonna be mad.'

The gloom in the big room was pronounced. Shades still closed, all lights off.

'He must be in the tanning bed,' Bobo said, and kept going across the room as I flipped on the central panel of lights with one hand. I reached for the ringing phone with the other.

'Body Time,' I said sharply, my eyes ranging from side to side. Something smelled wrong.

'I was able to get Bobo after you left,' Marshall said weakly. 'He can stay, Lily. I don't want you to miss work. Oops. Gotta . . .' He slammed down the phone.

I'd almost told Marshall something was wrong. But that would have been pointless, worrying him until I found out what was making the skin of my neck crawl.

I'd only switched on the central panel of lights, so the sides of the big room were still dark. Bobo had begun turning on lights and opening doors in the rear of the building. So I was by myself when I noticed the man lying on the bench in the far left corner.

I didn't for one minute think he was asleep, not with the barbell across his neck. His arms were dangling awkwardly, his legs spraddled. There was a stain. There were lots of stains.

I was scrabbling at the switch plate behind me, trying not to take my eyes off that still figure, when Bobo came from the hall that led to Marshall's office, the tanning beds, and the karate and aerobics room.

'Hey, Lily, you like Natural Morning Zap Tea? I didn't see Del, but I found this bag in Marshall's office . . .'

My fingers located the light switch for the left side of the room, and as Bobo looked to see what I was staring at, I flicked it up.

'Aw, shit,' said Bobo. We both stared at what was lying on the bench. We could see it all too clearly now.

Bobo scuttled sideways until he was behind me, looking over the top of my head. He put his hands on my shoulders, more to keep me firmly between him and It than to comfort me. 'Aw. . . shit,' he said again, gulping ominously. Just at that moment, Bobo came down hard on the 'boy' side of eighteen.

I had already encountered two nauseated males and it wasn't even seven o'clock.

'I've got to go check,' I said, 'If you're going to throw up, go outside.'

'Check what? He's dead as a doornail,' said Bobo, his big hands anchoring me firmly on his side of the service counter.

'Who is it, you reckon? Del?' Possibly I was stalling.

'Yeah, from the clothes. That's what Mr Packard was wearing last night.'

'You left him here by himself?' I asked as I began walking over to the body on the bench.

'He was doing chest when I left. He had his own key, to lock up. Marshall had told me that was okay. And Mr Packard said he had a spotter coming,' Bobo said defensively. 'I had a date, and it was closing time.' Bobo's voice got stronger and angrier as he saw he was going to have to justify leaving Del alone in the gym. At least he didn't sound nauseated anymore.

I finally got to the corner. It had been a long journey. Before I got there, I took a deep breath, held it, and bent over to check Del's wrist. I had never touched Del alive, and I didn't want to do it now that he was dead, but if there was any chance there was a spark of life left . . .

His skin felt strange, rubbery, or it might have been my imagination. The smell was not my imagination, nor was the lack of pulse. To make absolutely sure, I held my big watch in front of Del's nostrils. There were trails of dried blood running from them. I bit my lip hard, forced myself to hold still a moment. When I pulled my arm back to my side, the watch face was clear. I found myself backing up for the first two feet, as if it would be irreverent or dangerous to turn my back on poor Del Packard. I hadn't been scared of him when I'd been able to talk to him. It was absurd to be nervous around him now. But I had to tell myself that several times.

I picked up the phone again and punched in some numbers. I looked up at Bobo while I waited for the ring. He was staring at the body in the corner with a horrified fascination. Perhaps this was the first dead person he'd ever seen. I reached over and patted the back of his big hand, lying on the counter. He turned it over and clutched my fingers.

'Umhum,' rumbled a deep voice at the other end of the line.

'Claude,' I said.

'Lily' he said, warm and relaxed.

'I'm at Body Time.' I gave him a minute to switch gears.

'Okay,' Claude said cautiously. I could hear a creaking of bedsprings as the big policeman sat up in bed.

Maybe if I took this step by step it wouldn't be so bad? I glanced over at the still figure on the bench.

No way to ease up to this. I'd just plunge right in.

'Del Packard is here, and he got squashed,' I said.

I did make it to my first job on time, but I was still in my workout sweats, and still barefaced. So I was uncomfortable, and disinclined to do more than nod by way of greeting Helen and Mel Drinkwater. They weren't chatty people either, and Helen didn't like to see me work; she just liked seeing the results. She'd been giving me hard looks, since September when I'd been sucked into a notorious brawl in the Burger Tycoon parking lot – but she hadn't said anything, and she hadn't fired me.

I'd decided that she'd passed the point of most concern. Her pleasure in a clean house had outweighed her misgivings about my character.

Today the Drinkwaters went out their kitchen door at a pretty sharp clip, each sliding into a car to begin his/her own workday, and I was able to start my usual routine.

Helen Drinkwater doesn't want to pay me to do a total cleaning job on the whole house, which is a turn-of-the-century two-storey. She pays me for two and a half hours, long enough to change the sheets, do the bathrooms and kitchen, dust, gather up the trash, and vacuum. I do a quick pickup first because it makes everything easier. The Drinkwaters are not messy, but their grandchildren live just down the street, and they are. I patrolled the house for scattered toys and put them all in the basket Helen keeps by the fireplace. Then I pulled on rubber gloves and trotted up to the main bathroom, to start scrubbing and dusting my way through the house. No pets, and the Drinkwaters washed and hung up their clothes and did their own dishes. By the time I rewound the cord on the vacuum cleaner, the house was looking very good. I pocketed my check on the way out. Helen always leaves it on the kitchen counter with the salt shaker on top of it, as if some internal wind would blow it away otherwise. This time she'd anchored down a note, too. *'We need to pick a Wednesday for you to do the downstairs windows,'* said Helen's spiky handwriting.

Wednesday is the morning I reserve for unusual jobs, like helping with someone's spring cleaning, or doing windows, or occasionally mowing a yard. I looked at the calendar by the phone, picked two Wednesdays that would do, and wrote both dates on the bottom of the note with a question mark.

I deposited the check in the bank on my way home for lunch. Claude was walking up my driveway when I arrived.

Chief of Police Claude Friedrich lives next door to me, in the Shakespeare Garden Apartments. My small house is a little downhill from the apartments, and separated from the tenants' parking lot by a high fence. As I unlocked my front door, I felt Claude's big hand rubbing my shoulder. He likes to touch me, but I have put off any more intimate relationship with the chief; so his touches have to have a locker-room context.

'How was it after I left?' I asked, walking through the living room to the kitchen. Claude was right behind me, and when I turned to look up at him he wrapped his arms around me. I felt the tickle of his mustache against my face as his lips drifted across my cheek to fasten on a more promising target. Claude was my good friend but he wanted to be my lover, too.

'Claude, let me go.'

'Lily, when are you going to let me spend the night?' he asked quietly, no begging or whining in his voice because Claude is not a begging or whining man.

I turned sharply so my face was to the refrigerator. I

could feel the muscles in my neck and shoulders tighten. I made myself hold still. Claude's hands dropped to his sides. I got out some leftover dishes and opened the microwave, moving slowly, trying not to show my agitation with jerky gestures.

When the microwave was humming, I turned to face Claude, looking up at his face. Claude is in his midforties, ten years or more older than I, and he has graying brown hair and a permanent tan. After years of working in dark corners of Little Rock and dark places in people's hearts, Claude has a few wrinkles, deep and decisive wrinkles, and a massive calm that must be his way of keeping sane.

'Do you want me?' he asked me now.

I hated being backed into a corner. And there wasn't a simple answer to the question.

He touched my hair with gentle fingers.

'Claude.' I enjoyed saying his name, unlovely as it was. I wanted to lay my hands on each side of his face and return his kiss. I wanted him to walk out and never come back. I wanted him not to want me. I had liked having a friend.

'You know I'm just used to living my own life,' was what I said.

'Is it Sedaka?'

Oh, *hell*. I hated this. Marshall and I had been dating and bedding for months. Under Claude's scrutiny, I grew even more tense. Without my conscious direction, my hand crept under the neck of my sweatshirt, rubbing the scars.

'Don't, Lily.' Claude's voice was gentle, but very firm. 'I know what happened to you, and it doesn't make me feel anything except admiration that you lived through it. If you care about Sedaka I'll never say another word. From my point of view, you and I've been happy in the times we've spent together, and I'd like an extension.'

'And exclusive rights?' I met his eyes steadily. Claude would never share a woman.

'And exclusive rights,' he admitted calmly. 'Till we see how it goes.'

'I'll think,' I forced myself to say. 'Now, let's eat. I have to go back to work.'

Claude eyed me for a long moment, then nodded. He got the tea from the refrigerator and poured us each a glass, put sugar in his, and set the table. I put a bowl of fruit between our places, got out the whole-wheat bread and a cutting board for the reheated meat loaf. As we ate, we were quiet, and I liked that. As Claude was slicing an apple for himself and I was peeling a banana, he broke that comfortable silence.

'We sent Del Packard's body to Little Rock,' he told me.

'What do you think?' I was relieved at the change of topic.

'It's hard to say what might have happened,' Claude rumbled. He had the most comforting voice, like distant thunder.

'Well, he dropped the bar on himself – didn't he?' I hadn't been particularly friendly with Del, but it wasn't bearable to think of him struggling to get the bar back up to the rack, failing, all by himself.

'Why was he there alone, Lily? Sedaka was so sick I couldn't figure out what he was telling me.'

'Del was training for the championships at Marvel Gym in Little Rock.'

'The poster, right?'

I nodded. Taped to one of the many mirrors lining the

walls at Body Time, there was a poster giving the specifics of the event, with a picture of last year's winners. 'Del competed last year, in the men's middleweight division, novice class. He came in second.'

'How big a deal is this?'

'To a novice bodybuilder, pretty big. Del had never been in a competition before he got second place at Marvel Gym. If he'd won this year – and Marshall thought he had a chance – Del could've gone on to another competition, and another, until he entered one of the nationals.'

Claude shook his big head in amazement at the prospect. 'Is "posing" like the swimsuit part of Miss America?'

'Yes, but he'd be wearing a lot less. A monokini, like a glorified jockstrap. And he'd have removed his body hair . . .'

Claude looked a little disgusted. 'I wondered about that. I noticed.'

'He'd been working on his tan. And he'd grease up for the competition.'

Claude raised his eyebrows interrogatively.

'I don't know what they use.' I was getting tired of this conversation. But Claude was circling his hand in a gesture that meant 'Amplify'.

'You have a series of poses you go through, to emphasize the muscle groups.' I rose to give Claude a demonstration. I turned my body a little sideways to him, fisted my hand, arched my arms in pumped-up curves. I gave him the blank eyes and small smile that said, 'Look how superior my body is. Don't you wish you were me?'

Claude made a face. 'What's the point?'

'Just like a beauty contest, Claude.' I resumed my seat at the table. 'Except the focus is on muscular development.'

'I saw the poster of last year's winners. That woman was like nothing I've ever seen,' Claude said, wrinkling his nose.

'Marshall wanted me to enter.'

'You'd do that?' he asked, horrified. 'That gal looked like a small pumped-up man with boobs slapped on.'

I shrugged. 'I don't want to spend the time training. It takes months to get ready for a competition. Plus, I'd have to camouflage all the scars, which I think would be impossible. But that was what Del wanted to do, train and compete. Develop himself to his full potential, was the way he put it.' I'd watched Del stare at one of his muscles for a good five minutes, wrapped up in his own reflection to the exclusion of the other people in the gym.

'I think I could have lifted what he had on the bar,' Claude said, a question in his voice. He rinsed off the plates and put them in the dishwasher. 'It came to two hundred ninety pounds.'

I thought Claude was flattering himself, though I didn't say so out loud. Claude seemed to have a fair body, but he did not exercise and hadn't as long as I'd known him. 'Bodybuilding isn't exactly like competitive weight lifting,' I said. 'Training for a competition, some people use somewhat lower weights and lots of reps, rather than really heavy weights and a few reps. That was probably Del's highest weight.'

'Reps?' Claude said cautiously.

'Repetitions.'

'Would he be lifting so much by himself? Del wasn't that big a man.'

'That's what I don't understand,' I admitted, retying my New Balances. 'Del was so careful of himself. He wouldn't risk pulling a muscle or getting any injury this close to the competition. Surely he had a spotter. He told Bobo he was expecting someone.'

'What's a spotter?' demanded Claude.

'A spotter is a buddy,' I said, having to define a term so familiar to me I'd forgotten a time I hadn't known it. 'A workout partner. If you don't have someone to spot for you, you would have to ask whoever was working at the gym . . .' I could tell from Claude's frown that I wasn't being precise. 'It's someone who stands there while you're doing the hardest part of your workout. That person is there to act as your safety net: hand you the weights, or the bar, take them when you've finished your set, cheer you on, grab your wrists if they start to weaken.'

'So you won't drop the weights on yourself.'

'Exactly. And to help you do those last few you need to finish your set.'

'Example.'

'Like if I was doing forty-fives, and that was my top capability or close to it, I'd lie down on the bench holding the dumbbells, and the spotter would stand or kneel at my head, and when I was pushing the weights up, if my arms started to shake, the spotter would grab my wrists and help me keep them steady.'

'Forty-fives?'

'Two forty-five-pound dumbbells. Some people lift using the bar and adding weights, some people use different-weighted dumbbells. I happen to prefer dumbbells. Del liked the bar. He thought he got better chest development.'

Claude looked at me thoughtfully. 'You're telling me you can lift ninety pounds with your hands?'

'No,' I said, surprised.

Claude looked relieved.

'I can lift a hundred ten or a hundred twenty.'

'You.'

'Sure.'

'Isn't that a lot? For a woman?'

'In Shakespeare it is,' I said. 'At one of the bigger city gyms, probably not, you'd have a bigger pool of weight trainers.'

'So how much would a man serious about training be able to do?'

'A man about Del's build, under six feet, about one hundred seventy? After intense training, I guess he'd be able to lift maybe three hundred twenty pounds, more or less. So you can see strength wasn't Del's sole goal, though he was very strong. He wanted exceptional muscular development, for the look of it. I just like to be strong.'

'Hmmm.' Claude thought about the difference. 'So you knew Del?'

'Sure. I saw him almost every morning at Body Time. We weren't particularly friendly.' I was wiping off the table, since I had to go to work in ten minutes.

'Why not?'

I thought about it while I rinsed out the dishrag. I wrung it and folded it neatly and draped it over the divider between my sinks. I stepped across the hall to the bathroom, washed my hands and face, and slapped on a little makeup for my self-respect. Claude leaned against the kitchen doorframe to watch. He was waiting for an answer.

'Just . . . nothing in common. He was from here, had lots of family, dated a hometown girl. He didn't like blacks, he didn't like the Notre Dame football team, he didn't like big words.' That was as close as I could come to explaining.

'You think enjoying living in a small town is wrong?'

I hadn't meant this to be an analysis of my

'No, not at all. Del was a good guy in some
looked at my face, put on some lipstick, shrugged at my
reflection. Makeup didn't change the face underneath it, but
somehow I always felt better when I'd used it. I washed
my hands and turned to look at Claude. 'He was harmless.'
Right away I wondered what I meant. But I was too taken
aback by the expression on Claude's face to think it through
right then.

Claude said, 'I'll tell you something strange, Lily. There
weren't any fingerprints on that bar where there should
have been. There should have been lots, where a man would
normally grip the bar. Del's should have been on top. But
there weren't any. There were just smears. And you know
what, Lily? I don't think you'd put on your makeup in front
of me if you had any serious interest in me.'

He stopped at the front door to deliver his parting shot.
'And, I'd like to know, if Del Packard was in the gym by
himself, how he turned out the lights after he died.'

It was a day that had started out worst and moved up to
merely rotten.

I was cleaning in a spirit of anger, and the results were
not harmonious. I dropped papers, got paper cuts when I
picked them up, slammed the toilet lid down so hard that
a box of Kleenex plummeted from a flimsy rattan shelf in
the travel agent's bathroom, vacuumed up a few pushpins
at the base of the bulletin board, and developed a full-blown
hatred for the poster of a couple on the deck of a cruise
ship because they looked so simple. They looked like they
could say, 'Gee, we really get along well. Let's go to bed
together!' and it would actually work.

ast job of the day. I locked the
gh of relief.

detoured to Marshall's dumpy rented
me a key when we began 'seeing' each
used. So he had to stagger to the door to
agger right back to the ancient plaid couch
d from a friend when he'd separated from his
wife. is Body Time key ring on the equally dilapidated
coffee table, and went to sit on the floor near him. Marshall
was sprawled full length and obviously felt lousy. But he
wasn't groaning, and his fever was down, I thought as I
touched his forehead.

'Can you eat yet?' I asked, not knowing what else I could
do for him.

'Maybe some toast,' he said in a pitiful voice that sounded
very odd issuing from his extremely muscular throat. Marshall is one-quarter Chinese. He has skin that's just between
pink and ivory, and his eyes and hair are dark. His eyes have
a bit of a slant, just a hint. Other than that, he's Caucasian,
but since he's a martial arts teacher he enjoys emphasizing
the Oriental fraction of his heritage.

'Please,' he added, even more pitifully, and I laughed.

'Mean,' he said.

I got up and found his whole-wheat bread and waved a
butter knife over it, toasted it dry, and brought it to him
with some water.

He sat up and ate every crumb.

'You're going to live.' I took the plate from him and
carried it to the sink. I would coddle him to the extent of
loading his dishwasher, I decided.

Afterward I returned to sit by the couch. He'd slid down
to his original position. He took my hand.

'I guess I will live,' he admitted, 'though for a few hours I didn't want to. And finding out about Del, God! Who would have thought Del would be dumb enough to drop a weight on his neck?'

'I don't think he did.' I told Marshall about the lack of fingerprints on the bar, about the lights that should have been on.

'You think the spotter dropped the bar on Del by accident and then panicked?'

I shrugged.

'Hey, you don't think someone killed Del on purpose? Who would do that?'

'I'm not a doctor, so I don't know if this is possible . . . but if you felt a crushing weight on your neck and you knew you would die if it stayed there, and you were a grown healthy man, wouldn't you fight to heave it off?'

'If I wasn't killed instantly, I'd try as hard as I could,' Marshall said grimly. 'If you're saying someone held the bar down, who would be cruel enough to do that?'

I shrugged again. In my opinion, any number of people had that capacity for cruelty, even if they hadn't discovered it in themselves yet, and I told Marshall that. I just couldn't understand why anyone would indulge that cruelty by killing harmless, thick-headed Del Packard.

'You're cold sometimes, you know?' Marshall had said that more than once lately. I looked at him sharply. This cold woman had gotten her butt out at six in the morning to open his business.

He went on. 'Maybe Del was seeing someone else's wife – that got Len Elgin killed – or maybe Lindy got mad at his training so much.'

'Del was too self-involved to go to the trouble of

sneaking around,' I said. 'And if you think Lindy Roland can lift fifty pounds, let alone close to three hundred, you better find another job.'

'That's right, the one who dropped the weight had to be able to lift it first,' Marshall said thoughtfully. 'Who do we know that can lift that much?'

'Almost anyone we know that works out regularly could lift that. Especially the men. Maybe I could, if I had to.' But I said the last part doubtfully. It would take a mighty surge of adrenaline.

'Yeah, but you wouldn't kill Del.'

I could kill a man – I had killed a man – but I didn't think I could do it unprovoked. I began mentally reviewing the list of regular weight lifters at Body Time.

'I can think of at least twelve and I've only been trying for a minute or two,' I said.

'Me, too,' Marshall said, and sighed. 'Aside from feeling sorry for Del and his folks and Lindy, this isn't going to be good for business.'

'Who's cleaning up the mess?' I asked.

'Would you . . .'

'No.'

'Maybe the cleaning service from Montrose?'

'Phone them,' I said.

He looked at me accusingly. 'You're being cold about this.'

I felt a surge of irritation. There was that accusation again.

Marshall wanted me to yoke myself with him and his interests as though we were a permanent couple.

I wasn't willing.

I shifted my shoulders under my T-shirt, rolling the

muscles in an effort to relax. I reminded myself once again that Marshall was ill. I slid my hand from his.

'Marshall,' I said, keeping my voice quiet and even, 'if you wanted warm-fuzzy you came to the wrong woman.'

He laid his head back against his pillow and laughed. I made myself think of his having thrown up all night and some of the morning. I made myself remember an especially good time we'd had in that bed I could glimpse through his open bedroom door. There were several to choose from.

He'd been my sensei, my karate teacher, for four years now. We'd become friends. Then Marshall had left his terror of a wife, Thea. After that we'd shared a bed from time to time, and some good hours of companionship. Marshall was capable of moments of great compassion and sensitivity.

But as our relationship progressed, I'd discovered Marshall expected me to change, and swiftly; expected all my edges to be rounded off by that lust, companionship, compassion, and sensitivity . . . all my peculiarities to be solved by the fact that I had a steady guy.

Since having a steady guy, having Marshall, was nice in many ways, I found myself wishing it worked that way. But it didn't.

As I said a brief good-bye and left for home, I felt gloomy and restless. I'd rebuffed Claude, who was a proud man; now I was considering parting from Marshall. I couldn't read my own signals, but I could tell it was time for a change.

During the week after Del Packard's death, my life went according to routine once more.

I didn't catch the flu.

A woman who specialized in cleaning up crime scenes drove to the gym from Little Rock. She expunged the mess Del's passing had left. The gym reopened and Marshall resumed running it and teaching karate. He rearranged the workout equipment and mixed the bench Del had died on in with the others, so no one could say it was haunted, or try to reenact the crime.

I went to karate class, and I worked out. But I went to my home alone instead of to Marshall's after karate, contrary to my recent practice. Though Marshall looked a little angry and a little hurt as I wished him a good evening, he also looked a little relieved. He didn't ask me to explain myself, which was a pleasant surprise.

I didn't see Claude Friedrich. It took me a couple of days to register that I wasn't running into him and he wasn't dropping in for lunch, and after that it took me a couple more to decide that this was by design, his design. I missed Claude's company, but I didn't miss the pressure of his desire.

And I lost clients. Tom and Jenny O'Hagen, who'd lived next door to me in the Shakespeare Garden Apartments, moved to Illinois to manage a larger Bippy's. I wasn't too concerned at the opening in my schedule. I had a standby list. I began calling. The first two potential clients fobbed me off with a lame excuse, and I could feel the worry start somewhere in my gut. Ever since the Burger Tycoon parking lot fight, I'd been concerned that my clientele would drop off.

The third family had found another maid, so I crossed them off. The woman who answered at the fourth number said she and her husband had decided to get divorced, and she would be doing her own cleaning. Another X. The fifth name on the list was Mookie Preston. After puzzling over the entry, I remembered that when Ms Preston had called me a couple of months before, she'd said she'd just moved to Shakespeare. When I called her, she sounded delighted to hear that I could work for her on Friday mornings. She was renting a house, and she wanted longer than the hour and a half I'd given the O'Hagen apartment.

'Why don't I work from ten to twelve on Fridays?' I was trying to imagine why a young single woman would need me for that long.

'We'll see,' said the rich fruity voice. 'I'm a little messy.'

I'd never laid eyes on Mookie Preston, but she sounded . . . eccentric. As long as her checks were good, I didn't care if she raised catfish in the bathtub and wore a Barney the Dinosaur costume.

When I went to Body Time Thursday morning, I found Bobo sitting behind the counter to the left of the entrance. He looked as dispirited as an eighteen-year-old can look. I pitched my gym bag into an empty plastic cubicle, one of fifteen stacked against the east wall, after extracting my weight-lifting gloves. They were looking very shabby, and I knew I'd have to have a new pair soon; another item for my already tight budget. I began to pull them on, eyeing Bobo as I circled my wrists with the straps and Velcroed them tightly. Bobo stared back. He was even sitting depressed: shoulders sagging, hands idle on the counter, head sagging on his neck.

'What?' I asked.

'They've questioned me twice now, Lily,' he said.

'Why?'

'I guess the detective thinks I had something to do with Del getting killed.' He took a gulp of a repulsive-looking protein mixture that was the craze among the younger workout crowd. I wouldn't have touched it with a ten-foot pole.

'How come?'

'Del worked for my dad.'

Among his many financial pies, Bobo's father, Howell Winthrop, Jr., owned the local sports/exercise equipment/marine supplies store. Del had worked there, mostly in the exercise equipment and exercise clothing department, though he'd had to know enough about hunting and fishing to sell all the other products Winthrop Sporting Goods carried. Del himself had told me all about it at excruciating length when I'd been buying my punching bag.

'So do a lot of people in town,' I observed.

Bobo looked at me blankly.

'Work for your dad.'

Bobo grinned. It was like the sun coming out from behind a cloud. He was really a lovely boy.

'Yeah, but Mr Jinks seems to think that I decided Del knew something that would ruin Dad's business, so either I thought of killing him or Dad told me to.'

'Because you were the last one to see him here?' Dedford Jinks is a detective on the little Shakespeare police force.

Bobo nodded. 'Someone told the chief, who told Mr Jinks, that when people didn't bring their own spotters, they asked the staff to spot for them. Which, naturally, would be me.' He silently held out his plastic cup of goop. With a shudder, I shook my head.

I struggled with my guilt. It was I who had mentioned to Claude that sometimes a member of the staff was asked to fill in as spotter.

'I didn't know Mr Packard very well.' said the golden boy.

'But really, I don't think he could have found out anything illegal my dad was doing. This may not be respectful, especially now that Mr Packard's dead, but I never thought he was that smart, and if he knew something Dad was doing that was wrong, I think he'd just feel like he didn't really understand. Or he'd go talk to Dad about it.'

I thought Bobo was exactly right.

'You look nice, Lily,' Bobo said, changing the subject so abruptly that it took a minute for his words to sink in.

'Oh. Thanks.' I was wearing a teal-colored T-shirt and sweatpants, new and unstained but strictly Wal-Mart.

'Why don't you wear something like that?' Bobo pointed to the sportswear rack that Marshall kept stocked with expensive exercise clothing. The garment that had caught Bobo's eye was pale pink and blue swirled in a tie-dye pattern, cut low over the boobs and high in the legs, meant to be worn over coordinating tights.

I snorted. 'Right.'

'You'd look pretty. You've got the body for it,' he said self-consciously. 'I'd like to watch your back when you're doing lat pull-downs.'

'Thank you,' I said stiffly. 'But stuff like that just isn't my style.'

I went over to say hello to Raphael. He'd recovered from his flu, but he had something on his mind. His greeting was not the usual happy roar.

'What?'

'You askin' me what?' he said, rubbing the back of his head. Raphael kept his hair clipped so short that the passage of his mahogany hand made no change in the tight black curls. 'I tell you what, Lily.' His voice got louder than it should have been, and I knew immediately that I had spoken to him at the wrong moment.

'You're a good woman, Lily, but this place is not friendly to blacks.'

'Marshall—' I began. I was about to say Marshall was not a racist or some such thing, but I got interrupted.

'I know Marshall is not a bigot. But there are too many others here who are. I can't come to a place where I'm not welcome as a black man.'

I'd never heard Raphael speak so seriously and angrily in the four years I'd known him. He was glaring at two men who were working out together on the other side of the room. They paused, stared at him for a minute, then went back to their activity. One of them was Darcy Orchard, a massively built man with long, thinning beige hair and acne-scarred cheeks, a broad Slavic face and legs like trees. I didn't know the other man.

As I was trying to think what to say to Raphael, he just picked up his gym bag and walked out. I looked over at Darcy. He had his back turned, and his companion was lifting the bar. Everyone in the gym seemed to be looking somewhere else.

As I worked my way through my routine (today was legs and shoulders day) I tried not to brood about the little incident. I hated to think I might feel obliged to quit the gym, too. It meant so much to me, the daily workout. If I had to, could I buy my own gym equipment? No, not on my budget, not having already paid my annual fee here. I had to save so much each month, against the rainy day that would surely come. I already suspected Marshall discounted my Body Time membership.

Other users of the gym trickled in and began their

28

workout after waving a hand or calling hello to each other and to me. This was the only group of which I could call myself a member, except for my karate class. Until a few minutes ago, Raphael had been one of us. This fellowship of sweat had a wildly fluctuating membership as people made resolutions and broke them, lasting on an average three weeks into their exercise program. There was a hard-core group of members like me who came nearly every day, and we had gradually gotten to know each other. More or less.

Del Packard had been one of this group.

All the regulars except Del were here today: Janet Shook, who was also in my karate class, a short chunky woman with dark brown hair and eyes who'd had a crush on Marshall ever since I'd met her; Brian Gruber, silver-haired and attractive, the president of a mattress manufacturing plant; Jerri Sizemore, former wife of Dr John Sizemore, a local dentist; and Darcy Orchard, who worked at the sporting goods store, as Del had. Darcy usually worked out with Jim Box, another store employee, but today Jim was absent – probably home with the flu; he'd been sneezing yesterday. I wondered who Darcy's new partner was. Eventually Darcy's companion, whom I dimly recognized as someone I'd seen around the Shakespeare Garden Apartments, left. But Darcy lingered on.

Darcy was on the calf extension machine, which was my next station, so I watched as he did his second set. He had the pin pushed in at the two-hundred-pound mark, and as I waited he adjusted the shoulder pressure. Darcy, who was about six feet tall, had the rippling pectorals and ridged biceps of a workout fanatic. I thought there might be an ounce of subcutaneous fat on his body. He was wearing one of the ripped-up sweatshirts – arms chopped off, neck binding torn out – that were the mark of the committed, and his sweatpants were probably the same ones he'd worn in high school.

'Be through in a minute,' he panted, doing a set of twelve. He stepped down and walked around for a minute, relaxing the calf muscles that were taking such a beating. Darcy gathered himself, moved the pin down two more notches to add forty more pounds to his load, and stepped up on the narrow bar, his toes bearing his weight. Down went his heels, then up, for twelve more reps. 'Ow!' he said, getting off. 'Ow!' Staring at the floor with a scowl, Darcy relaxed the protesting muscles in his legs. 'Let me just burn out now,' he said, and moved the pin up to a more reasonable weight. He stepped back on the ledge and did twenty-four reps very rapidly, until the grimace of concentration on his face became a rictus of pain.

All together this took only minutes, and I was glad of the rest.

'How you doing, Lily?' Darcy asked, walking in place to work off the strain. He grabbed up a beige towel and patted his acne-pitted cheeks with it.

'Fine.' I wondered if he'd say anything about Raphael's exit. But Darcy had something else on his mind.

'Hear you found ole Del.' His small brown eyes scanned my face.

'Yeah.'

'Del was a good guy,' Darcy said slowly. It was a kind of elegy. 'Del was always smiling. That guy that was here with me a minute ago, that's the guy Howell hired to replace him. He's a big change.'

'Local fella?' I asked politely, as I adjusted the shoulder bars down for my five feet, five inches.

'Nope, from Little Rock, I think. He's one tough son of a bitch, 'scuse my language.'

I moved the pin up to eighty pounds. I stepped onto a narrow ledge, came up under the padded shoulder bars to take the weight, and dropped my heels down. I pushed up twenty times, very quick reps.

I stepped down to walk it off and shift the pin to a higher weight.

'You dating anybody now, Lily? I heard you and Marshall weren't such an item anymore.'

I looked up in surprise. Darcy was still there. Though Darcy had a wonderful body, it was the only thing about him that I found remotely interesting, and that wasn't enough basis for an evening together. Darcy's conversation bored me, and something about him made me wary. I never ignore feelings like that.

'I don't want to,' I said.

He smiled a little, like someone who was sure he'd misunderstood. 'Don't want to . . . ?' he asked.

'Date anyone.'

'Whoa, Lily! A fine woman like you doesn't want a man to take her out?'

'As of now, right.' I stepped up, took the hundred pounds on my shoulders, and did another set of twenty. The last five were something of a challenge.

'How come? You like women instead?' Darcy was sneering, as though he felt obliged to look contemptuous when lesbianism was mentioned.

'No. I'm going to finish here now.'

Darcy smiled again, even more uncertainly, though I'd been as civil as I was able. He couldn't seem to believe that any woman wouldn't want to date; specifically, date him.

But after a moment of waiting for me to take back my dismissal, he stalked over to the Roman chair, his narrow lips pressed together firmly in anger.

As I moved the pin to one hundred twenty pounds, once again I wondered whom Del might have asked to spot for him. Del would have trusted anyone in the room. Even Janet and I were just about strong enough to help him with some of the lower (but still formidable) weights that Del used for his bodybuilding. Janet was nearly as strong as I in the chest and arms, and had an edge on me in the legs since she taught two aerobics classes a day in addition to working at the Kids' Clubs, which provided community-sponsored after-school care for kids.

After I finished my calf workout, I drifted over to Janet, who was doing abdominal crunches. Sweat had darkened her short brown hair to a black fringe around her square little face.

'One hundred ten,' she gasped, as I stood over her. I nodded, and waited.

'One twenty-five,' she said after a moment, relaxing in a heap. Her eyes shut.

'Janet,' I said, after a respectful moment of silence.

'Umm?'

'Del ever ask you to spot for him?'

Janet's brown eyes flew open. They fixed on my face with some amusement. 'Him? He didn't think a woman could carry her own groceries, much less spot for him.'

'He'd seen female bodybuilders at those competitions. For that matter, he'd watched us work out many a morning.'

Janet made a rude noise. 'Yeah, but we're freaks to him,' she said, resentment in her voice. 'Well, we were,' she amended, more neutrally. 'He judged all women by that Lindy he went with, and Lindy couldn't cut a ham without an electric knife.'

I laughed.

Janet looked up at me with some surprise. 'That's good to hear, you laughing. You don't do that too much' she observed.

I shrugged.

'Now that you're over here,' she said, sitting up and patting her face with her towel, 'I've been wanting to ask you something.'

I sat on the closest bench and waited.

'Are you and Marshall a locked-in thing?'

I'd been expecting Janet to ask me to spot her, or to go over the fine points of the latest kata we'd learned in karate class.

Everyone wanted to know about my love life today.

I kind of liked Janet, so answering her would be harder than answering Darcy. Saying no meant Marshall was open game for any woman who wanted a shot at him; I was abdicating all claim to him. Saying yes committed me to Marshall for the foreseeable future.

'No,' I said, and went to do my last set.

On her way to the changing room, Janet stopped. 'Are you mad at me?' she asked.

I was a little surprised. 'No,' I said.

But I was really surprised when Janet laughed.

'Oh, Lily,' she said, shaking her head from side to side. 'You're so weird.' She said that as if being 'weird' was a cute little personality quirk of mine, like insisting my panties match my shoes or always wearing green on Mondays.

I left Body Time, vaguely dissatisfied with my workout

session. I'd had my first personal conversation with Darcy Orchard, and I hoped it would be my last. I had confirmed that Janet Shook lusted after Marshall Sedaka; not exactly stop-the-press news. I had confirmed that Del almost certainly wouldn't have asked a woman to spot for him. And I'd found out that Raphael felt he was getting a cold reception at a business he'd paid to patronize.

As I drove home, I tried to trace the reason for my dissatisfaction. Why did I think I should have gotten more out of the morning than a good workout? After all, it was as little my business what had happened in Body Time the night Del died as it was Janet's business whether or not Marshall and I were committed to each other.

I hadn't particularly liked Del. Why did I care whether he'd died accidentally or on purpose?

I'd told Claude that Del had been harmless. As I showered, for the first time I really considered Del Packard.

He hadn't made any of the jocular comments about my strength I occasionally got from other men. Del had been mildly pleased to see me when I was in front of him, hadn't missed me when I was gone, would have been glad to help me do anything I'd have asked him to help me with, was overwhelmingly proud of being Shakespeare's champion, would cheerfully have gone on doing his Del Packard thing the rest of his life . . . if his life had been allowed to run its natural course.

He loved his mama and daddy, sent his girlfriend Lindy flowers, performed his job adequately, and went his own way without bothering a soul. All he'd wanted with any passion was to be a champion again, this time a number-one champion.

If Del's spotter had killed Del through carelessness, he

should come forward. If he had murdered Del out of malice, that, too, should be paid for.

I toweled my hair dry and put on my makeup, still turning over the questions about Del's death to discover the source of my feeling I had a personal stake in the answers.

The police were working to discover how Del had met his death, and that should be enough to satisfy me. I certainly hadn't felt any urge to seek personal knowledge after the beating death of Darnell Glass early in the fall, or the shooting of Len Elgin weeks afterward, both of which cases remained unsolved.

An answer came to me as I was getting in the car to go to my first job. I cared about Del's death for two more reasons. Firstly, Bobo Winthrop was implicated, partly because of something I'd told Claude. Secondly, I was upset because Del had been killed *in the gym*, one of the few places I felt at home. So I cared about Del's death, and I cared about payment for it.

Chapter Two

As the plain days passed, I missed Claude more and more.

He'd taken care of me a few months before when I'd been hurt. He'd helped me take a sink bath, he'd helped me dress, he'd helped me get back in bed. It had seemed quite natural to put on my makeup in front of him, an act he'd construed as indicating a lack of interest in him as a man.

I'd figured he'd seen the worst. The makeup had not been for him, but for the rest of the world.

The only true thing I found hiding in my psyche was that I missed Claude, missed his dropping over to share my lunch, missed his occasional appearance at my doorstep with Chinese takeout or a video he'd rented.

And another true thing was that I didn't miss a dating relationship with Marshall. In fact, it felt good to slip back into comradeship and the teacher/student relationship we'd shared before. I found that disturbing.

I'd seen Del Packard's sweetheart, Lindy Roland, on the street today. Lindy was a strapping girl, with big brown hair and a ready smile. But when I'd seen her, Lindy's eyes had been red and her whole body seemed to sag. At Del's funeral, according to the grapevine at Body Time, Lindy had gone to pieces. Now, there was Del, under the ground at Sweet Rest Cemetery, and here was Lindy, alone and lonely.

After my solitary supper that night, after the dishes were washed and everything neat, I paced the house.

I took another shower and washed off all my makeup. I made sure I was shaved smooth and my eyebrows were plucked, and I put on all the usual lotions and a tiny dab of perfume.

I stood in my bedroom, naked and irresolute. I looked in my closet, knowing before I looked what I would see: blue jeans, T-shirts, sweats. A couple of dresses and a suit from my former life. Even thinking about a seduction seemed incredibly stupid as I saw how ill-equipped I was for one.

Suddenly I jettisoned the idea. It felt wrong. Claude deserved someone more – malleable, someone with a silk teddy and a Sunday dress.

I valued control over my life more than anything. With Marshall, and now with Claude, I was not willing to relinquish that control, to bind my life to either of theirs. Neither of them was necessary enough to me for me to take that frightening leap. This was a bitter acknowledgment.

Angry at myself, at Claude, I pulled on dark clothes and went out to walk. I wouldn't sleep much tonight. The light in Claude's window was on, a glance up at his apartment told me. If I'd found it in myself, I would be up there sharing that light with him, and he would be happy . . . at least for a little while.

I drifted through Shakespeare, merging with the night. In a while, I began to feel the chill and the wet. After shivering in my jacket for a few blocks, I was on my way home when I saw I had company.

On the other side of the street, walking as silently and darkly as I, went a man I didn't know, a man with long black hair. In the silence we turned our heads to look at each other. Neither of us smiled or spoke. I was not

37

frightened or angry. In seconds we were past each other, continuing on our ways in the chilly sodden night. I'd seen him before, I reflected; where? It came to me that he was the man who'd been working out with Darcy Orchard the day Jim Box had been out with the flu.

I went home to work out with my punching bag, which hangs from the ceiling in the middle of my empty extra bedroom. I kicked kogen geri, a snapping kick, until my instep burned. Then mae geri, the thrusting kick, until my legs ached. Then I just punched the bag, over and over, making it swing; no art, just power expended.

I slumped down to the floor and dried my face with the pink towel I kept hanging from a hook by the door.

Now, after I showered, I would probably sleep.

As I pulled up my covers and turned on my right side, I wondered where the man was, what he was doing, why he had been walking the night.

I felt too draggy to go to Body Time the next morning, even though I was due to do chest and biceps, my favorites. I forced myself to do fifty pushups and leg lifts as compensation. While I was on the floor, I had to notice that my baseboards needed dusting, and after I patted my face with the pink towel, I used it to do the job. I pitched the towel in the wash basket and went through my usual morning preparation.

My first job on Fridays was Deedra Dean's apartment in the building right next door, which coincidentally was upstairs by Chief of Police Claude Friedrich's. At the request of a local lawyer who represented the estate of Pardon Albee, I had been cleaning the public parts of the apartment building until Pardon's heir made some other arrangement.

So I noticed all the mud the tenants had tracked in after the recent rain, and decided I'd have to work in an extra vacuuming before its regular late-Saturday cleaning. Unclipping my work keys from my belt, I went up the stairs quickly.

But Deedra's dead bolt was on. She was still home. She'd be late for work again. I pocketed my key and knocked. There was a kind of scuffling noise on the other side of the door, then a sharp exchange between Deedra and someone else, an exchange I couldn't decipher.

I went on alert. Not because Deedra had company; that was no surprise. Deedra believes in the joy of indiscriminate giving. But scuffling, harsh words, these weren't things she was used to. As Deedra yanked open the door and stepped back, I saw that her guest was her stepfather, Jerrell Knopp. Jerrell had married 'up' when he wed the widowed, well-to-do Lacey Dean. Jerrell was attractive – lean, gray-haired, with dazzling blue eyes – and he treated his wife with courtesy and tenderness, if the little interaction I'd observed was the norm. But Jerrell had a mean side, and Deedra was bearing the brunt of it now. She had a bright red mark on her arm as if Jerrell had been holding her with a squeezing grip. He wasn't too pleased she'd let me in. Tough.

'The chief is right on the other side of this wall,' I lied. Claude was sure to be at work by now. 'He can be here in a split second.' I looked from the red mark to Jerrell. I'd cross him if I had to, but I didn't look forward to it.

'This here's a family talk, Lily Bard. You just butt out,' Jerrell said, very firmly. I thought it would make me feel pretty good to hit him.

'This is Deedra's apartment. I think she gets some say in who stays and who goes.' I was always hoping Deedra would show some backbone – or some sense – and I was always disappointed. This morning was no exception.

'You better start in my bedroom,' Deedra said in a small voice. There were tears on her face. 'I'll be all right, Lily.'

I gave her stepfather a warning look and carried my caddy of cleaning materials into Deedra's bedroom. It had a dismal view of the parking lot, and beyond that the embankment and the railroad track, and a bit of the Winthrop lumber-and-hardware business that backed onto the other side of the track. The most interesting thing about the view this morning was Deedra's beautiful red Taurus in the parking lot, halfway out of its stall. Someone had taken a can of white spray paint and carefully scripted, *'She fucks niggers'* on the hood.

I felt sick and old.

Deedra had apparently pulled out of her parking spot before she saw the writing. Then, I supposed, she'd run inside to call Mom, but Stepdad had come instead.

A tide of rage and fear rolled over me. My primary rage was directed at the bastards who'd ruined Deedra's car, and most likely her life. The story would be all over town in no time, and there wouldn't be any discreet lid on it, like there was on Deedra's bad reputation.

And then, less to my credit, I was angry with Deedra. She *had* been sleeping – from time to time – with Marcus Jefferson, who also lived in the apartment building, across the hall from Claude. And she'd told me it wasn't for any noble reason, such as love, or even a bizarre reason, such as a desire to cement race relations. She was screwing him for the fun of it.

You couldn't do that in Shakespeare unless you stood willing to pay the price. Deedra had received the bill.

I pointedly crossed through the living room a couple of times as Jerrell and Deedra continued their encounter. I couldn't call it a dialogue, since what one said made no difference to what the other responded. Jerrell was bawling Deedra out, up one side and down the other, for dragging herself (and her mother) through the mud, for polluting herself, for exposing all of them to the glare of gossip and the threat of danger.

'You know what happened to that black boy not two months ago?' Jerrell said hoarsely. 'You want something like that to happen to you? Or to that man you're going to bed with?'

I was polishing the mirror over Deedra's nine-drawer dresser when Jerrell said that, and I saw my reflection in the mirror. I looked sick. He was referring to Darnell Glass, who'd been beaten to death by person or persons unknown. I'd known Darnell Glass.

'But, Jerrell, I didn't do it!' Deedra persisted in stone-walling. 'I don't know where anyone would get that idea!'

'Girl, everyone but your mother knows you're just a whore that don't take money,' Jerrell said brutally. 'Lacey would kill herself if she knew black hands had been on your body.'

I made a face into the mirror as I dusted the top of the dresser. I dropped a pair of earrings into Deedra's earring box.

'I didn't do it!' Deedra moaned.

Childlike in many ways, Deedra believed that if you denied something often enough, it actually hadn't happened. 'Deedra, unless you change your ways right now, I mean this minute, worse things than that paint job are going to

41

happen to you, and I won't be able to stop them from happening,' Jerrell said.

'What do you mean?' Deedra asked, sobbing. 'What could be worse?'

Childlike and stupid.

'There's lots worse things than a little bit of white paint,' Jerrell said grimly, but with a somewhat milder voice. 'There's people in this town that take a situation like yours so seriously, you wouldn't believe it.'

He was threatening her.

Contrarily enough, I was all for it. As much as I now found I disliked Jerrell Knopp, any method that would scare Deedra into dropping her risky lifestyle was okay with me. The woman (and she was a woman in her twenties, though she often seemed much younger) would either contract HIV or another disease, or bring home someone who would brutalize her, if she didn't alter her ways.

'Now,' Jerrell was winding down, 'I've already called the car place to get your paint redone. Just drive it down there. Donnie'll give you a lift to work, I'll drop by to take you home, and your car'll be done in a couple of days.'

'I can't drive it down there,' Deedra whined. 'I'd die.'

'You may die if you don't stay away from black men,' he said, and there was stark warning in his voice. Jerrell wasn't just theorizing. He knew something.

I felt the hair on my neck stand up. I stepped into the living room, my dust cloth in my hand. Jerrell and I had a good ole look at each other.

'Would you drive my car to the paint shop?' Deedra asked, that little-girl look on her face that said she knew she was asking a lot, but it would be too much for *her* to do that thing.

42

'No,' I said briefly, and went back to work.

I don't know how Deedra and Jerrell settled it. I buckled down to cleaning, thinking hard thoughts about everyone involved, including Marcus Jefferson. I was willing to bet Marcus was running scared by now. He worked at the same factory as Jerrell Knopp, and if he hadn't seen Deedra's car when he left for work that morning, someone at the factory would let him know about it. I figured Marcus was going to be anxious, if not out-and-out terrified.

My oldest client, Marie Hofstettler, had told me it had been seven decades since Shakespeare had suffered a racially motivated lynching. If I'd been Marcus Jefferson, those seven decades would have seemed like yesterday.

Deedra and Jerrell cleared out without speaking to me, which was just fine. I finished my work in peace, or in the little peace they'd left behind them. The apartment still echoed with various gradations of anger and fear. It seemed to me that currents of bad feeling were drifting like smog through Shakespeare. My little adopted town had generally been quiet and predictable and pokey. I liked it like that. I loaded my arsenal of cleaning aids back into my car, trying to stave away a gnawing worry.

My new client, Mookie Preston, was next on my schedule, and I was able to feel a little more cheerful as I drove to her house.

I'd never worked on Sycamore Street before. It was lined with small white houses with neatly raked yards, in a neighborhood that had sprung up in the fifties, a neighborhood generally considered a starting-out point for newlyweds or an ending-up point for seniors.

The house Mookie Preston rented was in the middle of the block and indistinguishable from the others. A green

43

Toyota was parked in the driveway. It had an Illinois plate. If the car was any indicator of the condition of the house, Mookie Preston needed me. Badly. The Toyota was dusty and mud-streaked on the outside and littered with papers and fast-food debris on the inside.

I knocked briskly on the back door, and the same rich, fruity voice I'd heard on the phone called, 'Coming, coming!'

After a minute or so the back door opened and the woman on the other side of the screen door stood staring at me. She didn't speak. We examined each other.

Mookie Preston was younger than me, putting her somewhere in her midtwenties. She had very coarse, straight reddish hair skinned back into a ponytail, golden freckled skin, and big, dark brown eyes. Her face was round, and her teeth were perfect and white. If she was wearing any makeup, I couldn't see it.

And despite the fact that she was pretty, very pretty, and smiling in the friendliest way possible, this woman had thrown me off balance.

If her fading smile was any indication, she was feeling the same way about me.

'You're Lily Bard?' she said cautiously.

'I am.'

Slowly, she pushed open the screen door. She extended a plump golden hand. I shook it.

She stepped aside and I went in the house.

She began dithering around the filthy little kitchen. 'I should have been expecting you but I got caught up in my work,' she said over her shoulder, stacking plates by the sink in an effort to pretend she'd actually been engaged in doing so when I knocked.

'What do you do?'

'I'm a genealogist,' she said, her face turned away, which I thought was a lucky thing.

'Umm,' I said, which was the most noncommittal noise I could manage. 'You don't have to clean up for me. I'm the cleaning woman.'

She looked down at the plate in her hand as if she hadn't realized what she was doing, and very carefully deposited it on the drain board. 'Right.'

'What did you want me to do?' I asked.

'Okay.' That calmed her, as I'd intended. 'I want you to change my sheets – the clean ones are in the bathroom closet – and dust the house, and vacuum. There's only one bathroom, and it's in pretty bad shape. Clean the sink and tub, and wipe the kitchen counters. Mop the linoleum floors.'

'Okay. Anything else?'

'Not that I can think of right now.'

We discussed my pay, and my hours. She thought the house might take me until twelve-thirty to get in shape, and if the kitchen was any indication I agreed it would. I got to the Winthrops' at one, usually, so that didn't leave me much leeway. I figured I could stop by my house and grab a piece of fruit on my way to the Winthrops'.

I examined the house first, to plan my work. Mookie had retreated to the living room at the front of the house, which she had turned into a workroom. There was an old couch, an old chair, an old television, and a huge desk. She hadn't hung any curtains, and the blinds on the big windows were coated with dust. The wastebasket was overflowing, and cups from various fast-food places dotted the desk, the arm of the couch, the floor. I kept my face blank. I've learned to do that.

As Mookie sat down at her computer, I wandered down the hall (filthy baseboards, fingerprints on the paint) to the bigger bedroom. I wrinkled my nose. The sheets certainly did need changing, and the bed had probably never been made since the sheets had been put on. There was a thick layer of dust on every surface – every surface that wasn't already covered with something else, like paperbacks, makeup, snack wrappers, tissues, jewelry, hairbows and brushes, receipts. I could feel that little contraction between my brows that meant I was perturbed. Then I examined the bathroom, and I shook my head in disbelief.

The second bedroom was almost empty, only luggage and a few boxes strewn about the floor . . . at random.

Now I wondered if the allotted time would be enough.

I went out to my car to get my supplies, wondering how far I could get. I'd start with the bathroom, for sure . . . then the bedroom.

Cleaning is work that doesn't occupy your whole mind, which is something I occasionally enjoy. I was half-smiling to myself as I began scrubbing the bathtub. I'd expected Mookie Preston to be completely white, and she'd expected me to be black. We'd both been astonished.

In a better world, we wouldn't have even noticed that we were of different races – maybe if we'd even met each other in a big city, we would just have celebrated our ethnic diversity. But it wasn't a better world, at least not here and now. Not in Shakespeare. Not lately.

My astonishment about my new employer faded as I concentrated on the task at hand. After some determined scrubbing and mopping, I had the bathroom looking very respectable. I gave it a sharp nod and turned to start work in the bedroom. To my surprise, Mookie Preston was standing right behind me.

'I'm sorry I startled you,' she said, looking rather shocked herself as my hands fisted.

I relaxed with an effort. 'I didn't hear you,' I admitted, not happy at all about that.

'It looks great,' she said, looking past me into the small room. 'Wow, the mirror especially.'

Yeah, you could see your reflection now. 'Good,' I said.

'Listen, are you put off by my being mixed race?'

'What you are is none of my business.' Why did people always want to talk about every little thing? Even before a gang had held me down and drawn pictures on my chest with a knife, I hadn't been one for chatter.

'I didn't know you were going to be white.'

'Yeah.'

'So, can we make this work?' she persisted.

'*I* am working,' I said, trying to make a point, and began to strip the sheets off her bed. What I wanted Mookie Preston to get out of this was that if I'd seriously objected to her parentage, I would've hopped back in my Skylark and gone home to try the next name on my standby list.

Whether she got the point or not, I don't know. After waiting for me to say something else, she drifted back to her computer, to my relief.

She left once, to go to the grocery store. Other than that one period of peace, my new employer was in constant motion, jumping up to go to the toilet, drifting down the hall to get a drink from the refrigerator, always making some passing remark. Apparently, Mookie Preston was one of those people who can't be still when someone else is working. When she told me for the third time she was

47

leaving for the grocery, I decided it would be a good opportunity to clean the office area without her hovering presence.

At a closer examination of the nearly bare, dusty room, I realized the strips of paper fixed to the walls were genealogical charts. Some of them were printed really fancy with Gothic lettering, and some of them were dull-looking computer readouts. I shrugged. Not my thing, but harmless. There were a few books arranged on the old student standby of boards and cement blocks; three of them were about a woman named Sally Hemmings. I'd have to look her up at the library. There were stacks of software boxes, bearing titles like *Family Tree Maker* and *Family Origins*. I saw a list of Web sites taped beside the computer, and a list of phone numbers to places like the Family History Library and the Hidden Child Foundation.

But the more I dusted and straightened and vacuumed, the more questions I had about this woman. She'd been living here for at least five weeks, if she'd called me to get on my list right after she'd moved into this house. Why would a young woman like Mookie Preston move to a small southern town if she had no friends or relations in place here? If Mookie Preston was only a genealogical researcher, I was a sweet young thing.

She was gone a long time, which was fine with me. By the time she was toting in her plastic bags of Diet Pepsi and Healthy Choice microwave meals, I had the house looking much better. It would take a couple more sessions to finish clearing up the backlog of dirt and scrub down to a regular weekly accumulation, but I'd made a fighting start.

She looked around with her mouth a little open, stiff reddish hair brushing her shoulders as her head turned.

'This is really great,' she said, and she meant it, but she wasn't as enthusiastic about cleanliness as she was pretending to be. 'Can you come every week?'

I nodded.

'How do you prefer to be paid?' she asked, and we talked about that for a while.

'You work for a lot of the local upper crust, I bet?' she asked me, just when I thought she had about finished chattering. 'Like the Winthrops, and the Elgins?'

I regarded her steadily. 'I work for lots of different kinds of people,' I said. I turned to go, and this time Mookie Preston didn't detain me.

As I was assembling cheese, crackers, and fruit for a quick lunch in my own – thank God, spotless and silent – kitchen, the doorbell rang. I glanced out my living room window before answering the door. A pink van was parked in my driveway, with FANCY FLOWERS painted on the side.

It was surely the first time that particular vehicle had been to my place.

I opened the door, ready to tell the delivery person that she needed the apartment building next door, and the perky young woman on my doorstep said, 'Miss Bard?'

'Yes?'

'These are for you.'

'These' were a beautiful arrangement of pink roses, baby's breath, greenery, and white carnations.

'Are you sure?' I said doubtfully.

' "Lily Bard, Ten Track Street," ' the woman read from the back of the envelope, her smile fading a bit.

'Thank you.' I took the bowl and turned away, shutting the door behind me with one foot. I hadn't gotten flowers in . . . well, I just couldn't remember. Carefully, I set the bowl on my kitchen table and pulled the gift envelope out of the prolonged plastic holder. I noticed it had been licked and shut rather carefully, and after I extracted the card and read it, I appreciated the discretion. *'I miss you. Claude'*, it read, in a slanted, sprawling hand.

I searched inside myself for a reaction and found I had no idea how to feel. I touched a pink rose with one fingertip. Though I wear plastic gloves when I work, my hands still get rough, and I was anxious I would damage the delicate smoothness of the flower. Next I touched a white ball of baby's breath. I slowly positioned the bowl in the exact middle of the table, and reached up a hand to wipe my cheeks.

I fought an impulse to call the florist and send some flowers right back to him, to show him how he'd touched me. But Claude wanted this to be a purely masculine gesture, and I would let it be.

When I left to bring order into the Winthrops' chaos, I could feel a faint smile on my face.

Luck continued with me – up to a point – that afternoon. Since the weather was clear, I parked in front of the Winthrop house on the street. I only used the garage when it was snowing or raining, because my car had an apparently incurable oil leak and I didn't want to spot the immaculate Winthrop garage floor. I'd driven by the garage, which opened onto a side street, and seen it was empty. Good. None of the Winthrops were home.

Beanie, a lean, attractive woman somewhere in her midforties, was likely to be playing tennis or doing volunteer work. Howell Winthrop, Jr., would be at Winthrop

Sporting Goods or Winthrop Lumber and Home Supply, or even at Winthrop Oil. Amber Jean and Howell Three (that was what the family called him) were in junior high and high school. Bobo was at work at Body Time, or attending classes in the U of A extension thirty-five minutes away in Montrose. Though the Winthrops were very wealthy, no Winthrop child would consider going anywhere but the University of Arkansas, and my only surprise was that Bobo was going to the Montrose campus rather than the mother ship up north in Fayetteville. The razorback hog, symbol of the University of Arkansas, featured prominently in the Winthrops' design scheme.

On Fridays, I dusted, mopped, and vacuumed. I'd already done the laundry, ironing, and bathrooms on my first visit of the week on Tuesday morning. The Winthrop kids had gotten pretty good about washing any clothing item they just had to have between my visits, but they'd never learned to pick up their rooms properly. Beanie was pretty neat with her things, and Howell wasn't home enough to make a mess.

I paused in my dusting to examine the portrait of Beanie and Howell Jr. that had been their most recent anniversary present to each other. I could count on the fingers of one hand the number of times I'd seen Howell at home during the three years I'd worked for the family. He was balding, pleasantly good-looking, and perhaps twenty pounds over-weight. The artist had concealed that nicely. Howell was the same age as his wife, but not working quite as hard at concealing it. He spent a lot of time at the even more impressive home of his parents, Howell Sr. and Arnita, the uncrowned king and queen of Shakespeare. Howell Sr., though nominally retired, still had a say in every Winthrop enterprise, and the Seniors still led a very active role in the social and political life of the town. *They* had a full-time black housemaid, Callie Gandy.

As if thinking of Howell Jr. had conjured him up, I heard a key in the lock and he came in from the carport. Following behind him was the man who'd been out walking last night.

Now that I saw him in the daylight, I was sure he was also the man who'd been working out with Darcy Orchard the day Raphael had left Body Time.

The two men were each carrying a long, heavy black bag with a shoulder strap.

Howell stopped in his tracks. His face reddened, and he was obviously flustered.

'I'm sorry to disturb you at your work,' he said. 'I didn't see your car.'

'I parked in front.' Howell must have pulled into the garage from the side street.

'We won't get in your way,' he said.

My eyes narrowed. 'Okay,' I said cautiously. It was his house.

I looked past Howell at his companion. I was close enough to see his eyes. They were hazel. He was wearing a poly-filled vest, deep green, with a Winthrop Sporting Goods sweatshirt under it. The Winthrop sweats and tees, worn by all employees, were dark red with gold and white lettering. The man was eyeing me as intently as I was looking at him.

He didn't look like I would expect a friend of Howell's to look. This man was far too dangerous. I recognized that, but I also knew that I was not afraid of him, I nearly forgot Howell was there until he cleared his throat, said, 'Well, we'll be . . .' and walked into the living room to cross to his study. With a backward glance, the man in the red sweatshirt followed him, and the study door closed behind him. I was left to finish dusting the living room and bedroom, all the while trying to figure out what was going on. It crossed my mind that Howell might be gay, but when I recalled Black Ponytail's eyes, I jettisoned the idea.

I had to cross the living room one more time, and I saw that the door to Howell's study was still shut. At least, I thought with obscure relief, I'd already dusted and vacuumed Howell's study. It was one of my favorite rooms in the house. Its walls were paneled, with bookcases galore. A leather chair was flanked by a reading lamp, Ducks Unlimited prints were hanging on the walls, and a very important-looking desk that was hell to polish stood before the bay window with its window seat.

I didn't want to look nosy, so I worked hard and fast trying to finish and get out of there before they emerged, but I didn't make it. The study door opened and out they came, just as I was mopping the kitchen. They were empty-handed.

Howell and the stranger stood in the middle of the floor making footprints I'd have to mop over. I was wearing yellow plastic gloves, my nose was surely shiny, and I was wearing my oldest jeans and an equally ancient T-shirt. All I wanted was for them to leave, and all Howell wanted was to obscure the oddity of the situation by making conversation.

'I hear you're the one who found poor Del?' Howell was asking sympathetically.

'Yes.'

'You're going with Marshall Sedaka, I hear? You have a key to Body Time?'

'No,' I said firmly, without being sure which question I was answering. 'I opened that morning for Marshall as a favor. He was sick.'

'My son admires you a great deal. He mentions you often.'

'I like Bobo,' I said, trying to keep my voice very small and even.

'There was no indication that anyone was with him when the accident occurred?'

I stood perplexed, unable to follow. Then I made the leap. All the intervening conversation had just been waffling. Howell wanted to know about the death of Del Packard.

I wondered what 'indication' Howell imagined there might have been. Footprints on the indoor/outdoor carpet? A monogrammed handkerchief clutched in Del's fingers?

'Excuse me, Howell, I have to finish here and get to my next job,' I said abruptly, and rinsed out my mop. Though it took him a second, the man who signed so many local paychecks took the hint and hurried out the kitchen door. His companion lingered a moment behind him, long enough for me to meet his eyes when I looked up to see if they'd gone. I kept my gaze down until I heard the car start up in the carport.

After conscientiously mopping up their footprints, I wrung the mop and put it outside the back door to dry. With some relief, I locked the Winthrop house behind me and got into my car.

The Winthrops had irritated me, interested me, been a source of thought and observation for me for four years. But they had never been mysterious. Howell's sudden swerve from the straight-and-narrow of predictability made me anxious, and his association with the night-walking stranger with the black ponytail baffled me.

I discovered I had feelings ranging from tolerant to fond for the members of the Winthrop family. I had worked for them long enough to absorb a sense of their lives, to feel a certain loyalty to them.

Discovering this did not make me especially happy.

Chapter Three

Driving home from my last job of the day, I became acutely aware of how tired I was. I'd had little sleep the night before, I'd had a full working day, and I'd observed a lot of puzzling behavior.

But Claude's personal car, a burgundy Buick, was parked in front of my house. On the whole, I was glad to see it.

His window was rolled down, and I could hear his radio playing 'All Things Considered', the public-radio news program. Claude was slumped down in the driver's seat, his eyes closed. I wondered how long he had been waiting, since someone had stuck a blue sheet of paper under his windshield wiper. I could feel a smile somewhere inside me as I pulled into my carport and turned off the ignition. I'd missed him.

I walked quietly down the drive. I bent to his ear.

'Hey, hotshot,' I whispered.

He smiled before his eyes flew open.

'Lily,' he said, as if he enjoyed saying it. His hand went up to smooth his mustache, now more salt-and-pepper than brown.

'You going to sit out here or you going to come in?'

'In, now that you're here to offer.'

As Claude emerged from his Buick, I pulled the blue flyer from under his passenger-side wiper. I figured it was an ad for the new pizza place. I glanced at the heading idly.

'Claude,' I said.

He'd been retucking his shirtail. 'Yep?'

'Look.'

He took the sheet of blue paper from me, studied the dark print for a moment.

'Shit,' he said disgustedly. 'This is exactly what Shakespeare needs.'

'Yes indeed.'

TAKE BACK YOUR OWN, the headline read. In smaller print, the text read:

> The white male is an endangered species. Due to government interference, white males cannot get the jobs they want or defend their families. ACT NOW!! BEFORE IT'S TOO LATE!!! Join us in this struggle. We'll be calling you. TAKE BACK YOUR OWN. We've been shoved enough. PUSH BACK!

'No address or phone number,' Claude observed.

'Dr Sizemore got one, too.' I remembered the color, though naturally I hadn't extracted the sheet from the dentist's garbage can.

Claude shrugged his heavy shoulders. 'No law against it, stupid as it seems.'

Northern Arkansas had hosted several white supremacist organizations over the past few decades. I wondered if this was an offshoot of one of them, one that had migrated south.

Everywhere I went, in the grocery, in the doctor's office, the rare occasions I worked at one of the churches, people all complained about not having enough time, having too much to do in the time they had available. It seemed to me after reading 'Take Back Your Own' that some people just weren't busy enough.

I crumpled the thing in my hand, turned and went up the stepping stones to my front door, my keys already out and ready to turn in both locks. Claude stretched. It was a large stretch for a large man.

He followed me in. I tensed, thinking he'd try to kiss me again, but he just began a rambling monologue about the trouble he was having scheduling enough cars on the streets during Halloween, when the fun tended to get too rowdy.

I was occupied in emptying my pockets onto the kitchen counter, a soothing little ritual. I don't carry a purse when I'm working – it's just one more thing to tote in and out.

'Thank you for the flowers,' I said, my back still to him.

'It was my pleasure.'

'The flowers,' I began, and then stopped to take another deep breath. 'They are very pretty. And I liked the card,' I added, after another moment.

'Can I give you a hug?' he asked cautiously.

'Better not,' I said, trying to sound matter-of-fact.

On the card, he'd written that he missed my company. Of course, that wasn't true. Claude might enjoy my conversation, but his fundamental goal was getting me in bed. I sighed. So what else was new on the man/woman front?

I was more convinced than ever that intimacy wasn't a good idea for either of us.

I didn't say so, not just then; and that wasn't normal for me. But that evening, I wanted a friend. I wanted the company of a person I liked, to sit with me and drink coffee at my table. Though I knew it would prolong Claude's expectations, I temporarily bought into the illusion that it was only my companionship he wanted.

We did have coffee and a piece of fruit together, and a casual sort of conversation; but maybe because I was being in some sense deceptive, the warmth I'd hoped to feel didn't come.

Claude objected when I changed for karate class, but I never miss it if I can help it. I promised him that when I returned we'd go to dinner in Montrose, and I invited him to stay at my place and watch the football game on my TV while I was gone, since it had a bigger screen than his little portable. As I got in my car, I had a weary conviction that I should have told him to go on home.

I strode through the main room at Body Time, trying to look forward to the stress-reducing workout I was about to get. But mostly I felt . . . not very pleased with myself.

Though I'd been in there many times since Del had died, I always glanced at the corner where Del's body had rested on the bench. A smaller copy of Del's second-place trophy from the Marvel Gym competition the year before was still in its prominent position in the display case by the drinks cooler, since the gym where a winner trained was always recognized along with the winner.

I stopped to admire the shiny cup on its wooden stand, read the engraving. In the glass front of the display case, I could see the reflection of other potential champions as they went through their evening routines. I moved my hand up and down slightly to make sure I was there, too.

I shook my head at my reflection and continued down the hall to the open double doors of the aerobics/karate room. I bowed in the doorway to show respect, and entered. Janet Shook was already in her gi, its snowy whiteness setting off her dark hair and eyes. She was holding on to the barre, practicing side kicks. Marshall was talking to Carlton Cockroft, my next-door neighbor and my accountant, whom I hadn't seen in at least a week. There was a new woman limbering up, a woman with very long blond hair and a deep sun-bed tan. She was wearing a gi with a brown belt, and I regarded her with respect.

Raphael, who hadn't set foot in Body Time since the morning he'd left in a huff, was practicing the eight-point blocking system with Bobo Winthrop. I was glad to see Raphael, glad that whatever had eaten at him had eased up. As I watched the two spar, I noticed for the first time that Bobo was as tall as Raphael. I had to stop thinking of him as a boy.

'Yee-hah, Lily,' Bobo called cheerfully. I hadn't thought Bobo's naturally sunny nature would keep him down for long, and it was reassuring to see him smile and look less troubled. He and Raphael finished, and Bobo walked over to me as I finished tying my obi. I had time to think that Bobo looked like an all-American action hero in his white gi, when he simply reached over to place a large hand on each side of my waist, squatted slightly, and picked me up.

I had not been handled like that since I'd become an adult, and the sensation of being lifted and held up in the air abruptly returned me to childhood. I found myself laughing, looking down at Bobo, who was grinning up at me. Over his shoulder, I glimpsed the black-haired stranger, standing in the hall. His eyes were on me, and he was smiling a little as he patted his face with a towel.

Marshall, nodding at Black Ponytail, shut the double doors.

Bobo put me down.

I made a mock strike to his throat and he blocked me too late.

'Would've gotten you,' I warned him. 'You're stronger, but I'm quicker.'

Bobo was grinning at the success of his horseplay, and before I could move away, he gripped my wrists with his strong hands. As I stepped closer to him, I turned my palms up, bringing my hands up against his thumbs, and was free. I pantomimed chopping him in the neck with the sides of my hands. Then I patted him on his big shoulder and stepped away before he had any more ideas.

'Someday I'll get you,' Bobo called after me, shaking his finger.

'You get Lily, you're going to be sorry,' Raphael remarked. 'This gal can eat you for breakfast.'

Bobo turned dark red. I realized he'd read a double entendre into Raphael's remark. I turned away to hide my grin.

'Line up!' Marshall said sternly.

The blond woman was the highest-ranking student present. She took her place first in line. My belt is green, with one brown stripe. I took a deep breath, warned myself against unworthy feelings, and prepared myself to be pleasant.

'Kiotske,' Marshall said. We snapped to attention, our heels together.

'Rei.' We bowed to him, and he to us.

We worked through the familiar pain of three minutes in the shiko dachi position – pretty much like sitting on air – and calisthenics. Marshall was in a tough mood tonight. I didn't want to be petty enough to think he was giving us extra work because he was trying to impress the new class member; but he extended our sit-ups to one hundred. So we also did a hundred leg lifts and a hundred push-ups.

I was paired with the new woman, instead of Janet, for sit-ups. Her legs, hooked with mine, felt like bands of iron. She wasn't breathing heavily after eighty reps, though the next twenty were a little work. She broke into a light sweat after leg lifts, and was breathing a little hard after a hundred push-ups. But she had the energy to smile at me as she rose to her feet. I turned slightly to Raphael and gave him a look. He wiggled his eyebrows at me. We were impressed.

'Sanchin dachi blocking posture for jodan uki,' Marshall instructed. 'Komite!'

We assumed the correct position, right foot sweeping inward and forward, stopping when its heel was parallel with the toes of the left foot. I watched the blond out of the corner of my eye, wondering if she was from another discipline. She was, but she was also a quick study; watching Marshall intently, she swept her right foot in the correct half-arc and turned her toes in at a forty-five-degree angle to her body, her knees flexed slightly. Her left hand moved into chamber by her ribs, and her right formed a fist, as her right arm bent so that the fist faced her body at shoulder height.

As we went through kihon, practicing our strikes and blocks, I found myself distracted by my new neighbor. I made a determined effort to block her out of my consciousness. From then on, I felt more comfortable, and class went better. Marshall paired me with Carlton for practice. Between breaking free from each other and restraining each other, Carlton and I exchanged neighborhood news. He'd heard we were going to get new streetlights, and that the ownership of the empty lot at the corner – which I'd always thought was waste ground – had been decided among the five children of an elderly lady who'd passed away four years ago. What the new owner would do with the area, which would certainly be a challenge to fit a house on, Carlton hadn't yet discovered.

As I used one finger to jab the pressure point in Carlton's upper forearm, the one that made his knees crumple, he told me that he'd found a sheet of blue paper on his car when he'd come out to get his mail that afternoon. 'Nuts,' he commented.

I hoped everyone would dismiss the flyer so thoroughly. Then Carlton took his turn and pressed too hard, and from my position on the floor I looked up at him with my eyebrows raised.

When we had been dismissed, the blond drifted over to Marshall. Her hair flowed down to her butt, thick and straight, and though the youthful style didn't exactly match her apparent age, the effect was definitely enough to attract lots of attention. Janet was scowling as she sat on the floor to tie her shoes.

I was ready to go, having grabbed my gym bag and keys, when Marshall beckoned me over.

'Lily' he said, with a broad smile, 'this is Becca Whitley, Pardon's niece.'

Pardon Albee, the owner of the apartment building next to my house, had passed away the previous spring. Becca Whitley had taken her own sweet time in coming to check out her inheritance. One of the tenants in the apartment house, Marie Hofstettler, a very old woman who was one of my favorite clients, had told me the same lawyer who'd hired me to clean the halls had been collecting the rent for the past few months. And Deedra had told me that when her lease had expired her rent had gone up.

'I know I've been slow to get to Shakespeare to see to

settling Uncle Pardon's estate,' the blond said, chiming in on my thoughts in a way that focused my wandering attention firmly. I looked at her directly for the first time. She was narrow-faced, with strong but scaled-down features. The deep tan was freckled. Her eyes were a bright I-wear-blue-contacts sapphire, and heavily made up. She also wore candy-pink lipstick and lined her lips with a darker shade. The effect stopped short of vampiric; but it was definitely predatory.

Becca Whitley was saying, 'I had a divorce to settle in Dallas, and an apartment to clean out.'

'So you're moving to Shakespeare?' I asked, hardly able to conceal my amazement. I took in her long mane of Lady Clairol hair, and the cone-shaped breasts bulging at her gi, and thought she would surely stir the local roosters up. Marshall was strutting around practically wiggling his crest and crowing. No wonder tonight he'd spared me most of those wounded looks he'd been casting me the past two weeks. I had to repress an impulse to snort.

'I think I'll just live in Uncle Pardon's apartment, at least for now,' Becca Whitley was saying. 'It's so convenient.'

'I hope Shakespeare isn't too quiet for you after such a big city,' I said. I realized that when I thought about Marshall's interest in Becca Whitley, the pang I felt was very small, almost negligible, which was only right.

'Oh, I've lived in Austin, which is really just a big town,' Becca said. 'But the past few months I've been in Dallas, and I couldn't stand the traffic and the pressure. See, I just got divorced, and I need a new life for myself.'

'Any children?' Janet asked hopefully. She'd come up behind me.

'Not a one,' our newest Shakespearean responded happily. 'Just too busy, I guess.'

Marshall was trying to conceal his relief just as hard as Janet was trying to conceal her chagrin.

'I've been cleaning the apartment halls since Pardon died,' I said. 'Do you want me to keep on, or have you made other plans?'

'I expect I'll be doing it,' Becca said.

I nodded and gathered my things together. The extra money had been pleasant, but working late on Saturday hadn't.

Our sensei was still telling Becca how much we wanted her to come back to class as Janet and I bowed at the door on our way out.

'Screw her,' Janet said quietly and viciously after we'd reached the parking lot.

It seemed to me it wouldn't be too long before Marshall tried to do just that, and Carlton, longtime most eligible bachelor in Shakespeare, had seemed interested, too.

I liked Janet pretty well, and I could see she was chagrined at the sexy and striking Becca Whitley's appearance and Marshall's obvious approval. Janet had been waiting for Marshall to notice her for a couple of years.

'She'll never last in Shakespeare,' I told the disappointed woman. I was surprised to hear my own voice.

'Thanks, Lily,' Janet said, sounding equally surprised. 'We'll have to wait and see.' To my amazement, she gave me a half-hug before unlocking her Trooper.

When I came in through the kitchen door, I could hear my television. Claude was parked in the double recliner watching a football game. He looked unnervingly at home. He waved a casual hand when I called 'Hello,' so I didn't hurry as I showered and dressed. When I emerged, once again made up and polished, Claude was in the kitchen drinking a glass of iced tea.

'What do you think of your new landlady?' I asked.

'The Whitley woman? Looks like a raccoon, don't she, with all that eye makeup?' he said lazily.

I smiled. 'Ready to eat?' I asked.

Soon we were driving toward Montrose, the nearest large town. It lay west and slightly north of Shakespeare, and it was the retail hub for many small towns like Shakespeare. Montrose, which boasted a population of around forty thousand year-round, more during college sessions, was where Shakespeareans went when they didn't want to make the somewhat longer northeast drive to Little Rock.

I'd never been enthusiastic about Montrose, a town which could have been dropped anywhere in the United States without its visitors knowing the difference. Montrose had no character; it had shopping. There were all the usual fast-food places and all the usual chain stores, and a five-screen movieplex, and a Wal-Mart Super Center. In my view, the main attractions of Montrose were its superior library, its one good independent bookstore, and perhaps four fairly good nonchain restaurants. And a couple of decent chain ones.

In the months I'd been seeing Marshall, I'd spent more time in Montrose than I had in the four years I'd lived in Shakespeare. Evenings at home had little charm for Marshall.

We'd tried every restaurant, sat through Jackie Chan and Steven Seagal movies, visited every sporting goods store to compare their prices to Winthrops', and done our weekly shopping at the Super Center.

This evening, Claude suggested a movie. I almost agreed out of courtesy. But remembering the uncomfortable hours with Marshall, I admitted, 'I really don't like going to the movies.'

'That so?'

'I don't like sitting with a lot of strangers in the dark, having to listen to them shift around and rattle paper and talk. I'd rather wait until it comes out on video and see it at home.'

'Okay,' he said. 'What would you like to do?'

'I want to eat at El Paso Grande and go to the bookstore,' I said.

Silence. I looked over at him out of the corners of my eyes.

'What about Catch the Wave and the bookstore?' he countered.

'Done,' I said, relieved. 'You don't like Tex-Mex?'

'Ate there last week when I had to come to Montrose to the courthouse.'

As we waited on our order in the seafood restaurant, Claude said, 'I think Darnell Glass's mother is going to bring a civil suit against the Shakespeare Police Department.'

'Against the department?' I asked sharply. 'That's unfair. It should be against Tom David.' Tom David Meicklejohn, one of Claude's patrolmen, had long been on my black list, and after the Darnell Glass incident, he'd moved to the number-one spot.

Suddenly, I wondered if this was the real reason for the flowers, the evening out: this conversation.

'Her lawyer's also naming Todd Picard. You think you could remember the timing just once more?'

I nodded, but I heaved an internal sigh. I was reluctant to

recall the warm black night of The Fight. I'd been interviewed and interviewed about The Fight: That's what all the Shakespeareans called it. It had taken place in the parking lot of Burger Tycoon, a locally owned hamburger place that competed valiantly with Burger King and McDonald's, which were both down Main Street a piece.

I'd only come in on the crisis, but I'd read and heard enough later to flesh out what I'd actually seen.

Darnell Glass was sitting in his car in the Burger Tycoon parking lot, talking to his girlfriend. Bob Hodding, trying to pull into the adjacent parking space, hit Glass's rear bumper. Hodding was white, sixteen years old, a student at Shakespeare High School. Glass was eighteen and in his freshman year at UA Montrose. He had just made the first payment on his first car. Not too surprisingly, when he heard the unmistakable grinding crunch of the two bumpers tangling, Glass was enraged. He jumped out of his car, waving his hands and shouting.

Hodding was instantly on the offensive, since he knew the reputation of the young man whose car he'd just hit. Darnell Glass had attended the Shakespeare schools until he enrolled in college, and had a reputation as a bright and promising young man. But he was also known to be aggressive and hair-trigger sensitive in his dealings with white peers.

Bob Hodding had been raised with a Confederate flag flying in front of his house. He remembered Glass overreacting to situations at the high school. He wasn't afraid, since he had three of his buddies in his car, and he wasn't about to apologize in front of them, or admit his driving had been less than adequate.

A couple of witnesses told Claude later, privately, that Hodding pushed every emotional button he possibly could to further enrage Darnell Glass, including a jibe about Glass's mother, a junior high school teacher and well-known activist.

It was no surprise to anyone when Glass went ballistic.

And that was where I came in. I hadn't ever met Darnell Glass or Bob Hodding, but I was there when The Fight began.

So were two policemen.

I'd just pulled into the parking space on the other side of Glass's, having picked that night of all nights to buy a hamburger instead of cooking for myself, an event so rare it later seemed to me that a cosmic joke had placed me at the punch line. It was a very warm evening in early September; of course, in Shakespeare we have to mow our yards until well into November.

I was wearing my usual T-shirt and baggy jeans, and I'd just finished work. I was tired. I just wanted to get my carry-out food and watch an old movie on television, maybe read a chapter or two of the thriller I'd checked out of the library.

Off-duty Shakespeare patrol officer Todd Picard was in Burger Tycoon picking up his family's supper. On-duty patrol officer Tom David Meicklejohn had pulled in to get a Coke. But I didn't know there were two serving officers of the law present.

Not that their presence had made any difference. Though, of course, it should have.

I'd seen wiry Darnell wisely get in the first punch, and I saw the taller, more muscular Bob Hodding gag and double over, and then I watched his friends swarm over Darnell like angry bees.

If I'd had a gun or a whistle, maybe the sudden noise would have halted them, but I only had my fists. These were strong high school boys full of adrenaline and I had my work cut out for me. Not wanting to seriously hurt the little bastards made my job more difficult: I could drop them fairly easily if I was inclined to cause some lasting damage. Since Bob Hodding was temporarily out of the picture, puking his guts out in the crepe myrtles lining the parking lot, I concentrated on his buddies.

I moved up behind the tallest boy, who was raining punches on Darnell Glass. First I pinched a pressure point in the upper shoulder of the boy, who was standing between the other attackers, with my right hand. With my left, I pressed a point in his upper arm. The boy shrieked. Though he began to crumple, he still provided me with cover from the black-haired kid on my right, who was swinging blindly at me, but standing legs a-spraddle . . . someone who'd never fought in the street. I kicked him in the balls, just a glancing blow, a pretty neat kogen geri.

That took care of him.

The boy I'd disposed of first finally hit the ground wailing. He tried to scramble back, out of the way, to figure out what had happened.

From the corner of my eye I finally noticed the patrol car. I saw Deputy Tom David Meicklejohn climb out of it. He did nothing but smile his mean redneck smile and extend his arms to bar spectators from joining in the brawl. A man in civilian clothes, a bag and a cardboard tray with five cups in holders bogging him down, was yelling at Tom David. I later learned this was off-duty officer Todd Picard.

Meanwhile, the third boy grasped Darnell around the waist and tried to lift him off his feet, a wrestling move. Losing patience and temper, I hook-kicked him behind his knee, and of course his legs folded. But the parking lot sloped, and he brought Darnell down with him. Darnell rolled rapidly to the side. I slipped on a wrapper on the pavement and hit the ground myself, and the boy's flailing foot, shod in a boot, caught me painfully right at the joint of my right hip. I rolled away and jumped to my feet before the pain could get its teeth into me. When the wrestler struggled to his knees, I pulled his arm up behind him. 'I'll break it if you move,' I said. Most people recognize absolute sincerity. He didn't move.

Being on the ground is most often bad in a fight, but Darnell, though bleeding in several places on his face and badly bruised, had not lost his spirit. Bob Hodding, slightly recovered from the punch to the stomach and frantic with rage, staggered toward Darnell for another try. Darnell kicked up at Bob, who staggered back into the arms of a Marine who happened to be on leave and visiting his family. This huge young man, right out of basic training, stepped around Tom David to grip Bob Hodding with a hold like handcuffs and give him some sound, if unprintable, advice.

I stood panting, scanning the group for another adversary. I was feeling pain in my lip, and I noticed a few spots of bright blood staining my gray T-shirt; an elbow had caught me in the mouth somewhere along the way. I straightened up, evaluated the remaining fight left in the boy I was restraining, decided it was practically nil. The Marine, whose name I never learned, caught my eye and gave me an approving nod.

'Sorry I didn't get out here earlier,' he said. 'That Tae Kwon Do?'

'Goju. For close fighting.'

'My drill sergeant would love you,' he said.

I tried to scrape together a smile.

At that point a noise like a siren went off a few feet away.

It was coming from the mouth of Darnell Glass's girl-friend, Tee Lee Blaine. She'd watched the fight from inside the car. Now she scrambled out to help Darnell rise. She was floundering through a spectrum of emotions, from fear for her own safety and Darnell's, to anger over the dent in the car, to rage that Darnell had been ganged up on. She knew each of the white boys by name, and she gave each of them a few new ones.

I caught Tom David Meicklejohn's eye. I wanted power-fully to kick him.

He smiled at me. 'Keeping back the crowd,' he said succinctly. By then, Todd Picard had deposited the food in his car and was standing by Tom David's patrol vehicle. Todd looked ashamed. I'd finally recognized him, and if I'd had the energy I'd have slapped him. I expected no better from Tom David, but Todd could have given me a hand.

For the first time, I realized there was quite a crowd. Burger Tycoon is on Main Street (Shakespeare's not too imaginative about street names) and the restaurant had been full. It was true that if Tom David had not kept the crowd back the incident could have turned into a full-fledged riot; but he had allowed most of this to happen, as I saw it.

Suddenly the hip that had taken the kick began to throb. I'd run out of adrenaline. I eased myself down into a sitting position and leaned my head back against the car.

'Lily! You okay?' a voice called from the crowd, and I saw my neighbor. Carlton, neatly groomed as always, was accompanied by a bosomy brunette with a headful of curls. I remember thinking about his companion for longer than the topic deserved, trying to recall where the woman worked.

It had been nice to have someone ask about my welfare. I was feeling distinctly flat and a little shaky.

'I'll be fine,' I said. I closed my eyes. I would have to get up in a minute. I couldn't sit here looking hurt.

Then Claude was bending over me, saying, 'Lily! Lily! Are you hurt?'

'Sure,' I said angrily. I opened my eyes. 'Having to do your cops' jobs for them. Help me up.'

Claude extended his hand and I gripped it. He straightened and pulled, and I came up. Maybe not gracefully, but at least I was steady on my feet once I got there.

Darnell Glass was standing by that time, too, but leaning heavily against his car, Tee Lee supporting him on his other side. The Marine let go of his captive, and the white boys were getting into Tom David's patrol car.

'You have a problem with your officer there,' I told Claude.

'I have more problems than that right now,' he answered quietly, and I observed that the crowd was restless, and hot words were being exchanged among a few young men in the parking lot.

'Get in my car,' he said. 'I'll get the boy and the girl.'

So we all took a ride down to the police station. The rest of the evening was completely miserable. The white boys were all juveniles. Their parents descended in a cloud of buzzing, like angry African bees. One father snapped at me that he ought to sue me for hurting his boy – the one I'd kicked in the groin – and I used his prejudice against him. 'I would love to tell the court how a woman beat up your boy and two others,' I said. 'Especially when they were ganging up on one young man by himself.' I heard no more comments about suing.

Until now. And I wasn't the target of the lawsuit.

As our waitress left, Claude spread his napkin in his lap and speared a shrimp. 'Tom David was there and did nothing,' he said, just a hint of question in his voice. 'Todd was there and did nothing.'

I raised my brows. 'That's right,' I said. 'Do you doubt it?'

He shot a look at me from under his heavy brows. 'Tom David says he had to keep the other people from joining in. Todd says he was afraid he wouldn't be recognized as an off-duty officer and would be seen as joining the brawl.'

'Of course they're going to say that, and there may even be some trace of truth to it. But they also let two other people do their job, me and the Marine. Tom David, for sure, wanted Darnell Glass to get beat up. At the very least, Todd didn't care if that happened.'

Claude avoided my eyes, clearly unhappy with the idea that a member of his force would let violence go unchecked, even though to my certain knowledge, Claude bore no love whatsoever for Tom David Meicklejohn.

'And Darnell struck the first blow,' he said, again in the tone of one confirming an unpleasant truth.

'Yes. It was a good one.'

'You never met any of those boys beforehand,' Claude said.

'No.'

'Then why so partisan?'

I stared over at him, my fork suspended midway to my mouth with a bit of flounder impaled on the tines. 'I didn't care until they all jumped him,' I said after a moment's thought. 'I would have done the same if Darnell had been white and the other guys black.' I thought about it. Yes, that was true. Then the familiar tide of anger surged up. 'Of course, as it turned out, I might have saved my strength and let them go on and stomp him.'

A dull red flush crept up Claude's face. He believed I was accusing him of something. But I wasn't, at least not consciously.

Darnell Glass hadn't lived long after that evening in the Burger Tycoon parking lot.

Four weeks later, he'd been beaten to death in a clearing in the woods north of town.

No one had been arrested for the crime.

'If the rumors are true and Mrs Glass does bring a suit, you're sure to be called as witness.' Claude felt obliged to point that out to me, and he wasn't happy about it, any more than I was.

'I wish we hadn't started talking about this,' I said, knowing it was futile to say. 'If you're really worried about the future of your police department, thinking it'll rest on my testimony . . . I can't change or shade what I saw. You may not want to be around me.' This wasn't the right place. I said it too bluntly. And I felt a funny pang when the words left my mouth.

'Is that what you want?' Claude said. His voice was very quiet.

Truth time. 'I want to see you if you're going to be my friend, but I don't see us becoming lovers. I don't think that's right for us.'

'And if I do?' I could see the distance growing in his eyes.

'Claude, I feel comfortable when I'm in your company, but if we have sex that'll be ruined. I don't think we can carry this to another dimension.'

'Lily, I'll always like you,' he said after a long pause. 'But I'm at the age and disposition where I'm thinking, I can't be in law enforcement forever. I want a wife, and a home, and someone to go camping with, someone to decorate the Christmas tree with. That was what I was thinking might happen with you. As I hear it, you're telling me it's not gonna.'

God, I hated explaining my emotions.

'I can't see my way to that, Claude. I just can't make that leap with you. And if I use up your time trying, you might miss something better.'

'Nothing can be better, Lily. I may find something different, something good. But nothing better.'

'So,' I said quietly. 'Here we are in Montrose, have to drive home, have to be with each other. We should have done this in Shakespeare, huh? Then you could go over to your apartment and I could lock my door and we could lick our wounds.'

'I wish I could believe that you have wounds to lick, Lily,' he said. 'Let's go look at some books.'

Of course after the restaurant discussion, the bookstore wasn't much fun.

I read biographies, mostly; maybe I'm hoping I'll find the key to make my life lighter by finding out how someone else managed. Or maybe I loved company in my miserable past; I could always find a tougher life than mine. But not tonight.

I found myself thinking not about Claude and myself, but about Darnell Glass.

I glanced at the true crime books, which I cannot stomach any more than I can watch the news on television.

No one would ever write a book about Darnell Glass.

A beating death in Arkansas, especially the beating death of a black male, was not newsworthy, unless whoever'd killed Darnell got arrested and generated some lurid publicity – if the murderer was one of the local ministers maybe, or if Darnell's death was the first escapade of a flamboyant serial killer.

I had managed to make my way through the newspaper account. The Shakespeare paper did its best to defuse tense situations, but even its brief references to the young man's long list of injuries made my stomach lurch.

Darnell Glass had suffered a broken jaw, five broken ribs, multiple arm fractures, and the blow that had mercifully killed him, a crushing strike to the skull. He had suffered massive internal injuries consistent with a determined beating.

He'd died surrounded by enemies – in rage, in terror, in disbelief – in an unremarkable clearing in the piney woods.

No one deserved that. Well, I had to amend that thought. I could think of a few people I wouldn't weep over if they met an identical end. But Darnell Glass, though no saint, was a very smart young man with no criminal record, whose worst crime (apparently) was a bad temper.

'Let's go,' I said to Claude, and he looked surprised at the shortness of my tone.

All the way back home I kept silent, which Claude perhaps interpreted as regret. Or sulking. Anyway, he gave me a brusque cheek peck on the doorstep that had a sort of chilly finality to it. It seemed to me, watching his broad back retreat, that I'd never see him again. I went inside and looked at the flowers, still beautiful and sweet. I wondered if Claude regretted sending them now. I almost pulled them from the vase to throw away. But that would have been silly, wasteful.

As I prepared for bed, thankful to be alone, I wondered if Marshall's charge was true. Was I a cold woman?

I could never see myself as cold; self-protective, maybe, but not cold. It seemed to me that underneath the surface, I was always on fire.

I tossed and turned, tried relaxation techniques.

I got up to walk. It was chilly outside now, midnight in late October, and it was windy; before morning it would rain again. I wore a T-shirt, a sweatshirt, sweatpants, and Nikes, all dark shades: I was in a hateful mood, and didn't want anyone to see me. The streetlights at each corner of my street, Track Street, were dispensing their usual feeble nimbus. Claude's window was dark, as was every window in the apartment building; an early night for tenants old and new. The Shakespeare Combined Church, or SCC as the members called it, was dark except for some security lights. There was very little movement in the town, period. Shakespeare rises early and goes to bed early, except for the men and women who work the late shift at one or two of the fast-food places, and the people who work nights at the mattress factory or the chicken processing plant, which run round the clock.

I went as far as the lower-middle-class neighborhood in which Darnell Glass had grown up, one of Shakespeare's few mixed-race areas. I passed the little house Glass's mother, Lanette, had bought when she moved back to Shakespeare from Chicago. It, too, was dark and silent. None of these homes had garages or porte cocheres, so it was easy to see Lanette Glass was not at home.

But I found out where she was.

She was at Mookie Preston's house.

While I'd been thinking about my curious cleaning stint at Mookie's that day, I'd drifted in that direction without conscious thought. So I was opposite the house when Lanette Glass emerged. I wasn't close enough to see her expression, which the deep shadows of the streetlight behind her would have made difficult anyway, but from the way she walked – shoulders hunched, head shaking slightly from side to side, purse clasped hard against her side – Lanette Glass was a woman in trouble, and a troubled woman.

More and more I wondered about the purposes of the mysterious Mookie Preston.

As a cold breeze stirred my hair, I felt some of its chill creep down my spine. Something was brewing in Shakespeare, something sick and dangerous. I'd always felt comfortable about the state of race relations in my adopted town. There were still taboos, plenty of them, probably several of which I wasn't even conscious. But there were also blacks in managerial positions, blacks who owned comfortable homes. Several clubs and one church were integrated. The public school system seemed to be functioning with little friction, and Lanette Glass was only one of many black teachers.

The habits and prejudices of over a century weren't going to vanish overnight, or even in thirty years; and I'd always felt that progress, quiet and slow, was being made.

I wondered now if I'd been in a fool's paradise. I had

assumed that my approval of this change was shared by most people of both races, and I still thought so. But something evil was slithering through Shakespeare, had been for months.

Perhaps three weeks after Darnell Glass had been killed, Len Elgin had been found shot dead in his Ford pickup, on a little-traveled country road just within the city limits. Len, a prosperous white farmer in his fifties, was a genial and intelligent man, a pillar of his church, father of four, and an avid reader and hunter. Len had been a personal friend of Claude's. Failure to solve Len's murder had been eating at Claude, and the rumors that spread like wildfire had made handling Len Elgin's death investigation even more delicate.

One school of thought had Elgin being killed in retaliation for the death of Darnell Glass. Of course the guilty parties, in this version, would be black extremists, even as Glass's death was ascribed to white extremists.

Another rumor had it as fact that Len was being unfaithful to his wife, Mary Lee, with the wife of another farmer. According to this rumor, the murderer was either Mary Lee, the other farmer (who was named Booth Moore), or Moore's wife Erica. Those who accused Erica were assuming that Len had terminated their relationship.

Somehow the fight – The Fight – in the Burger Tycoon parking lot had triggered all this.

We were all losing our sense of community; we were subdividing into groups not only by race but by the degree of our intensity of feeling about that race. I thought about the ugly scrawl on Deedra's car. I thought about Tom David Meicklejohn's scarcely concealed glee that September night in the parking lot. I remembered glimpsing, through the windows of the limousine following the hearse, Mary

Lee Elgin's face as the funeral cortege passed by. And then, banal in its wrongheadedness, but no less vicious for its banality, the sheet of blue paper under Claude's windshield wiper.

Surely it was stretching credulity to think that Del Packard's death in the gym was totally unrelated to the deaths of Darnell Glass and Len Elgin. How could three men be done to death in a town the size of Shakespeare in a space of two months and the killings all be mysterious? If Darnell Glass had been knifed behind a local bar during a fight over a girl, if Len Elgin had been shot in Erica Moore's bed, if Del had been in the habit of lifting alone and maybe had some undiagnosed physical weakness . . .

I was making another circuit by the apartments. I looked up at Claude's window, thinking sadly about the man inside. Would I change my mind about what I'd said, given another chance? I was genuinely fond of Claude, and grateful to him, and he had a lot on his shoulders.

But that was his chosen job. And Darnell Glass's death had taken place in the country, so that investigation was Sheriff Marty Schuster's headache. I didn't know too much about the sheriff, except that he was good at politicking and was a Vietnam veteran. I wondered if Schuster could calm the rising storm that was rattling Shakespeare's windows.

I had to walk another hour before I could sleep.

Chapter Four

I woke up and looked out at sheets of rain, a chilly autumnal gray rain. I'd slept a little late since I'd had such a hard time getting to bed the night before. I'd have to hurry to make it to Body Time. Before I dressed, I poured myself a cup of coffee and drank it at the kitchen table, the morning paper unopened beside me. I had a lot to think about.

I worked out without talking to anyone. I drove home feeling a lot better.

I showered, dressed, put on my makeup, and fluffed my hair.

I wondered if the black-haired man had been out walking in the night, too.

As my car lurched slowly along the driveway that led to the back of the small Shakespeare Clinic, an uninspiring yellow brick office structure dating from the early sixties, I was betting that Carrie Thrush would be working today.

Sure enough, Carrie's aging white Subaru was in its usual place behind the building. I used my key and called 'Hi!' down the hall. Carrie's clinic was depressing. The walls were painted an uninspiring tan and the floors were covered with a pitted brown linoleum. There wasn't enough money yet for renovation. The doctor had massive debts to pay off.

Carrie's answer came floating back, and I stepped into the doorway of her office. The best thing you could say about

Carrie's office was that it was large enough. She did a lot of scut work herself, to save money to pay back the loans that had gotten her through med school. The doctor was in black denims and a rust-red sweater. Carrie is short, rounded, pale, and serious, and she hasn't had a date in the two years since she's come to Shakespeare.

For one thing, she's all too likely to be interrupted in any free time she might manage. Then, too, men are intimidated by Carrie's calm intelligence and competence. At least that was what I figured.

'Anything interesting happen this week?' she asked, as if she wanted to take her mind off the heap of paper. She shoved her brown chin-length hair behind her ears, resettled her glasses on her snub nose. Her beautiful brown eyes were magnified many times by the lenses.

'Becca Whitley, the niece, is living in Pardon's apartment.' I said, after some thought. 'The man who's taken Del Packard's place at Winthrop Sporting is living in Norvel Whitbread's old apartment. And Marcus Jefferson moved out in a hurry after the Deedra Dean car-painting incident.' I'd seen the U-Haul trailer attached to Marcus's car the morning before.

'That was probably a good move,' Carrie said. 'Sad though that state of affairs is.'

I tried to think of other items of interest. 'I ate out in Montrose with the chief of police,' I told her. Carrie hungered for something frivolous after being a sober, God-like decision-maker all week.

'Is that the niece everyone was talking about, the one he left everything to?' Carrie had fastened on the first item. But she would get around to all of them.

I nodded.

'What's she like?'

'She's got long blond hair, she wears heavy makeup, she works out and takes karate, and she probably features in the wet dreams of half the guys she meets.'

'Smart?'

'Don't know.'

'Has she rented out Marcus's apartment yet? A lab tech at the hospital is looking for a place to live.' Shakespeare had a tiny hospital, perpetually in danger of being closed.

'I don't think the dust has had time to settle on the windowsill yet. Tell the lab tech to get on down there and knock on the apartment to the rear right.'

'So what's with the chief? He show you his nightstick?'

I smiled. Carrie had a ribald sense of humor. 'He wants to, but I don't think it's a good idea.'

'He's been hanging around you for months like a faithful hound, Lily. Cut him loose or give in.'

I was reminded yet again of how much people in a small town knew about you even when you tried to keep your life private.

'He's cut loose as of last night,' I said. 'I just enjoy his company. He knows that.'

'Do you think you can be comfortable with him now?'

I thought of a quick answer and a longer truer one. I sat down in one of the two patient chairs and said, 'It was possible until Claude started talking about the Darnell Glass lawsuit.'

'Yeah, I hear Mrs Glass is talking to a lawyer from Little Rock about bringing a suit. You'd be a witness, huh?'

'I reckon.'

'Tom David Meicklejohn is such a jerk.'

'But he's Claude's jerk. She'd be suing the Shakespeare Police Department, not just Tom David or Todd.'

Carrie shook her head. 'Rough waters ahead. Think you and Claude can weather it as friends?'

I shrugged.

Carrie's smile was wry. 'It's uphill work being your confidant, Bard.'

I sat silent for a minute. 'I expect that's from being Victim of the Year after I got raped. Too many people I talked to, people I'd known all my life, turned around and told everything I said to the press.'

Carrie looked at me, her mouth slightly open in surprise. 'Gosh,' she said finally.

'Got to work.' I got up and pulled on my yellow rubber gloves, prepared to tackle the patients' bathroom first, since it was always the nastiest.

When I left the room, Carrie was bending over her paperwork with a little smile on her lips.

Another favorite woman of mine was Marie Hofstettler, and I was sorry to see today was not one of her 'limber' days. When I used my key to enter her ground-floor apartment, I could see at a glance that she wasn't in her usual chair. Marie had been living in the Shakespeare Garden Apartments, next door to me, for years. Her son, Chuck, who lives in Memphis, pays me to clean once a week and take Mrs Hofstettler wherever she wants to go on Saturdays.

'Mrs Hofstettler,' I called. I didn't want to scare her. Lately, she'd been forgetting when I was due to come.

'Lily.' Her voice was very faint.

I hurried back to her bedroom. Marie Hofstettler was

propped up, her long silky white hair in an untidy braid trailing over one shoulder. Somehow she seemed smaller to me, and her myriad wrinkles looked deeper, chiseled into her fine skin. Her color was bad, both pale and gray-tinged.

She looked like she was dying. The effort of calling out to me had clearly exhausted her. She gasped for breath. I picked up the phone on the bedside table, jammed between a framed picture of her great-grandchild and a box of Kleenex.

'Don't call,' Marie managed to say.

'You have to go to the hospital,' I said.

'Want to stay here,' she whispered.

'I know, and I'm sorry. But I can't . . .' My voice trailed off as I realized I'd been about to say 'be responsible for your death.' I cleared my throat. I thought about her courage in the face of the pain she'd endured for years, from arthritis and a bad heart.

'Don't,' she said, and she was begging.

As I knelt by the bed and held Mrs Hofstettler's hand, I thought of all the people in this apartment building I'd seen come and go from its eight units. Pardon Albee had died, the O'Hagens had moved, the Yorks were gone, and Norvel Whitbread was in jail for forging a check: this, out of the tenants that had been in the Garden Apartments this time last year. And now Marie Hofstettler.

She was gone in an hour.

When I judged the end was near, and I knew she no longer heard me, I called Carrie.

'I'm at Marie Hofstettler's,' I said. I heard paper shuffling around on Carrie's desk.

'What's up?' Carrie knew something was wrong by my voice.

'She's leaving us,' I said very quietly.

'I'm on my way.'

'She wants you to drive slow.'

A silence. 'I hear you,' Carrie said. 'But you have to call nine-one-one to cover your ass.'

I put down the phone with the one hand I had free. I'd been holding Marie's thin bony fingers with the other. When I focused on Marie's face, she sighed, and then her soul left her body. I gave a sigh of my own.

I punched in 911. 'I've been here cleaning Marie Hofstettler's apartment,' I said. 'I left the room for a while to clean the bathroom and when I checked back on her, she was . . . I think she's dead.'

Then I had to move quickly. I grabbed some glass cleaner to give the bathroom a very quick once-over. I left the spray bottle and some paper towels by the sink and I stuck the bowl brush in the toilet, hastily pouring some blue cleanser in the water.

Carrie Thrush knocked on the door, and she was barely bending over Marie when the EMTs got there.

As I let them in, the door across the hall and to the back opened, and Becca Whitley looked out. She was dressed to kill, in tailored red slacks and a black sweater.

'The old lady?' she asked me.

I nodded.

'She having a crisis?'

'She died.'

'Should I call someone?'

'Yes. Her son, Chuck. The phone number is right here.'

While Carrie and the EMTs consulted over Mrs Hofstettler

and then loaded her onto a gurney, I fetched the pad of telephone numbers the old lady had kept by the living room phone, and handed it to Becca Whitley.

I was relieved beyond words to be spared calling Chuck, not only because I didn't like him but because I was feeling guilt. As Marie was wheeled out to the ambulance, I thought of the things I should have done; I should have called Carrie, or 911, immediately, called Marie's best friend – the older Mrs Winthrop, Arnita – and then talked Marie into wanting to go on. But Marie had been in more and more pain, more and more dependent, the past few months. There'd been many days I'd had to dress her, and times I wasn't scheduled to come and found later she'd stayed in bed all day because she couldn't do otherwise. She'd refused her son's proposal to move her to a nursing home, she'd refused to have a nurse in the apartment, and she'd made up her own mind when to let go.

Suddenly I realized how much I would miss Mrs Hofstettler, and the impact of witnessing her death hit me broadside. I sat down on the stairs up to the second floor's four apartments, sat down and felt the wetness on my cheeks.

'I got Chuck's wife,' Becca said. She was in her stocking feet, I noticed, trying to figure out how she'd crept up on me. 'She didn't exactly sound torn up.'

I didn't look up at her.

'They wrote her off a few years ago,' I said flatly.

'You're not in her will, are you?' Becca asked me, her voice calm.

'I hope not.' And then I did look up at her, and she stared back at me with her contact-blue eyes, and after a minute she nodded and went back into her place.

I was scared to finish my work in Mrs Hofstettler's apartment without permission. If anyone came asking me questions about her death, I didn't want my staying to clean afterward to look suspicious, as though I was clearing away evidence or stealing valuables. So I locked the door behind me, and turned my key over to Becca, who took it without comment.

As her own door closed behind me, I heard another one above me slam shut. I looked up the stairs. Down came the man who'd rented Norvel Whitbread's apartment, the man who'd come into the Winthrops' with Howell the day before. He was maybe my age, I now conjectured, about five foot ten, with a prominent straight nose, straight black brows over those hazel eyes. Again, his hair was pulled back in a ponytail. He had narrow, finely chiseled lips and a strong chin. There was a thin scar, slightly puckered, running from the hairline by his right eye down to his jaw. He was wearing an ancient leather jacket, dark green flannel shirt, and jeans.

I was able to take all this in so minutely because he stopped at the bottom of the stairs and looked at me for a long moment.

'You've been crying,' he said finally. 'You all right?'

'I don't cry,' I said furiously and absurdly. I met his eyes. It seemed to me I was full of fear; it seemed to me I could feel something inside me cracking.

He raised his straight brows, stared for an instant longer, and then went past me, out the back door to the tenants' parking area. The door didn't sigh shut for a long moment. I could see that he sat in his car for a beat or two before he pulled out of his space and drove away.

89

*

Mrs Hofstettler's funeral was Monday, quick work even for Shakespeare. She'd planned the service two years before; I remembered the Episcopal priest, a tiny man almost as old as Marie, coming by to talk to her about it.

I hadn't entered a church in years, so I had a long struggle with myself. I'd already said good-bye to Marie, but it came to me very strongly that she would have wanted me to be at the funeral.

Stiffly, reluctantly, I called two of my Monday afternoon regulars to reschedule. I brushed and pressed my long-stored, expensive black suit (which I'd retained from my former life as being all-purpose). I'd bought a pair of panty-hose, and now I wriggled into the nasty things. Grimacing with distaste, I slid my feet into high-heeled black pumps. Two of my scars were visible, thin and white, because of the square neckline of the suit. I was so pale that the scars weren't conspicuous, I decided; anyway, there was nothing to be done about it. I wasn't about to buy another dress. This one still fit, but not exactly the way it used to. Working out so consistently had resculpted my body.

The black suit seemed dreary unadorned, so I put my grandmother's diamond earrings in my ears, and added her diamond bar pin to the ensemble. I still had a good black purse; like the suit, it was a relic of my former life.

Shakespeare police always escort local funerals, and one of the cars is always stationed at the church. I hadn't anticipated this, especially that the police car attending to the church traffic would be manned by Claude. He watched me get out of my Skylark, and stood drop-jawed as I came down the sidewalk to enter the church.

'Lily, you look beautiful,' he said, unflatteringly amazed. 'I've never seen you dressed up before.'

I shot him a glance and passed in to the warm dimness of tiny Saint Stephen's. The dark old Episcopal church was absolutely jam-packed with friends and connections from Marie Hofstettler's long life; her contemporaries, their children, other members of the church, volunteers from her favorite charity. Only two pews had been marked off at the front for the family. Chuck, now in his late fifties, was Mrs Hofstettler's only living child.

It was obvious what sitting room there was left should be saved for the older people who formed the majority of the mourners. I stood at the back, bowing my head as the coffin was brought in draped with the heavy church pall, staring at the sparse hair on the back of Chuck Hofstettler's head as he followed behind the coffin. He was looking at the embroidered pall with a kind of grieved fascination. To me, the container and its contents were uninteresting. The essential Marie was elsewhere. The casket was only there to provide a focus for grief and meditation, the way a flag provided a focus for patriotic upswelling.

Marie's best friend, Arnita Winthrop, was seated near the front of the church with her husband, Howell Sr., her son, and his wife. Old Mr Winthrop was holding his wife's hand. Somehow I found that touching. Beanie, chic as always, had lightened her hair a couple of shades, I noticed. Beanie and Howell Jr. were not holding hands.

The unfamiliar service progressed slowly. Without a prayer book, I was at a loss. There were quite a few of us standing, and more people crowded in even after the service began. It took at least five minutes for me to realize who was a little behind me. As if some inner radar had blipped, I turned my head slightly to see the man who'd come down the apartment building stairs the day Marie died, Howell's mysterious friend.

He was as duded up as I was. He was wearing a suit with a vest, a navy-blue pinstripe. Instead of Nikes, he was shod in gleaming wing tips. His shirt was white and his tie was a conservative navy, green, and gold stripe. The black ponytail and the puckered scar contrasted oddly with the banker's costume.

As I located him, he turned his head to look at me. Our eyes met. I looked forward again. What was he doing here? Was he some long-ago army buddy of Howell's? Was he Howell's bodyguard? Why would Howell Winthrop need a bodyguard?

When the interminable service was over, I left the church as quickly as I could. I refused to look around me. I climbed back into my car and went home to change and go to work. Even for Marie, I wasn't going out to the cemetery.

When I went in to Body Time the next morning, Darcy Orchard greeted me with, 'Is it true you're working for a nigger?'

'What?' I realized I hadn't heard that word in years. I hadn't missed it.

'You working for that gal who rented the house on Sycamore?'

'Yes.'

'She's gotta be half black, Lily.'

'OK.'

'What's she doing here in Shakespeare, she told you?'

'No.'

'Lily, it's not my business, but it don't look right, a white woman cleaning for a black.'

'You're right. It's none of your business.'

'I'll say this for you, Lily,' Darcy said slowly. 'You know how to keep your mouth shut.'

I turned to stare at Darcy. I'd been doing lat pull-downs, and I didn't rise, just swiveled on the narrow seat. I looked at him thoroughly, from magnificent physique to acne-marked cheeks, and I looked beyond him at his shadow, Jim Box, a darker, leaner version of Darcy.

'Yes,' I said finally. 'I do.'

I wondered what Darcy's reaction would be if I told him that the last time I'd cleaned at Mookie Preston's house, I'd found a rifle under her bed, along with a bundle of targets. Nearly every target was neatly drilled through the middle.

The next day I stayed at Body Time longer than I usually do. I keep Wednesday mornings open for cleaning emergencies, and the only thing I had scheduled was my semiannual turnout of Beanie Winthrop's walk-in closet.

Bobo was working that morning, and once again he seemed depressed. Jim and Darcy were attacking triceps work with determination. They both gave me curt hellos before diving back into their schedule. I nodded back as I stretched.

Jerri Sizemore fluttered her fingers at me. I decided it must be the effect of my new outfit. I'd unbent enough to buy a pair of calf-length blue spandex workout pants and matching sports bra, but I'd mitigated the bare effect by pulling on an old cutoff T-shirt.

I finished my regular routine and decided to try some chin-ups, just to see if I could. I'd turned to face the wall instead of the room, because the T-shirt came up when I raised my arms, exposing a stretch of scarred ribs. I'd pulled over a stool to help me grip the high bar initially, but after that I'd shoved it away with a dangling foot so I wouldn't be tempted to cheat.

The first chin-up went fairly well, and the second and third. I watched myself in the mirror on the wall, noticing with irritation that the T-shirt certainly did expose a lot of skin. I should never have listened to Bobo's flattery.

By the fourth rep, I wouldn't have cared if the shirt fell off, I was in so much pain. But I'd promised myself I'd do at least seven. I shut my eyes to concentrate. I whined out loud when I'd achieved the fifth, and dangled from the bar, despairing of finishing my set. I was taken by surprise when big hands gripped me at the hipbones and pushed up, providing just enough boost to enable me to finish the sixth chin-up. I lowered myself, growled, 'One more,' and began to pull up again. The hands gave a trifle more boost, enabling me to accomplish the seventh.

'Done,' I said wearily. 'Thanks, Bobo.' The big hands began lowering me to the stool he'd shoved back into position.

'You're welcome,' said a voice that wasn't Bobo's. After a moment, his hands fell away, leaving an impression of heat on my stomach and hips.

I pivoted on the stool. My spotter had been the black-haired man. He was wearing a chopped-off gray sweatshirt and red sweatpants. He hadn't shaved that morning.

He walked away, and began doing lunges on the other side of the room. Picking an exercise almost at random, I hooked my feet under the bar on the lat pull-down machine and did stomach crunches, my arms crossed over my chest. I kept an eye on the stranger as he did leg presses. After he'd warmed up, he pulled off his sweatshirt to reveal a red tank top and a lot of shoulder. I turned my back.

As I was leaving, I almost asked Bobo if he knew the man's name. Then I thought, I'll be damned if I ask anybody anything, least of all Bobo. I gathered my gym bag and my jacket and started to the door.

Marshall entered as I reached it. He threw his arm around my shoulders. I leaned away from him, startled, but he pulled me close and hugged me.

'Sorry about Marie Hofstettler,' Marshall said gently. 'I know you cared about her.'

I was embarrassed at mistaking his intention, and his concern and tenderness reminded me of the reasons I'd hooked up with him initially. But I wanted him to let go. 'Thanks,' I said stiffly. The black-haired man was looking at us, as he stood with Jim and Darcy, who were chattering away. It seemed to me now that something about him was familiar, an echo of long ago, from the darkest time in my life. I couldn't quite track the trace of the memory back to its origins.

'How's your hip been?' Marshall asked professionally.

'A little stiff,' I confessed. The kick that I'd taken in The Fight had proved to be a more troublesome injury than I'd guessed at the time. Standing on my left foot, I swung my right leg back and forth to show Marshall my range of motion. He crouched before me, watching my leg move. He told me to raise my leg sideways, like a male dog about to pee, the position the karate class assumed for side kicks. It was very uncomfortable. Marshall talked about my hip for maybe five more minutes, with other people contributing opinions and remedies like I'd asked for them.

None from the black-haired man, though he drew close

to listen to the discussion, which ranged from my hip to The Fight to Lanette Glass's civil suit to some upcoming meeting at one of the black churches.

While I showered and dressed, I thought how strange it was that this black-haired man was cropping up everywhere.

It could be a coincidence. Or maybe I was just being paranoid. He could have his eye on someone else other than me; maybe Becca Whitley? Or maybe (I brightened) the finances of the Shakespeare Combined Church had attracted the interest of some government agency? The church pastor, Brother Joel McCorkindale, had always alerted that sense in me that detected craziness, twistedness, in other people. Maybe Mr Black Ponytail was after the good brother.

Then why the secret tryst with Howell? The black bags? I hadn't opened the window seat when I'd been cleaning the day before, because I hadn't any business in Howell's study.

Of course, I could be attributing all sorts of things to a regular working guy, who also liked to keep fit, and go to funerals of old women he didn't know, and have secret meetings with his employer.

What with Mookie Preston, Becca Whitley, and this scarred man with his long black hair, in no time at all I was going to lose my standing as the most exotic imported resident of Shakespeare.

It was a chilly day, almost visible-breath temperature. Though I don't like to work in long sleeves, I pulled on an old turtleneck I wore when it was too cold to do without. I'd bought it before I started muscle-building, and it was tight in the neck, the shoulders, the chest, the upper arms . . . I shook my head at my reflection in the mirror. I looked as obvious as Becca Whitley. I'd throw it out after I wore it today, but it certainly would do to clean Beanie's closet. I pulled on my baggy jeans and some old Converse high-tops, and after checking my mirror one more time to verify that my hair was curling and fluffy and my makeup was smooth and unobtrusive – evaluating Becca's cosmetics had made me more aware of the dangers of overdoing it – I went out to my car.

It wouldn't start.

'Son of a *bitch*,' I said, and a few more things. I raised the hood. One of the legacies of my gentle upbringing is that I don't know shit about cars. And since I became ungentle, I have been too busy making a living to learn. I stalked back into my house and called the only mechanic I trusted in Shakespeare.

The phone was picked up to a mind-numbing blast of rap music.

'Cedric?'

'Who you want?'

'Cedric?'

'I'll get him.'

'Hello? Who wants Big Cedric?'

'Cedric, this is Lily Bard.'

'Lily, what can I do for you this fine cold day?'

'You can come find out what's wrong with my car. It was running smooth this morning. Now it won't start.'

'I won't insult you by asking if you got gas in it.'

'I'm glad you're not going to insult me.'

'Okay, I tell you what. I got this car up on the rack I got to finish with, then I come by. You gonna be there?'

'No, I got a job. I can walk to it. I'll leave the keys in the car.'

97

'Okay, we'll get this problem taken care of.'

'Thank you, Cedric.'

The phone went down without further ado. I sighed at the thought of the expense of fixing the car – again – on a tight budget like mine, detached the car keys from my ring and put them in the ignition, and started walking to the Winthrops'.

Nothing in Shakespeare is really far away from anything else. But it was a considerable hike to the Winthrops' neighborhood in the northern part of town, especially in the cold.

At least it wasn't raining.

I reminded myself of that frequently. I promised myself something extra good for lunch, maybe a whole peanut butter-and-jelly sandwich with my homemade soup. I deserved another treat, too. Maybe a new pair of boots? Nope, couldn't do that if I had to pay for the car repairs . . .

Finally, about nine-thirty, I got to the Winthrops', the jewel of the most opulent new neighborhood in Shakespeare. This neighborhood, not coincidentally, was farthest away from the southwestern black area and my own slightly-less-southern patch to the east.

The Winthrop lot was a corner lot. Today I used the kitchen door at the back of the garage, which was a wing on the side of the house opening onto Blanche Street, since I didn't have my oil-spotting car. The front door of the house faced Amanda Street. To compensate for the small trees in front (this was a new subdivision) the landscaper had made the backyard a veritable jungle enclosed by a wooden privacy fence. There were several gates in the privacy fence, always kept carefully locked by the Winthrops so neighborhood children wouldn't trespass for a dip in the pool or a game of hide-and-seek. The Winthrop house backed up to an equally large home that had employed the same landscape planner, so in the greener seasons their block resembled the tropical bird enclosure at a good zoo. There was a narrow alley in between the back gates of the two houses. It ran the length of the block and allowed passage for the Shakespeare garbage trucks and the lawn service that maintained almost every lawn in the neighborhood.

I stepped into the Winthrop kitchen, for once feeling positively happy to be there. The kitchen was dim and warm, wonderfully warm. For a couple of minutes I stood under a vent, enjoying the rush of heated air, restoring my circulation. I pulled off my old red Lands End squall jacket and hung it on one of the chairs at the round table where the family ate most of their meals. I strolled out of the kitchen, still rubbing my hands together, to the huge family room, stylishly carpeted in hunter green and decorated in taupe, burgundy, and gold. I picked up a couch pillow and fluffed it, replacing it automatically in the correct corner of the couch, which could easily seat four.

Still trying to reach a normal temperature, I stood staring out the sliding glass doors. The backyard looked melancholy in the late autumn, the foliage thinned out and the high fence depressingly obvious. The gray pool cover was spotted with puddles of rainwater. The warm colors of the big room were more pleasant, and I roamed around it picking up odds and ends as I stretched chilled muscles.

The pleasure of being warm made me feel like singing. I'd only rediscovered my voice recently; it was as though for years I'd forgotten I had the ability. At first the memories had wrenched at me – I remembered singing at weddings as a teenager, remembered church solos . . . remembered what my life once was. But I'd gotten past that. I began humming.

Though it wasn't my regular cleaning day, from habit I walked through the whole house, as I always did when I came in. Upstairs, Bobo's room was picked up and the bedspread was actually pulled straight. No such epiphany had inspired Amber Jean and Howell Three, but then they'd never been as sloppy as Bobo. The two upstairs bathrooms were more or less straight. Downstairs, Beanie always made the king-size bed in the huge master bedroom, and she was meticulous about hanging up her clothes because she had paid a lot for them. Beanie's family had a great regard for money.

I began singing 'The First Time Ever I Saw Your Face' as I went to the 'cleaning stuff' closet in the kitchen to select what I'd need: dust cloths, the vacuum cleaner, glass cleaner and rags, shoe polish.

Twice a year, for extra pay of course, I performed this odd little service for Beanie. I took everything out of her huge walk-in closet, every single thing. Then I cleaned the closet, reorganized her clothes, and checked to make sure all her shoes were polished and ready to wear. Any clothes that needed mending or were missing buttons I put to one side for Beanie's attention, or rather her seamstress's.

I had sung my way to the end of the ballad when I took all my cleaning paraphernalia into the big dark bedroom – Beanie kept the drapes drawn – and dumped it on the floor to one side of Beanie's closet. I opened the mirrored door and reached inside to switch on the light.

Someone grabbed my wrist and yanked me in.

I fought immediately, because Marshall had taught me not to hesitate; if you hesitate, if you falter, you've already lost psychological ground. In fact, I almost went crazy and lost all my training, but hung on by a little rag of intelligence. I formed a good fist and hit with my free left hand, striking for anything I could hit. I couldn't place my assailant exactly, had no idea who had grabbed me.

My blows made contact with flesh, I thought a cheek. He grunted but didn't lessen his formidable grip on my right wrist, and it was only with an effort that I kept the left hand free. I knew it was a man from the sound of the grunt, so I went for his balls, but he twisted to one side and evaded my fingers. He'd been wanting to catch that free hand, and this he finally did; bad news for me. I tried breaking loose by stepping into him and bringing my hands, palms up, against his thumbs, the same move that had worked against Bobo; once I was free, I would slap him over the ears or gouge his eyes, I wasn't particular, I would kill him or hurt him however I could.

The move didn't work because he'd been expecting it. His hands slid down from my wrists to hold me right below the elbows. I slammed my head forward to break his nose but got his chest instead. As I threw my head back up I heard his teeth click together, so I'd clipped his chin, but that wasn't enough to effect any major damage. I tried for the groin again with my knee and this time managed to make some contact because I got the grunt again. Elated, I tried to bring him down by hooking my leg between his legs and kicking the back of his knee. This was incredibly stupid on my part, because I succeeded. I brought him down right on top of me.

He pinned me to the floor with his body, his strong hands gripping my arms to my sides, his legs weighting mine. I lost my mind. I bit him on the ear.

'Goddamn! Stop it!' He never lessened his grip, which was what I was working for, but brought his forehead down on mine, using my own trick against me. He hadn't used full force, not by a long shot, but I gasped with pain and felt tears form in my eyes.

He moved his head down to my ear, so his cheek was against mine, an oddly intimate contact. I heaved and bucked against him, but I could feel the weakness in my movements. 'Listen,' he hissed. And then as I opened my mouth to scream, hoping to throw him off guard for a second, he said the one thing that could have achieved a truce.

'They're breaking in,' he whispered. 'For God's sake, just shut up and be still. They'll kill us both.'

I know how to shut up and I know how to be still, though I couldn't stop quivering. My eyes finally adjusted to the near-darkness of the closet, and by the faint light coming in through the partly open door, I saw that the man on top of me was Mr Black Ponytail.

After a second, I wasn't too surprised.

Those eyes were not focused on me, but staring out the closet door as the man listened to the faint sounds that were just now penetrating my tangled state of fear and rage.

He bent back so his mouth was by my ear, his newly shaven cheek again resting against mine. 'It's gonna take them a while. They don't know shit about breaking and entering,' he said in a voice so low it seemed to come from somewhere inside my own head. 'Now, who the fuck are you?'

Through clenched teeth I said, 'I am the fucking *maid*.' Every muscle in my body was tensed, and the shivering would not stop no matter how I willed myself to be still.

I began to make myself relax, knowing that if I didn't, I would remain weak and disadvantaged.

'That's better. We're on the same side,' whispered the man as he felt my body soften and still beneath him.

'Who are you?' I asked him.

'I,' he told my ear, 'am the fucking *detective*.' He shifted on top of me. He wasn't as calm or cool as he was trying to sound. His body was reacting to its proximity with mine, and he was getting uncomfortable. 'If I let you go, are you gonna give me any trouble? They're much more dangerous than I am.'

I thought about it. I had no idea if he really was a detective. And whose detective? FBI? Private? ATF? The Shakespeare police force? Winthrop County?

I heard glass shattering.

'They're in,' he breathed into my ear. 'Listen, the game plan has changed.'

'Huh,' I said contemptuously and almost inaudibly. I hated sports metaphors. I felt much better almost immediately. Angry is better than scared or confused.

'They'll kill us if we're caught,' he told me again. His lips, so close to my ear, suddenly made me want to shiver again in a completely different way. His body was talking to mine at great length, no matter what his mouth was saying.

'Now, what I want you to do, when they're all in the house,' he whispered breathlessly, 'is start screaming. I'm going out the front door, circling around to the alley to get their license plate number, identify the car, so I can try to find where they go after this.'

I wondered what his original plan had been. This one seemed awful haphazard. His hands, instead of gripping my arms, were rubbing them slowly.

'They'll know it was me and come after me.'

'If you're never in their sight, they won't believe you saw them,' he breathed. 'Give me three minutes, then scream.'

'No,' I said very softly. 'I'll turn on the vacuum cleaner.'

I sensed a certain amount of exasperation rolling off Mr Ponytail. 'OK,' he agreed. 'Whatever.'

Then he slid off me, and rose to his feet. He held out his hand and I took it without thinking. He pulled me up as easily as he'd helped me do chin-ups that morning. He gave me a sharp nod to indicate the clock was running, and then he was gone, easing himself out of the closet, through Beanie's bedroom, and presumably down the little hall that led to the foyer of the house. His exit was much more subtle than the burglars' entrance.

I peered at my big-faced man's watch, actually timing the self-proclaimed detective, trying not to wonder why I was doing what he said. At two and a half minutes, I risked stepping out of the closet. I could hear the intruders clearly now. Once they'd gotten into the house, they'd abandoned all attempts at silence.

After plugging in the vacuum cleaner, I suddenly began belting out 'Whistle While You Work'. Without waiting to assess the reaction, I stepped on the 'On' button and the vacuum cleaner roared to life. I was careful to keep my back to the bedroom door as I began industriously vacuuming, because I could see in Beanie's dressing table mirror if I was being stalked. I caught a shadow swooping across the mirror, but its owner was in the act of departure. I'd spooked them.

When I felt sure they were gone, I turned off the vacuum cleaner. Watchfully, I once again toured the Winthrop house. One of the sliding glass doors leading to the pool area was broken. Looking across the covered pool, I saw one of the wooden gates standing ajar. The Winthrops needed a full-fledged security system, I thought severely. Then I realized I would have to clean up all the glass, and I found myself irrationally peeved.

Also, I had to call the police.

There was no way around it.

Should I tell them about Black Ponytail? If it weren't for Claude, I'd lie in a jiffy. All my contacts with the police had been painful. But I trusted Claude. I should tell him the truth. But what could I tell him?

I was fairly sure Howell Jr. must have admitted Black Ponytail to the house or given him the keys. My doubts about their relationship recurred. But no matter what that relationship was, it seemed to me I'd be violating whatever loyalty I was supposed to have to the Winthrop family if I told the police Black Ponytail had been already concealed in the house, anticipating this very break-in.

This was knotty.

I called the police station and reported the break-in, and had a few moments to think hard.

The safest thing was a straight break-in. I don't know nothin', boss.

It helped immensely that Claude didn't come. Dedford Jinks, the detective who'd so frightened Bobo, and two patrolmen responded to my call. Claude was in a meeting with the county judge and the mayor and had not been told about the incident, I gathered from listening to the patrolmen.

Dedford was a good ole guy with a beer gut hanging over a worn belt buckle he'd won in his calf-roping days. He had thin graying hair, a thin compressed mouth, and a ruddy complexion. Dedford was nobody's fool.

My story was this: I'd heard little noises, but thought that a member of the family had come in. From then on, I told the truth: I'd plugged in the vacuum and turned it on, I'd heard a big commotion, I hadn't seen anyone.

After they'd checked out the backyard and found a gate unlocked, and many footprints in the flower beds, the police said I could go.

'I have to clean up,' I said, gesturing to the glass on the Winthrops' thick hunter-green carpet. They'd gathered up the biggest pieces for fingerprint testing, but there were lots of fragments.

'Oh,' said one of the patrolmen, disconcerted. 'Well, OK.'

Then Howell burst into the house, moving faster than I'd ever seen him move. His face was red.

'My God, Lily, are you all right?' He actually took one of my hands and held it. I reclaimed it. This was strange. I could feel the policemen looking at each other.

'Yes, Howell, I'm fine.'

'They didn't hurt you?'

I gestured wide with my hands to draw his notice to my uninjured body.

'But the bruise on your forehead?'

I touched my face carefully. Sure enough, my forehead was tender and puffy. Thanks, Mr Ponytail. I hoped his ear hurt.

'I guess I ran into the doorframe,' I said. 'I got pretty excited.'

'Well, sure. But one of the men didn't . . .'

'No.'

'I had no idea you were going to be here today,' Howell said, taking his snowy white handkerchief out of his pocket and patting his face with it. 'I am so glad you weren't harmed.'

'I came to do your wife's closet. It's just a twice-a-year thing,' I explained. For me, I was talking too much. I hoped no one would notice. I was rattled. I knew now that Howell was directly involved in this day's peculiar doings. At least it was Howell who had let Ponytail in, so he had been here legitimately. I guessed Howell was now wondering where the hell his man was and what part he'd played in this fiasco.

'I'll just clean up this mess and go,' I suggested again.

'No, no, you need to go home after this,' Howell exclaimed, his handsome, fleshy face creased with anxiety. 'I'll be glad to clean it up.'

Definite glances between all police personnel within earshot. Shit.

'But I'd like to . . .' I let my sentence trail off as Dedford raised an eyebrow in my direction. If I insisted longer, so would Howell, drawing more attention to his unusual preoccupation with my condition. He was obviously guilt-stricken. If he kept this up, everyone present would figure something strange was going on, and they might think it was more than Howell having an affair with his maid, which was bad enough.

'Where's your car?' Howell asked suddenly.

'It wouldn't start this morning,' I said wearily, by now tired of explaining myself. 'I walked.'

'Oh my God, all that way! I'm sure one of these boys will be glad to give you a ride home!'

One of the 'boys', the older paunchier one with a dis-believing mouth, said he sure would be glad to do that.

So I got delivered to my house in style. My car was still in my carport, but with a sheet of yellow legal paper stuck under the windshield. It read, *'I fixed it. You owe me $68.23.'* It was a lot more direct and honest than the blue sheets that were suddenly papering the town. I turned to the patrolman, who was waiting to see me enter my house safely. 'Do you know anything about those flyers that are turning up under everyone's windshield wipers?'

'I know they ain't no ordinance against it,' he replied, and his face closed like a fist. 'Likewise they ain't no ordinance against the blacks meeting to talk about it, which they aim to do tonight.'

'Where?'

'The meeting? At the Golgotha A.M.E. Church on Castle Road. We got to maintain a presence, case there's any trouble.'

'That's good,' I said, and after thanking the man for giving me a ride home (and being willing to part with information without asking any questions) I sat in my recliner and thought.

Chapter Five

I don't know what I expected of the rest of the day. I think I expected the man in the closet to pop up any minute; to tell me what had happened when he left, to ask me if he'd hurt me in our struggle, to explain himself.

After seeing him everywhere I turned, now he was nowhere. I passed through being worried, to being angry, and back through worried. I made my feelings cool down, concentrated on chilling them; I told myself the fear and rage engendered by our silent struggle in Beanie Winthrop's walk-in closet – what a location – had nudged me past some internal boundary marker.

Out of sheer restlessness, that night I attended the meeting at Golgotha A.M.E. Church. I found it with a little difficulty since it was in the center of the largest black residential area in Shakespeare, which I seldom had reason to visit. The church itself, redbrick and larger than I expected, was set up on a knoll, with cracked concrete steps bordered by a handrail leading up to the main doors. It was on a corner lot, and there was a big streetlight shining down those steps. Golgotha was so centrally located that I saw many people walking to the meeting despite the gusty cold wind.

I also saw two police cars on the way there. One was driven by Todd Picard, who gave me an unhappy nod. It was easy to tell that every time he saw me, I reminded him of something he wanted to forget. I felt the same way about him.

I went up the steps of the church at a fast clip, anxious to get out of the wind. It seemed to me I'd been cold all day. There were double doors at the top of the steps, and inside those, a large foyer with two coatracks, a table spread with lots of free literature on Planned Parenthood and Alcoholics Anonymous and the practice of daily prayer, and the doors to two rooms, one on each side, that I guessed were vesting rooms or perhaps served for choir practice. Ahead, there were two sets of doors into the body of the church. I picked the right set of doors and followed the flow of people into the sanctuary. There was a long center set of pews and a shorter set on each side, with wide aisles in between, the same conformation I'd seen in many churches. I picked a long central pew at random, and scooted toward the center to give later arrivals easy access.

The meeting was scheduled to begin at seven, and surprisingly enough it did. The high attendance on a cold school night was a measure of how strong feeling was running in the African-American community. Mine was not the only white face in view. The Catholic sisters who ran a preschool for disadvantaged children were seated some distance away, and Claude was there: a good public relations move, I thought. He gave me a curt nod. Sheriff Marty Schuster was sitting beside Claude on the dais. To my surprise, he was a small wizened man you would've thought couldn't arrest a possum. But his appearance was deceiving; I'd heard more than once that Sheriff Schuster had cracked his share of skulls. Schuster's secret, Jim Box had told me one morning, was to always strike first and hardest.

Claude and Marty Schuster shared the platform with a man I supposed was the church's pastor, a short, square man with great dignity and angry eyes. He was holding a Bible.

Another light face caught my eye. Mookie Preston was there, too, sitting by herself. When Lanette Glass came in, the two women exchanged a long look before Lanette sat by another teacher.

I saw Cedric, my mechanic, and Raphael Roundtree, who was sitting with his wife. Cedric gave me a surprised smile and wave, but Raphael's greeting was subdued. His wife just stared.

The meeting went like many community meetings with an ill-defined goal. It opened with a prayer so fervent that I half expected God to touch everyone's heart with love and understanding on the spot. If He did, the results were not immediate. Everyone had something to say, and wanted to say it simultaneously. They were all angry about the blue pieces of paper, and wanted to know what the chief of police and the sheriff were doing about them. At tedious length, the lawmen explained that they couldn't do anything about them; the handouts were not obscene, did not contain a clear and overt incitement to violence. Of course, this was not a satisfactory response to most of the people in the church.

At least three people were trying to speak when Lanette Glass stood up. There was silence, gradually; a deep silence.

'My son is dead,' Lanette said. Her glasses caught the harsh fluorescent light and winked. Darnell's mother was probably still in her forties, with a pleasant round figure and a pretty round face. She was wearing a brown, cream, and black pantsuit. She looked very sad, very angry.

'You may talk about "we don't know this" and "we can't

guess that," but we all know good and well that Darnell was murdered by the same men that are passing around this paper.'

'We can't know that, Mrs Glass,' Marty Schuster said helplessly. 'I sympathize with your grief, and your son's is one of the three homicides the city and county police are working on – believe me, we're working on it, we want to find out what happened to your son – but we can't go haring off and accuse people who don't even have an identity.'

'I can,' she said unanswerably. 'I can also say what everyone here is thinking, blacks and probably whites, too: that if Darnell hadn't been killed, Len Elgin would not have died, and maybe Del Packard, too. And I want to know what we, the black community, are supposed to do about these rumors of armed militia in our town, armed white men who hate us.'

I awaited a reply with interest. An armed militia? The problem was, just about every white man – and black – in town was already armed. Guns were not exactly scarce in this area, where lots of citizens felt you were wise to carry a weapon if you traveled to Little Rock. You could buy arms at Winthrop Sporting Goods, if you wanted a top-of-the-line piece. You could buy a gun at Wal-Mart, or at the pawn-shop, or just about anywhere in Shakespeare. So the 'armed' part wasn't exactly a shocker, but the 'militia' part was.

I wasn't too surprised when Claude and Marty Schuster protested ignorance of any knowledge of an armed militia in our fair city.

The meeting was effectively over, but no one wanted to admit it. Everyone had had his or her say, and no solution had been reached, because a solution to this problem was simply unreachable. A few die-hards were still trying to get the lawmen to make some kind of statement committing the law to eradicating the group apparently inciting white Shakespeareans to some kind of action against dark Shakespeareans, but Marty and Claude refused to be pinned.

People rose and began to shuffle toward the two exits: I saw Marty Schuster, Claude, and the minister go toward the aisle on my left. I stood admiring the carved pulpit, at the end of the aisle to the right, before I stepped into the aisle. I had zipped up my coat and was pulling on my black leather gloves when I felt a hand on my arm. I turned to meet the magnified eyes of Lanette Glass.

'Thank you for helping my son,' she said. She looked at me unwaveringly, but her eyes suddenly swam in tears.

'I wasn't able to help when it counted,' I said.

'You can't blame yourself,' she said gently. 'You can't count the times I've cried since he died, thinking I could somehow have warned him, somehow rescued him. I could have gone out for milk myself, instead of asking him to run to the store. That was when they got him, you know, in the parking lot . . . at least that was where his car was found.'

His new car, still with its crumpled fender.

'But you, you fought for him,' Lanette said quietly. 'You bled for him.'

'Don't make me better than I am,' I said flatly. 'You're a brave woman, Mrs Glass.'

'Don't you make me any better than I am,' Lanette Glass said quietly. 'I thanked the black Marine the day after the fight. I never thanked you until tonight.'

I looked down at the floor, at my hands, at anything but

Lanette Glass's large brown eyes; and when I looked up, she had gone.

The crowd continued to exit slowly. People were talking, shaking their heads, pulling on their own coats and scarves and gloves. I moved along with them, thinking my own thoughts. I pushed up my sleeve to check my watch: It was 8:15. Through the open doors ahead of me, I could see that the crowd was thick in the church's foyer. People were hesitating before stepping out into the cold. There were about three people between me and the sanctuary doors, and there were at least six people behind me.

The stout woman on my left turned to me to say something. I never found out what it was. The bomb went off.

I can't remember if I knew what had happened right away or not. When I try, my head hurts. But I must have turned. Somehow I had a sense of the pulpit disintegrating.

I was pushed from behind by a powerful wind and I saw the head of the woman beside me separate from her body as a collection plate clove through her neck. I was sprayed with her blood as her body crumpled and her head and I went flying forward. My thick coat and scarf helped absorb some pressure. So did the bodies of the people behind me. The wooden pews also blocked some of the blast, but they splintered, of course, and those splinters were deadly . . . some of them were as big as spears, just as lethal.

The roar deafened me and in silence I flew through the air. All this happened at the same time, too much to catalog . . . the woman's head flew with me, we flew together into kingdom come.

I was lying halfway on my right side, on something lumpy. Something else was lying on me. I was soaking wet. There were cold winds blowing in the church, and flames were flickering here and there. I was in hell. I watched the flames and wondered why I was so cold. Then I realized if I turned my head a little, I could see the stars, though I was in a building. This was remarkable; I should tell someone. The lights were out, but I could see a little. I could smell smoke, too, and the sharp smell of blood, and even worse things. And there was a heavy chemical smell overlaying everything, an odor that was completely new to me.

My situation isn't good, I thought. I need to move. I want to go home. Take a shower.

I tried to sit up. I couldn't hear a thing. That made my state even more surrealistic. With some senses so drenched with input and others totally deprived, it was easy to convince myself I was in a nightmare. I lost my place for a few minutes, I think. Then I reoriented, after a fashion. Someone was near me, I could tell, I could feel movement but not hear it. I turned painfully onto my back, put my hands on whatever was lying on my chest, and shoved. It moved. I tried to sit up, fell back. That hurt. A face appeared through the gloom in front of me. It was the face of Lanette Glass. She was talking, I could tell, because her mouth was moving.

At last she seemed to realize that she wasn't getting through. She moved her lips slowly. I decided she was saying, 'Where – is – Mookie?'

I remembered who Mookie was, and I remembered seeing her earlier. She had been on the other side of the church – that was where I was, in the Golgotha A.M.E. Church – and I'd glanced across at Mookie as she'd passed from the sanctuary into the foyer.

'Can you hear me?' I asked Lanette. I couldn't hear

myself. It was overwhelmingly strange. I thought of going to the dentist, not being able to feel your own lips after he filled a tooth. I went off course, for a minute. Lanette shook me. She was nodding frantically. It took me another moment to realize she was letting me know she could hear me. That was great! I smiled. 'Mookie is on the other side of the church,' I said. 'In the foyer.'

Lanette vanished.

I wondered if I could stand up and go to a warm place and shower. I tried to roll onto my knees; I pushed against the thing underneath me, to flip from my back to my stomach. When I'd gotten that done, I saw the lump underneath me was the body of a girl, about ten or twelve years old. Her hair was elaborately decorated with beads. There was a sharp splinter protruding from her neck. Her eyes were blank. I closed my mind to that. I pulled up on a bench upended and aslant, propped against another bench. I wondered at the multitude of benches. Then I thought, church. Pews.

I stood erect. Everything swung around me, and I had to hold on to the back of the pew, actually a leg, since it was upside down. I suspected that all the flashing I could see meant I was losing my vision; but it was blue flashing. I was looking through the sanctuary doors to the foyer, through the foyer door to the outside; all the doors were open. No. The doors weren't there anymore. Maybe I was seeing police cars? Surely, in an emergency like this, they would help?

I wondered how I might get out of this place. Though the electricity had gone out, there was that big streetlight right outside, and its light was coming through the holes in the roof. There were flames in several spots around me, though I couldn't hear them crackle.

I remembered I was strong. I remembered I should be helping. Well, there was no helping the girl beneath me. I had helped Lanette by telling her where Mookie had been the last time I'd seen her. And look at what happened. Lanette had left. Maybe I should just fend for myself, huh?

But then I thought of Claude. I should find him and help him. It seemed to me it was my turn.

I took a shuffling step, now that I had a purpose. My left leg hurt very badly, but that was hardly a big surprise. Didn't make it hurt any the less, though. I looked down unwillingly, and saw there was a cut in my leg, a very long slicing cut down the side of my thigh. I was terrified I'd see another splinter protruding, but I didn't. I was bleeding, though. Understatement.

I took another step, over something I didn't want to identify. I could feel my throat moving and I knew I was making sounds, though I couldn't hear them, which was fine. They were better unheard. The beams of the streetlight that came through the roof had a surrealistic air because of the dust, which swam and floated in their light.

I stepped carefully through debris where there had been order just minutes before; the dead and dying and terribly injured where there had been whole clean living people. My leg collapsed once. I got back up. I could see other people moving. One man had gotten to his knees as I neared him. I held out my hand. He looked at it as if he'd never seen a hand. His eyes followed the line of my arm up to my face. He flinched when he looked at me. I figured I looked pretty bad. He didn't look so great himself. He was covered with dust, and he had blood flowing from a deep cut in his arm.

He'd lost the sleeve of his coat. He took my hand. I pulled. He came up. I nodded to him and went on.

I found Claude in the far aisle of the church, where I'd last seen him talking to the sheriff and the minister. I'd been closer to the bomb on the east side of the church, but the sheriff and the minister were dead. One of the big bar-shaped lighting fixtures had fallen from the ceiling and hit them square. They'd been much the same height. Claude must have been a step ahead of them. His legs were under the long heavy bar and he was lying on his stomach. His hands and arms and the back of his head were covered with white powder and debris and dark red blood. He was motionless.

I touched his neck, couldn't remember why I was doing that, and began to push the long lighting fixture that was pinning his legs. It was very heavy. I was in terrible pain, and wanted desperately to lie down. But I felt there was something wrong about that, something bad, and I had to keep on pushing and pulling at the light fixture.

I finally got it off Claude's legs. He was stirring, heaving up on his arms. I made a connection in my mind between the flashing blue light and Claude. I saw a group of lights swinging around catching millions of dust motes, thought it was in my head. But I gradually worked out that these were flashlights in the hands of rescuers.

It seemed to me they would want to move the most seriously injured first; at the same time, I had to admit, I really wanted to go home and shower. Maybe an ambulance would drop me off at home. I was sure sticky and smelly, and I was so sleepy. Maybe Claude and I could drive together, since we lived side by side. I knelt down by him and leaned over to look in his face. He was in agony, his eyes wide. When he saw me, his lips began moving. I smiled at him and shook my head, to show I couldn't hear. His lips drew back from his teeth, and I knew that Claude was screaming.

Oh, I had to get up again, I realized wearily. I made it, but I was pretty sick of trying to walk. I shuffled a few steps, saw an upright figure ahead of me in the uncertain gloom. He swung around, and my eyes dazzled in the sudden blast of the flashlight. It was Todd Picard, and he was talking to me.

'I can't hear,' I said. He ran the flashlight up and down my length, and when I could see his face in its glow again, he looked sick.

'I know where Claude is,' I said. 'You need him, right?'

He illuminated himself with the flash. 'Where – is – he?' Todd mouthed. I took his free hand and pulled, and he followed me.

I pointed down at Claude.

Todd turned in another direction, and I could see his hand go up to his mouth, his lips moving; he was screaming for help. Claude was still alive; his fingers were moving. I bent down to pat him reassuringly, and I just fell over. I didn't get back up.

I don't remember being loaded onto the stretcher, but I do remember the jolt of being carried. I remember the brilliance of the lights of the emergency room. I remember Carrie, all in white, looking so clean and calm, and I remember her trying to ask me questions. I kept shaking my head, I couldn't hear anything.

'Deaf,' I said finally, and her lips stopped moving. People were busy around me; there was near-chaos in the hospital corridor. Since I wasn't the most seriously injured, I had to wait my turn, and that was fine, except I couldn't have any pain medication until Carrie had looked me over.

I blanked in and out, waking to see people moving up and down the hall, gurneys rolling past, all the doctors in town and most all the medical personnel of any kind.

And then, very oddly, I felt fingers on my wrist. Someone was taking my pulse, and while that was not so extraordinary, I knew I had to open my eyes. With an effort, I did. The detective was bending over me. He was so clean.

I could not hear much, I found, but I could hear a little, and I could lip-read.

'Is your head hurt?' he asked.

'I don't know,' I said slowly, every word an effort. 'My leg is.'

He looked down. 'They'll have to stitch it up,' he told me, and he looked very angry. 'Who can I call for you? Someone should be here with you.'

'No one,' I said. It was an effort to talk.

'There's blood all over your face.'

'The woman next to me was . . .' I couldn't think of *decapitated.* 'Her head came off,' I said, and closed my eyes again.

When I opened them some time later, he was gone.

I hardly woke up when Carrie stitched on me, and it was a surprise to find myself in the X-ray room. Other than these travels, I was out in the hall all night, which was fine. All the rooms were filled with the more seriously injured. And I could tell by the constant flow of ambulance personnel that some people were being sent to Montrose or Little Rock. Carrie came by and shook me awake every so often to check my eyes, and the nurses took my pulse and blood pressure, and I wanted most of all to be left alone. Hospitals are not places for being left alone.

The next time I opened my eyes, it was daylight. I could see a pale watery morning through the glass doors of the emergency room. A man in a suit was standing by my gurney. He was looking down at me. He, too, was looking a little squeamish. I was really tired of people looking at me that way.

'How do you feel, Miss Bard?' he asked, and I could hear him, though his voice was oddly beelike.

'I don't know. I don't know what happened to me.'

'A bomb went off,' he said. 'In Golgotha Church.'

'Right.' I accepted that as the truth, but it was the first time I had thought of the word *bomb*. Bomb, man-made. Someone had actually done that on purpose.

'I'm John Bellingham. I'm with the FBI.' He showed me some identification, but my brain was too scrambled for it to make sense.

I absorbed that, trying to make sense of it. I thought that since Claude and the sheriff were down, the FBI had been called in to keep the peace. Then I cleared up a little. Church bombing. Civil rights. FBI.

'OK.'

'Can you describe what happened last night?'

'The church blew up as we were leaving.'

'Why did you attend the meeting, Miss Bard?'

'I didn't like the blue sheets.'

He looked at me as if I were insane.

'Blue sheets . . .'

'The papers,' I said, beginning to be angry. 'The blue sheets of paper they were putting under everyone's windshield wipers.'

'Are you a civil rights activist, Miss Bard?'

'No.'

'You have friends in the black community?'

I wondered if Raphael would consider himself my friend. I decided, yes.

'Raphael Roundtree,' I said carefully.

He seemed to be writing that down.

'Can you find out if he's okay?' I asked. 'And Claude, is Claude alive?'

'Claude . . .'

'The police chief,' I said. I couldn't remember Claude's last name, and that made me feel very odd.

'Yes, he's alive. Can you describe in your own words what happened in the church?'

I said slowly, 'The meeting went long. I looked at my watch. It was eight-fifteen when I was leaving, walking down the aisle.'

He definitely wrote that down.

'Do you still have your watch on?' he asked.

'You can look and see,' I said indifferently. I didn't want to move. He pulled the sheet down and looked at my arm.

'It's here,' he said. He pulled out his handkerchief, wet it with his tongue, and scrubbed at my wrist. I realized he was cleaning the watch face. 'Sorry,' he apologized, and when he pocketed the handkerchief again I could see it was stained.

He bent over me, trying to read the watch without shifting me.

'Hey, it's still ticking along,' he said cheerfully. He checked it against his own watch. 'And right on time. So, it was eight-fifteen, and you were leaving . . . ?'

'The woman next to me was about to say something,' I said. 'And then her head wasn't there.'

He looked serious and subdued, but he had no idea what it had been like: though when I thought about it, I had little idea myself. I could not remember exactly . . . I could see the shiny edge of the collection plate. So I told John Bellingham about the collection plate. I recalled Lanette Glass speaking to me, and I mentioned that, and I remembered helping the man up, and I knew I'd journeyed across the church to find Claude. But I refused to recall what I'd seen on that journey, and to this day I do not want to remember.

I told John Bellingham about finding Claude, about leading Todd to him.

'Was it you that moved the fixture off his legs?' the agent asked.

'I believe so,' I said slowly.

'You're one strong lady.' He asked me more questions, lots more, about whom I'd seen, white people in particular of course, and where I'd been sitting . . . ta da ta da ta da.

'Find out about Claude,' I told him, wearying of the conversation.

Instead, he sent me Carrie.

She was so tired her face had a gray cast. Her white coat was filthy now, and her glasses smeared with fingerprints. I was glad to see her.

'You have a long cut on your leg. Some stitches and some butterfly bandages are holding it together. You have a slight concussion. You have bruising all across your back, including your butt. A splinter evidently grazed your scalp, one reason you looked so horrendous when they brought you in, and another splinter took off a little of your earlobe. You won't miss it. You have dozens of abrasions, none of them serious, all of them painful. I can't believe it, but you have no broken bones. How's your hearing?'

'Everything sounds buzzy,' I said with an effort.

'Yeah, I can imagine. It'll get better.'

'So I can go home?'

'As soon as we're sure about the concussion. Probably in a few hours.'

'Are you gonna charge me for a room since I was out in the hall all night?'

Carrie laughed. 'Nope.'

'Good. You know I don't have much insurance.'

'Yeah.'

Carrie had arranged for me to be in the hall. I felt a surge of gratitude. 'What about Claude?' I asked.

Her face grew more serious. 'He's got a badly broken leg, broken in two places,' she began. 'Like you, he has a concussion, and he's temporarily deaf. He has a serious cut on one arm, and his kidneys are bruised.'

'He's going to be okay?'

'Yes,' she said, 'but it's going to take a long time.'

'Did you treat my friend Raphael Roundtree, by chance?'

'Nope, or I did but I don't remember the name, which is entirely possible.' Carrie yawned, and I could tell how exhausted she was. 'But I'll look for him.'

'Thanks.'

A nurse came a few minutes later to tell me Raphael had been treated and released the night before.

A few hours later, a hospital volunteer gave me a ride back to my car, still parked a couple of blocks away from the ruin of Golgotha Church. She was civil enough, but I could tell she thought I'd mostly deserved what happened to me because I'd gone to a meeting in a black church. I was not surprised at her attitude, and I didn't care a whole lot. My coat was in a wastebasket at the hospital because the back of it was shredded, and the hospital gave me a huge ancient jacket of sweatsuit material, with a hood, which I was grateful to wrap around me. I knew I looked pretty disreputable. Bits of my shoes were missing and my blue jeans had been cut off to treat my leg. I was wearing even older sweatpants.

The wound was in my left leg, which was fortunate, because it meant I could drive. It was painful to walk – hell, it was painful to move – and I wanted to be home locked inside my own place so bad that I could just barely endure the process of getting there.

I parked my car in my own carport and unlocked my own kitchen door with a relief so great I could almost taste it. My bed was waiting for me, with clean sheets and firm pillows and no one shaking me awake to check my pupils, but I could not get into it as filthy as I was.

When I looked into my bathroom mirror, I was amazed that anyone had been able to endure looking at me. Though I'd been swabbed at some, the hospital had been so flooded with injuries that cleaning up the victims had had low priority. I had speckles of blood all over my face and clotting my hair, my neck had a dried river where my ear had bled, my shirt and bra were splotched in blood and smelled to high heaven of all kinds of things, and my shoes would have to go. It took a long long time to get all this off me. I threw the remains of my clothes and shoes into a plastic bag, set it outside the kitchen door, and hobbled laboriously to the bathroom to sponge myself. It was impossible to get in the bathtub, and my stitches were supposed to be kept dry, too.

I stood on a towel by my sink, and soaped with one washrag and rinsed with another, until I looked and smelled more like my own self. I even did that to my hair; all I can say of my hair after that is that it was clean. I dabbed more antiseptic ointment on the scalp wound. I threw away the earring still in my right ear – the left earring had been removed in the hospital when they'd treated my ear, and I had no idea where it was and cared less. I did look at my left ear to make sure I could still wear a pair of pierced earrings. I could, but I needed to grow my hair longer to cover the place about midway down the edge of my earlobe where there was, and would always be, a notch.

Finally – barely able to walk, full of medicine, and still oddly numb emotionally – I was able to lower myself into my bed. I flipped the volume of the telephone ring to its lowest setting, but left it on the hook. I didn't want anyone breaking in to see if I'd died. Then I lay back very very carefully and let the darkness come.

I had to miss two and a half days of work, and I had Sunday as a free day anyway. I should have stayed home Monday (and maybe Tuesday), too, but I knew I had to pay the hospital for the emergency room visit, and Carrie for treatment. I always cleaned for Carrie to pay her, but I didn't want my debt to mount too high.

That Monday, it was much easier to clean for the clients who weren't present when I got to work. Otherwise, they tried to send me home.

Bobo had come by the evening of the day I went home.

'How'd you find out?' I asked.

'That new guy said you might need some help.'

I was too exhausted to ask questions, and I was too depressed to care.

Bobo came every day after that, too. He brought in my mail and my paper, and made me sandwiches so thick they were almost impossible to chew. Carrie ran by one evening, but I felt guilty because she looked so tired. The hospital was still full.

'How many dead?' I asked, lying back in my recliner.

She was in the blue wing-back chair. 'So far, five,' she said. 'If it had gone off five minutes later, there would maybe have been no fatalities and few injuries. Five minutes earlier, and the death toll would have been very high.'

'Who died?' I asked.

Carrie fetched the local paper and read me the names. I hadn't personally known any of them, and I was glad of that.

I asked about Claude, and she told me he was better. But she didn't sound comfortable about his progress. 'And I'm worried about him going home by himself, anyway. He lives upstairs.'

'Move all his stuff to the empty downstairs apartment,' I said wearily. 'They're just alike. Tell all the officers they have to show up and help. Don't ask Claude if that's what he wants. Just get it done.'

Carrie looked at me with some amazement. 'All right,' she said slowly.

Carrie had suggested I use a cane for a few days until the swelling and pain in my leg subsided, and I was glad to have the one she loaned me. Marshall came the same evening after she'd left, and he was horrified to see me hobble. He brought three movies he'd taped off HBO for me to watch, and a take-out meal from a local restaurant. I was glad for both. Thinking and standing were not things I wanted to do. When Marshall left, I noticed that he walked next door to the apartments. I figured he was going to see Becca Whitley. I didn't care.

To my amazement, Janet Shook dropped by about lunchtime on Sunday. I'd never seen Janet in a dress before, but she'd been to church and was all decked out in a deep blue dress that looked very nice. She had made me a pot of stew and a loaf of bread, and while she was there she helped me shave my legs and wash my hair properly, two problems that had been bothering me to the point of distraction.

When I went back to work Monday, I can't say I did a good job, but I did my best: That would have to do. I would do extra things, I promised myself, to atone for leaving some chores not well accomplished this time.

I tried all day to save some energy, and at the end of it I drove to the hospital. I was really hurting by then, but I knew if I went home first and took a pain pill I wouldn't persuade myself to go back out. I was looking forward to taking the strongest ones, the ones Carrie had said to take if I knew I wasn't going anywhere.

I had some flowers in a bud vase in my right hand, and my cane in my left, so I was glad the doors were automatic. I made my way to Claude's room, resting here and there. I couldn't knock with both hands occupied, so I called out through the partially open door, 'Claude? Can I come in?'

'Lily? Sure.' At least he seemed to be hearing better.

I butted the door open with my head and hobbled in.

'Damn, girl, I better move over and let you in with me,' he said wearily.

I was shocked when I had a good look at Claude. His face was not its normal healthy color, and his hair was spiky. He was shaven, at least. His right leg and his right arm were engulfed in bandages and casts. He had visibly lost weight.

To my horror, I felt tears crawling down my cheeks.

'Didn't know I looked that bad,' Claude murmured.

'I just thought . . . when I saw you that night . . . I thought you were gone.'

'I hear you did me a favor.'

'You've done plenty for me.'

'Let's call us even, then. No more rescuing each other.'

'Sounds good.'

I sank into the chair by the bed. I felt like hell.

Carrie trotted in then, moving fast as always, her professional face on.

'Two-for-one visit,' she remarked. 'I just came to check in on you, Claude, before I leave for the day.'

Claude smiled at her. Carrie suddenly looked more like a woman than a doctor. I felt extra.

'I ain't feeling as bad as yesterday,' Claude rumbled. 'You get on out of here and get some rest, or you'll end up looking as ragged as Lily. And she hasn't been at work all day.'

'Yes, I have.'

They both looked at me like I was the biggest fool they'd ever encountered. I could feel my face hardening defensively.

'Lily, you'll end up back in bed if you don't rest,' Carrie said, keeping her voice even though it obviously cost her a great deal of self-control.

'I've got to go,' I said, hauling myself up with an effort I didn't want to show. I had counted on sitting longer before I walked back out to my car.

I hobbled out, trying not to limp, failing, getting angry and sad.

For the first time in years, as I stood at the front doors of the hospital and looked at how far away my car was parked, I wanted someone to make my life easier. I had even thought of calling my parents and asking for help, but I hadn't asked them for anything for so long that I'd gotten out of the habit. They would have come, I knew. But they'd have had to book a room at the motel on the bypass, they'd have looked at everything in my house and gotten a close-up of my life. It seemed more trouble, finally, than the help was worth. And I knew from their letters that my sister Serena was heavily involved in engagement parties and showers; the wedding would be just after Christmas. Serena would resent me even more than she already did if I horned in on her spotlight.

Well, this was too close to wallowing in self-pity. I jerked my shoulders straight. I set my eyes on my car, I gripped the cane and started walking.

Two nights later I got an unexpected summons.

The phone rang when I'd finally gotten warm and comfortable, curled up in my double recliner watching TV, covered by an afghan my grandmother had crocheted for me. When the shrill of the bell jolted me into awareness, I realized I hadn't registered anything I was supposed to be watching. I stretched out a hand to lift the receiver.

'Miss Bard?' An old voice, an empress's voice.

'Yes.'

'This is Arnita Winthrop. I wonder if you could come by the house. I would surely like to talk to you.'

'When did you have in mind?'

'Well, young woman, would now be inconvenient for you? I know you're a working woman, and I'm sure you're mighty tired by the evening . . .'

I was still dressed. I hadn't taken a pain pill. Tonight would be as good a time as any. Though I could tell my body was healing, since the night of the explosion I'd been gripped by an apathy that I could not shake. It seemed a great deal of trouble to get out again, but that was no good reason to refuse.

'I can come now. Could you tell me what this is about? Are you thinking of replacing your maid?'

'Oh, no. Our Callie is part of our family, Miss Bard. No, there's something I need to give you.'

'All right. I'll come.'

'Oh, wonderful! You know where we live? The white house on Partridge Road?'

'Yes, ma'am.'

'We'll see you in a few minutes, then.'

I hung up. After powdering my nose I got my better coat from the closet, the one with no stains or holes, and buttons instead of a zipper. It was all I had left. I was tired, so I took the cane, though I'd managed that day without it.

In a few minutes, I was a little out of town but still within the city limits at the white house on Partridge Road. *House* was a belittling term to apply to the senior Winthrops' dwelling. *Mansion* or *estate* would be more accurate. I turned onto the semicircular drive that swept opulently through a huge front yard. The drive was illuminated by lampposts stationed at intervals on either side of the paved surface. Pools of water from an afternoon shower glistened with reflected light.

I went up the shallow front steps as quickly as I could.

The wind was biting through my coat and jeans. I limped across the stone flags of the front portico, too cold to even think about standing back to admire the facade of the house. I punched the doorbell.

Mrs Winthrop opened the door herself. I had to look down at her. I judged Arnita Winthrop to be in her mid-seventies. She was beautifully turned out in chestnut brown, which made the rich white of her hair glow. She was lightly made up, and her nails were manicured and coated in clear polish. Her earrings would have paid six months' electric bills for my house. She was absolutely charming.

'Come in, come in, it's freezing out there!' As I stepped past her into the glowing warmth of the entrance hall, she took my hand and clasped it lightly and briefly.

'I'm so glad to meet you at last,' she said with a smile. She glanced at my cane and courteously did not mention it.

Her southern accent, laced with the flat vowels of southern Arkansas, was the thickest I'd heard in years. It made everything she said sound warm and homey.

'Marie talked about you all the time,' Mrs Winthrop continued. 'You were so helpful to her, and she thought so highly of you.'

'I liked her.'

'Here, let me take your coat.' To my discomfort, Mrs Winthrop eased the coat off my shoulders and hung it in a convenient closet. 'Now, come on in the family room. My husband and son are in there, having a drink.'

The family room, predictably, was as large as the ground floor of the Shakespeare Garden Apartments. I had never seen a room that amounted to an investment. There were animal heads on the dark paneling, which had never been on sale at Home Depot. The colors in the upholstery and wallpaper were deep and rich. On top of the wall-to-wall was a rug that I could have stared at for hours, its pattern was so intricate and beautiful.

The two men in the room weren't nearly as appealing.

Howell Winthrop, Sr., was a little rat terrier of a man, with thin gray hair and a thin sharp face and an alert expression. He was wearing a suit and tie, and looked as if that was his casual wear. I thought he was older than his wife, perhaps eighty. Howell Jr. looked much less at ease than his father; in fact, he looked terrible.

'Honey, this is Lily Bard,' Arnita Winthrop said as if her husband should be happy to hear it. At least her equal in manners, he tried to look delighted I'd come, and he and his son both rose without hesitation.

'Pleased to meet you, young lady,' the older man said, and I could hear his age in his voice. 'I've heard a lot of nice things about you.' But his tone said 'interesting stories' rather than 'nice things.'

Howell Jr. and I nodded at each other. I hadn't seen Howell since the day of the break-in. He was giving me the strangest, most intense look. I could see he was trying to transfer some thought directly to my brain.

This was becoming more complex by the second. Now, what might he want me to say, or not say? And why? Could I manage to care?

'Lily and I will just go into the other room for a minute,' Arnita Winthrop excused us. Underneath her courtesy and the mask of her expensive turnout, I realized the older woman was anxious. Very anxious. That made three of us.

Her husband looked cool as a cucumber.

'Now, sugar, wait a minute,' Howell Sr. said, with the greatest good nature. 'You can't just whisk the prettiest woman I've seen in ages out of the room before I have a chance to get a good look at her.'

'Oh, you!' said Arnita with an excellent imitation of perfect good humor. She relaxed visibly. 'Sit down, then, Miss Bard.' She set an example by easing into the couch opposite the two men, who were in higher wing chairs. I had to comply or look like a clod.

I was sorry I'd come. I wanted to go home.

'Miss Bard, weren't you in the church during the explosion, *and* at my son's house at the time of this very mysterious break-in?'

My senses went on full alert. The older Winthrop knew full well I had been there.

'Yes.'

He waited a second for me to say more, saw I wasn't going to.

'Oh my goodness,' Arnita murmured. 'I know you were scared to death.'

I cocked an eyebrow.

Howell Jr.'s forehead was beaded with sweat.

I didn't want to talk about the church. 'Actually, I didn't know anyone was breaking into the house until he left. I probably scared him more than he scared me.' I hoped making the burglar singular would make me sound more ignorant. Howell Jr. looked off at a stag's head, but I could read relief in his posture. I'd given the correct response.

Looking at the three other people in the room, I had the strangest feeling: It seemed so unlikely that I was in this house, in their company. It was like falling down the rabbit's hole in *Alice in Wonderland*. I wondered if I was suffering some strange aftereffect of the explosion.

Howell Sr. found my last remark quite amusing. 'You got

any idea what they were after, young lady? You even know if they were niggers or whites?'

I was used to taking people in their context, but I felt my back stiffen and probably my face, too. I felt Howell Sr.'s tone was contemptuous and hectoring. But if I'd been tempted to upbraid the old man, that temptation passed from me when I saw the anxiety in my hostess's face.

'No,' I said.

'My goodness, a woman of few words, ain't that unusual,' Howell Sr. cackled. But his faded blue eyes were not amused. The oldest living Winthrop was used to more respect.

'A break-in in broad daylight,' Arnita said, shaking her head at the evils of the modern world. 'I can't think what was going through their minds.'

'Oh, Mama,' said her son, 'they could have taken the VCRs and the camcorder and even the television sets and gotten enough money to buy drugs for days.'

'I guess you're right.' Arnita shook her head in dismay. 'The world's just not getting any better.'

It seemed a strange point to make with me, but perhaps the older Winthrops were the only two people in Shakespeare who didn't know my history.

'Honey, Miss Bard knows how bad the world is,' her husband said, his voice sad. 'Her past, and this terrible bombing . . .'

'Oh, my dear! Forgive me, I would never want to—'

'It's all right,' I said, unable to keep the weariness from my voice.

'How's your leg, Miss Bard?' the old man asked. He sounded just as tired as I was. 'And I understand you lost part of your ear?'

'Not the important part,' I said. 'And my leg is better.'

All the Winthrops made commiserating noises.

Arnita seized the ensuing pause to tell her husband and son firmly that she and I had something to discuss, and I heaved myself to my feet to follow her erect back down a hall to a smaller room that appeared to be Arnita's own little sitting room. It was decorated in off-white, beige, and peach, and all the furniture was scaled down for Arnita Winthrop's small body.

Again I was ensconced on a comfortable sofa, again Arnita sat, too, and she got down to business.

'Lily, if I may call you that, I have something of Marie's to give you.'

I digested that in silence. Marie hadn't had much at all, and I'd assumed Chuck would be handling whatever little odds and ends of business Marie had left to be completed. I nodded at Arnita to indicate she could continue when she chose.

'You came by on days you weren't supposed to work at Marie's.'

I looked off. That was no one's concern.

'She appreciated it more than you will realize until you get old yourself, Lily.'

'I liked her.' I looked at an oil painting of the three Winthrop grandchildren. Somehow it felt even odder seeing Bobo's young face in these unfamiliar surroundings. Amber Jean looked more like her mother in the picture than she did in the flesh. Howell Three looked gangly and charming.

'Of course, Marie was always conscious that she didn't have much, and Chuck was helping her live in a tolerable way.'

'As he damn well ought to,' I said flatly.

Our eyes met. 'We certainly agree on that,' Arnita said, her voice dry. I almost found myself liking her. 'The point is, Marie couldn't leave you money to thank you for your kindness to her, so she told me she wanted you to have this little ring. No strings. You can sell it or wear it, whatever.'

Arnita Winthrop held out a shabby brown velvet ring box. I took it, opened it. Inside was a ring so pretty and feminine that I smiled involuntarily. It was designed to look like a flower, the petals formed of pinkish opals, the center a pearl circled by tiny diamond chips. There were two leaves, suggested by two dark green stones, which of course were not real emeralds.

'It's a pretty little thing, isn't it?' my hostess said gently.

'Oh, yes,' I said. But even as I spoke, it was occurring to me that I didn't remember seeing the worn velvet box among Marie's things, and I'd been familiar with her belongings for years. I could tell my smile was fading. Marie could have concealed it somewhere clever, I supposed, but still . . .

'What's the matter?' Arnita leaned forward to look at my face, her own deeply concerned.

'Nothing,' I said, quite automatically hiding my worry. 'I'm glad to have it to remember her by, if you're sure that's what she wanted.' I hesitated. 'I can't recollect ever seeing Marie wear this ring.'

'She didn't, for years, thought it looked too young for an old wrinkled woman like the ones we'd turned into,' said Arnita, with a comic grimace.

'Thanks,' I said, there being nothing else to do that I could think of. I stood and pulled my car keys out of my pocket.

Arnita looked a bit startled.

'Well, good night,' I said, seeing I'd been too abrupt.

'Good night, Lily.' The older woman rose, pushing a little on the arms of her chair. 'Let me see you out and get your coat.'

I protested, but she was adamant about fulfilling the forms of courtesy. She opened the beautiful doors to the family room so I was obliged to say good-bye to Howells Sr. and Jr. I hadn't brought a purse so the ring box was in my hand. Howell Jr.'s eyes registered it, and suddenly he turned white.

Then his eyes met mine, and he looked as though he were going to be sick. I was bewildered, and I am sure I looked it.

What was wrong with these people?

I said the minimum courtesy demanded, and I left the room, taking my coat from Arnita at the door. She saw me to the porch and stood there while I climbed into my car. She waved, called out admonitions to drive carefully on the wet streets, thanked me for coming, hoped she would see me again soon. At last she closed her doors behind her.

I shook my head as I turned my keys in the ignition, switched on my headlights. Then my head jerked, following a movement I'd caught out of the corner of my eye. I was out of the car as quickly as I could manage, staring through the dark shapes of the bushes lining the drive, trying to figure out what I'd just seen. I wasn't about to run from the lamplight illuminating the drive into that outer darkness, and I wasn't really sure that I'd seen an actual living thing. Maybe it had been shadows shifting as I turned on my lights. Maybe it had been a dog or cat. As I began to ease down the drive, I scanned the shrubbery for movement, but I saw nothing, nothing at all.

My summons and visit to the Winthrop mansion had been peculiar and strangely off-kilter, and I was tempted to think over the problems this family obviously had. But getting involved in the internecine squabbles of the most powerful family in the county was no way to earn a living. Head low, go forward; I needed to go home and write that a hundred times.

I had a bad feeling. I was already enmeshed in more trouble than I could imagine.

The next day was so normal it was a relief. Though I couldn't stop myself from looking side to side when I was out driving from one job to another, at least I didn't have that jumpy feeling that something – or someone – was about to leap out in front of me in challenge.

The assorted minor bruises on my face and arms had faded to a dusty eggplant shade, and the worst ones on my back were at least less painful. My leg felt much better. The cut on my scalp was almost healed and the notch in my ear was somewhat less disgusting.

I had no appetite for lunch, so after eating a piece of fruit at home I decided to go make a necessary purchase, one I'd been putting off for a few days. My workout gloves were falling apart at the seams, literally. Maybe if I got new gloves, I would go back to Body Time. I hadn't worked out or been to karate since the explosion. I knew I was hardly up to my former routine, but I could be doing abdominal crunches or some biceps work. All my energy seemed to be absorbed in just making my body get through the move-ments of life, and sometimes I swear I had to remind myself to breathe, it felt like so much trouble. New gloves, a little treat, might set me back on my former track.

Since my street is the bottom stroke of a U-shaped dead end, I had to take a circuitous route to Winthrop Sporting Goods. If I'd wanted to walk up the hill and cross the railroad tracks behind my house, I'd have reached the chain-link fence enclosing the huge back lot of Winthrop Lumber and Supply, which abutted directly onto the equally huge fenced back lot of the sporting goods store. But the fences and the rough ground made walking impractical, especially in my weakened state, so I had to make a ten-minute drive that routed me through a portion of downtown Shakespeare, then off to the right on Finley.

I had too much time to think as I drove, and was scowling when I walked in the front door of Winthrop Sporting Goods. Darcy Orchard looked up, flushed nearly the color of the red store sweatshirt, and flinched in exaggerated terror as I came in.

'You better smile, girl!' he called. 'You gonna crack any mirror if you walk by.'

I looked around me. I was always staggered by the sheer size and complexity of Winthrop's. The building had been remodeled inside any number of times, until now it consisted of a huge central cavern with specialty rooms lining the walls on either side of the store. There was a room for rifles, and one for bows – bow hunting is very popular in Shakespeare. There was a room over on the left wall just for fishing paraphernalia, and another for camping accessories. There was at least an acre of open yard out back for Jet Skis, boats, deer stands, and four-wheelers.

But the main room was full of everything else. There were high racks of camouflage gear in every conceivable shade of green and brown, in sizes down to infant sleepers. There were hunting caps, and insulated socks, and special gloves, and thermoses, and coolers. Life vests screamed in neon orange, deer corn was piled in fifty-pound bags, and oars were arranged in upright racks. There was a display of bottles containing fluids that made you smell like raccoon pee or a doe in heat or a skunk.

There were other clothes for every sport, even a small section for skiing outfits, since the wealthy of Shakespeare went to Colorado when the snow was deep. Every time I came to Winthrop's, it was to be amazed all over again that a place this size could thrive in a town as small as Shakespeare. But the surrounding area was known for its hunting, and sportsmen came from all over the region to the numerous hunting camps in the deep woods. Engaged couples were known to keep a list of desirable gifts hanging behind the counter. Whole families came from Little Rock to shop at Winthrop Sporting Goods, and there had been a rumor Howell Jr. was going to start sending out a catalog.

I realized as I looked around that the Winthrops must be incredibly rich, on paper at least. I'd seen the evidence in the size of the houses the family lived in, their clothes and jewelry and toys: But seeing the vastness of the store, thinking of the huge lumber and home supply store right next to this place, remembering all the fences I'd seen across areas containing working oil wells marked WINTHROP OIL, NO ENTRANCE, the amount of money the family must have in the bank just winded me.

Well, I didn't want it. All I wanted was gloves.

I would have to safari into the camouflage jungle to reach the little area I wanted, a far hike to the rear if I remembered the store layout correctly. Darcy Orchard seemed to feel I wanted his company, and when he found out what I needed he led me down the narrow middle aisle and veered to the left. I lifted a hand to Jim Box, who was explaining to a teenager why he needed a gun case that would float. The young woman who worked in boating accessories came up and gave me a half-hug and asked about my leg, and one of the men who'd worked in the store for over twenty years – his sweatshirt said so – patted me on the back in the friendliest way, though I hadn't a clue who he was. These were nice people, and their kindness and their courtesy in not asking questions reminded me of why I'd liked Shakespeare in the first place.

'You can meet the new guy, if you haven't already. He's 'bout as mean as you,' Darcy said in that jocular tone some men reserve for insults they don't want you to take them up on. I suddenly remembered who the new man was, suddenly and for the first time realized . . . Just as a jolt of alarm went through me, I made myself pay attention to Darcy.

Darcy's voice had been offhand, but something in his tone had made the hair on my neck stand up. 'You sure turn up in funny places,' he said now. 'You in the Winthrop house when it's not your day to work, you in the church when everyone going to that meeting is black.'

'Did your wife tell you everything she was going to do, Darcy?'

I recalled he been married for six years or so, though he'd been divorced as long as I'd known him.

'My wife had more plans than the Pentagon,' Darcy said grimly, but he seemed to relax.

We rounded a corner consisting of men's jumpsuits (very popular in Shakespeare) which led us into the small open area devoted to workout equipment and workout clothes.

Reading the instructions for an abdominal exerciser

gadget, with a skeptical sideways pull to his lips, was the detective, Black Ponytail. I'd just figured out who I was going to see, but he didn't have any warning. I admired the calm with which he took me in. His hands tightened on the brochure, but that was the only outward sign that we weren't seeing each other for the first time.

'Lily, this is Jared Fletcher,' Darcy said. 'He's got those abs of steel, don't you, Jared?'

His name wasn't Jared. I knew him now. He'd had the same skeptical look in the newspaper photos. I could feel my breath shorten.

'Jared, this is Lily, the toughest woman in Shakespeare.' Darcy completed the introduction with relish. 'You two ought to hit it off great.'

Even Darcy seemed to realize there was something tense in the ensuing silence.

'You two already know each other?' he asked, his beige head turning from me to 'Jared' and back again.

'I've seen Lily at the gym,' the new man said easily. 'But we've never actually met.'

'Oh, sure.' Darcy's face cleared. 'I'll leave you two to it, then. Jared, Miss Lily here needs herself some new gloves. Might oughta sell her some body armor, too, since she seems to always be in the wrong place at the wrong time.'

'What size?' the dark man asked as Darcy reluctantly went back to his work area.

I held out my hand. 'What do you think?' I asked, meeting his eyes.

He took my hand with his right and stepped closer to me. This area of the store seemed isolated and silent, suddenly, though I knew there were people just through the dense racks of clothes. His other hand reached up to touch the bruise on my forehead. Among my other injuries, the place he'd bopped me had paled into insignificance.

'Sorry,' he said. He was so close I was afraid he could hear my pulse. I laid my finger on his wrist. I felt his blood leap. The apathy that had lain on my shoulders like a fog seemed to be lifting.

'Gloves,' I reminded him. My voice was scratchy.

'Right,' he said, stepping away. He looked around him like the new employee he was. 'Jared' hadn't had much time to get acclimated.

'There,' I pointed. 'Women's mediums?'

'We have some in black,' he said.

'Black is okay.'

He pulled down a plastic container and popped it open. 'You better try them on.'

Again I held out my hand, and he wriggled the glove over my fingers, wrapping the strap around my wrist and Velcroing it snugly. I flexed my fingers, made a fist, looked at him. He smiled, and deep arcs appeared on each side of his mouth. The smile changed him totally, threw me off balance.

'Don't hit me here. Save it for later,' he murmured. 'You're quite a fighter.' I remembered I'd bitten him on the ear. I looked at it. It looked better than mine.

It had been a long time since I'd met someone new. It had been even longer since I'd met someone who apparently didn't know who I was.

'Lived here long?' he asked, as if we'd just seen each other for the first time and he was introducing a standard conversational gambit. I looked down at the glove on my right hand, considered the fit.

'Over four years,' I said, holding out my left hand.

'And you have your own maid service?'

'I clean houses and run errands,' I said a little sharply. 'I work by myself.'

His fingers stroked my hand as he pulled the other glove on.

'Do you think they're too tight?' I asked, pantomiming a *seiken zuki* strike to get the feel of the glove. I was able to curl my fingers more easily than I'd thought. I practiced a hammer fist strike. I'd looked at the price tag. The gloves were very expensive, and I'd better be sure they suited me. I picked up one of the twenty-pound barbells, gripped it, raised it over my head. It was a very unpleasant surprise to find it felt heavy.

'They'll loosen a little. Lily is a pretty name.'

I shot him a look.

He looked back steadily. 'I know you live next to my apartment building. But if I wanted to call you, how are you listed in the phone book?'

As if he couldn't ask Howell. Or anyone else in town, for that matter. I put down the barbell very gently. I'd enjoyed a few minutes of feeling normal.

'Bard,' I said. 'My name is Lily Bard.' I knew he would remember.

Because I didn't want to see the look on his face, I took the package the gloves had come in from his suddenly still hands, walked out of the area stripping off the gloves. I paid for them at the front counter, exchanging a few idle words with Al Ferrar, a big, friendly redheaded man whose fingers seemed too large to punch the cash register keys. The hunting bows were behind him, and I stared at them as he rang up the purchase. The arrowheads hung in bubble containers on the wall behind him some so wickedly sharp, like four razors joined together, that I could hardly believe the user wouldn't be frightened to fit them on the shafts. When Al handed me the plastic bag with the gloves in it, I stared at him blankly for a minute and then left the store.

I stood looking up into the sky when I'd reached my car, lost in the gray emptiness of an overcast November day. Wet leaves had piled up in the lower parts of the parking lot. It was going to rain again that evening, the weatherman had predicted. I heard footsteps behind me. The apathy washed back over me, a wave that pulled me under. I was so tired I could scarcely move. I wished the coming scene to be over and done with, wished I could go somewhere else while it was accomplished.

'Why'd you run out like that?'

'You'd better go back to your area, or you'll blow your cover.'

'I'm working,' he said harshly.

'Night and day. At the store and elsewhere, Jack.'

There was a moment of silence.

'Look at me, dammit.'

It would have seemed too affected not to, so I stopped looking at the bleak sky and looked instead at Jack Leeds's bleak face.

'I get a hard-on every time I see you,' he said.

'Try sending me roses. It's a little more subtle.'

He gazed off at a corner of the asphalt. He'd come out without a jacket. I was meanly glad to see him shiver.

'OK. I'll start over,' he said through gritted teeth. 'You know I'm working, and you know what I am.'

He waited for me to nod. To get it over with, I did.

'I am not seeing anyone right now. I've been divorced twice, but you may remember that from the papers.'

I leaned against my car, feeling far away, glad to be there.

With the speed of a snake, he ran his hand under my jacket and T-shirt, placing it flat on my ribs. I gasped and flinched, but his hand stayed there, warm and firm.

'Move your hand,' I said, my voice ragged.

'Got your attention. Listen to me. This job in Shakespeare will come to an end. I want to see you then.'

I shivered, standing stock-still, rigid, taken by surprise. His fingers moved against my skin, touching the scars gently. A silver pickup pulled into the space two vehicles away and the driver gave us a curious look. I chopped down on Jack Leeds's wrist, knocking his hand from its intimate lodgment.

'I have to go to work, Jared,' I said numbly, and got in my car and backed up, avoiding looking at him again.

Carrie was coming to supper tonight and I thought about what I'd fix, not one of my usual frozen-ahead dishes that I prepared on Sundays to carry me through the week. Maybe fettuccine with ham . . . or chili would be good, on such a chilly gray day, but I didn't have enough time to let it simmer.

Keeping my thoughts to a simple minimum, I managed my afternoon well. It was a relief to go home, to allow myself ten minutes in my favorite chair reading a news magazine. Then I set to work, tossing a salad, preparing the fettuccine, heating some garlic bread, chopping the ham. When Carrie knocked on the front door, I was ready.

'Those morons at the hospital!' she said, sliding out of her coat, tossing her gloves on the table.

'Hello to you, too.'

'You'd think they could see the handwriting on the wall.

Everyone else can.' The tiny Shakespeare Hospital was in perpetual crisis trying to maintain its accreditation, with no adequate budget to supply its lacks, which were legion.

I let Carrie bear the brunt of the conversation, which she seemed quite willing to do. There were few people Carrie could talk to, as a woman and a doctor and an outlander from northern Arkansas. I knew from previous talks with Carrie that she had gotten a loan to attend medical school. The terms of the loan stipulated that she had to go to somewhere other doctors didn't want to go and stay there for four years; and other doctors didn't want to go to Shakespeare. Carrie was one of four local GPs, who all made a decent living, but for more specialized medical care Shakespeareans had to travel to Montrose, or in dire need, Little Rock.

'Where'd you get the ring?' Carrie asked suddenly.

I'd been feeling a warm hand on my skin. It took me a second to reorient.

'The older Mrs Winthrop says Marie Hofstettler left me this,' I told Carrie.

'It's a pretty ring,' she said. 'Can I see it?'

I slid the ring off and handed it to Carrie. I thought of my strange visit to the Winthrop house the night before, the pallor of Howell Winthrop's face as he saw the ring box in my hand.

Some things that were supposed to be free actually came mighty expensive. I wondered if this little ring was one of them.

Then I wondered why that thought had crossed my mind.

I took the ring back from Carrie and slid it on my right

hand, then took it back off and dropped it in my pocket. Carrie raised her thick dark brows, but didn't say anything.

We washed the dishes, talking in a companionable way of whatever crossed our minds: the price of milk, the vagaries of dealing with the public, the onset of hunting season (which would have a certain impact on Carrie's job *and* mine, since hunting engendered both injuries and dirt galore), and the recuperation of Claude, which continued at too slow a pace to suit him, and, I suspected, Carrie. She told me she'd gotten the green light to move Claude from an upstairs to a downstairs apartment, but that he wanted to be on the scene to direct the move, so a date hadn't been set yet.

When Carrie left, it was a little later than usual, and I was worn out. I took a quick shower, put on my favorite blue nightgown, laid out my clothes for the next morning. I went through my nightly routine of checking the locks at the windows and doors. I felt more relaxed, more content. Tomorrow might be a regular day.

Chapter Six

My heart was hammering. The bad time was back again. I sat up in bed, gasping, my nightgown damp against my breasts. I'd been sweating in my sleep. Horrible dreams, old dreams, the worst: the chains, the shack, the rhythmic thud of the iron headboard against the wall.

Something had wakened me, something besides the dream; or maybe something had sparked the dream. I scrambled out of bed and pulled on the white chenille robe I keep draped across the footboard. As I tied the sash tightly around my waist, I glanced at my digital clock. One-thirty. I heard a sound: a quick, light rapping at my back door.

I crept out of my bedroom. It's next to that door. I put my ear against the wood. A voice on the other side of the door was saying something over and over, and as my hand reached for the switch, I realized the voice was saying, 'Don't turn on the light! For God's sake, don't turn on the light!'

'Who is it?' I asked, my ear pressed to the meeting of door and frame so I could hear better.

'Jack, it's Jack. Let me in, they're after me!'

I heard the desperation in his voice. I pushed the dead bolt back and opened the door. A dark form hurtled past me and crashed on the hall floor as I slammed the door shut and relocked it.

I knelt beside him. The faint radiance provided by the

nightlight burning behind the nearly shut bathroom door was almost useless. His breathing was ragged and loud; no point in asking him questions. I moved my fingers up Jack's legs first: wet boots, damp blue jeans – it was raining again. My hands moved higher, running over his butt and crotch; then I felt his chest, his back, under his padded waterproof vest.

The detective rolled to his right side. He groaned when my fingers found the sticky patch on his left shoulder, I flinched, too, but I made my hand return to the wound. There was a hole in the vest. I probed further. There was a big hole in the vest, and the shirt underneath was ripped. It seemed plain enough that Jack Leeds had been shot high in the shoulder.

'I need to look at this in some light,' I said. His breathing seemed closer to normal. He was shaking now, from cold and perhaps relief.

'If you turn on a light, they'll know I woke you. They're gonna knock on your door any minute.' He took a deep breath, let it out slowly, trying for control. He made a little sound through clenched teeth.

I'd have to turn on the outside light, then. I thought about Jack's wet boots and the little roof over the back porch.

'Crawl into the first door on your left,' I said. I hurried into the kitchen, glad my leg was so much better. I washed my hands in the dark. I filled a saucepan with water. Returning to the back door, I edged it open and listened; not a sound beyond the cool patter of the rain. I opened the door wider. The security light in the parking lot to the rear of the apartment building also benefited my backyard, at least a little. I could see the dark wet footprints Jack had left on the boards. I poured water over the porch and steps, wiping out the marks of his entrance. I could only hope 'they' (whoever they were) wouldn't be observant enough to wonder why my sheltered porch was soaking wet.

Shutting and locking the door again, I automatically placed the inverted pan in the kitchen drainer. I stood in the middle of the room, thinking furiously. No, there was nothing more I could do. Jack had surely left tracks on the wet ground, but it was beyond my power to obliterate them.

I padded silently into my bedroom. 'Where are you?' I whispered. This was like playing hide-and-seek, in a scary kind of way.

'By the bed, on the rug,' he said. 'Don't want to mess up your sheets or your floor.'

I appreciated the consideration. 'How'd you get here? To the house?' I asked, ashamed of the anxious undertone I could hear in my own voice.

'Over the fence, from the back lot of the lumber place. But I went further down to the vacant lot at the corner, then cut back here on the pavement. I started to come to your front door, but then I figured they might have a car cruising the neighborhood by now, if they've stopped to think. So I went up your driveway, around your carport, and took the stepping stones to the back door.' He paused. 'Oh, shit, the porch! Footprints!'

'I took care of it.'

I could sense his movement as he turned to stare in my direction. But all he said was 'Good.' His eyes closed, I thought, and he shifted positions painfully.

My eyes had done some adjusting, enough to make him out. He hadn't cut all his hair off, as it had looked at first. He was wearing a black knit watch cap and he'd tucked all his hair up under it. I eased it off. Of course the cap hadn't done anything to keep his head dry. The released strands spread in rat's tails across the white bedside rug.

He opened his eyes and regarded me steadily. I found myself running my fingers through my hair to fluff it out. Ridiculous. I couldn't postpone dealing with the wound any longer.

'Let's get your vest off,' I said, trying to sound matter-of-fact. I scooted closer. 'Hold out your hand. I'll help you sit up.'

Jack had better night vision than I did. His hand was on mine instantly. I gripped and pulled, automatically giving the 'Huh!' of heavy exertion. I leaned him against the side of the bed and unzipped the vest. I pulled it down his right arm first. I eased it across his back, leaning almost against his chest to accomplish the maneuver. I smelled the wet of his vest and his shirtsleeves, and the scent of his skin, the faintest trace of some aftershave. Then I scuttled over to his left side, held up his left arm with one hand while I tugged at the vest with the other. He gave a deep groan, and I sucked my breath in sympathetically. But I didn't stop. The vest wasn't actually stuck; it was the movement of his arm and shoulder that was causing him pain.

His flannel shirt, now, *that* was stuck. I fetched my heavy kitchen scissors and began to cut through the thick material. This proved impossible and dangerous in the darkness. I left to push the bathroom door wide open. I'd worried about the nightlight, but I figured a nightlight in a bathroom was no big wonder, and it was my habit. Suddenly switching it off might be even more suspicious.

With the slightly improved visibility I could just see

enough to cut off the shirt without hurting Jack worse. He was leaning back against the bed with his eyes closed.

I wanted to call Carrie, but her arrival would be a dead giveaway. Jack was still shivering, but it didn't seem to be as teeth-chattering a tremor as before.

There was a single loud knock at the back door. Jack's eyes flew open and stared into mine, only a few inches away.

'They won't come in,' I promised. I looked down at my robe. It was streaked with dirt and damp and blood. I unbelted it and draped it over Jack, wiping my hands on its hem. I went into the hall and up to the back door, as noisily as I could.

'Who is it?' I asked loudly. 'I'm going to call the police!'

'Lily, hey! It's Darcy!'

'Darcy Orchard, what the hell are you doing knocking at my door in the middle of the night? Go away!'

'Lily, we just want to make sure you're all right. Some-one broke in over at the store.'

'So?'

'He took off running across the back lot. He scaled the fence and went into the lumber yard lot. We think he climbed out and came across the tracks.'

'So?'

'Let us lay eyes on you, Lily. We gotta be sure you're not being held hostage.'

That was clever.

'I'm not letting you in my house in the middle of the night,' I said baldly, figuring that would be congruent with my history and character. And it was the simple truth. They would not come into my house.

'No, that's fine, honey. We just want to see you're okay.' Darcy did a good job of sounding concerned.

I switched on the light above the back door, which I'd been hoping to avoid in case Jack had left traces I hadn't anticipated. I stuck my head out the door and glared at Darcy up on my back porch and the group of men in my backyard. Darcy wasn't dressed for the weather; he looked exactly like he'd run out the door in whatever he had on. His thinning hair was plastered to his head. His pale eyes glistened in the porch light. Darcy was enjoying himself.

I swept my eyes over the four bundled figures clustered together behind him, enduring the light rain and chill wind. I was trying to gather in a look at the posts supporting the little porch roof while I was at it.

Dammit all to hell. Jack had left a bloody handprint on one of them; but it was on the inside toward me, thank God.

To make sure their attention didn't wander, I stepped out on the tiny porch in my nightgown, and five pairs of eyes bugged out.

I heard a reverent 'Wow,' which Darcy instantly suppressed by turning to glare at the offender. Despite the fact that all the men had pulled up their collars and pulled down their hats, I could recognize the exclamation had come from the boy who worked at the loading dock of the lumber supply house. I wondered how they'd picked Darcy to be the one who got his name on the record, so to speak.

'See, I'm fine,' I said, not having to work at sounding furious. 'I'm under no duress, and I could walk away from this house right now if I wanted to freeze. How come all of you are out in the rain chasing a burglar, anyway? Don't you have an alarm system that calls the police?'

As I'd hoped, going on the offense made them begin to back away.

'We were having a little . . .' Darcy paused, clearly unsure how to end the sentence.

'Inventory,' said one of the men. His voice was oddly muffled since he was trying to keep his face buried in his collar. I was pretty sure it was Jim Box, Darcy's work out buddy and coworker. Jim had always thought quicker than Darcy, but without the panache. Behind him, a figure crouched with a hood covering most of his features, but I would recognize that thin, mean mouth anywhere. Tom David Meicklejohn, in mufti. Hmmm.

'Right, we have to do pre-Christmas inventory,' Darcy said, relieved. 'Takes all night. We'd turned off the alarm because we were going in and out.'

'Um-hmm,' I said, neutrally. As I'd anticipated, they began to back off even more quickly, though still keeping their eyes on my nightgown. I decided to burn it.

'Aren't you going to go wake up Carlton, too?' I demanded, jerking my head toward Carlton's little house, almost identical to mine. 'Maybe *he's* a hostage.'

The bedraggled group began to herd toward Carlton's house, where I'd noticed a light burning in the bedroom. I figured Carlton had company and would give them as warm a reception as I had. I slammed my back door shut, turned the locks as loudly as I could, and switched off the porch light quickly, hoping they would fall in a puddle in the sudden darkness.

Fools. Dangerous fools.

It made me sick that I had exposed myself to them. I crossed my arms over my chest, tried to feel warmer.

I went into my bedroom and padded past Jack to get to

the window. Opening the shades a trifle, I peered out. Yes, Carlton was standing at his back door now, in an attractive velour bathrobe and nothing else, looked like. He was very angry.

Even as I watched, he slammed his own back door and switched out his light. I'd closed my eyes the second before, so when I thought my vision had adjusted, I peered into the darkness again. I could make out vague shapes, trailing back across my yard and up the steep embankment to the railroad tracks. They'd given up the chase.

'They've gone,' I said.

'Good,' Jack said. His voice was a little steadier, but hoarse with suppressed pain. I shut the shades again, tightly, and loosened the tiebacks on the curtains so they fell shut, too. Instead of switching on the overhead light, I used the bedside lamp. I knelt down by Jack again. His eyes had closed against the sudden light. I stared at him for a long moment. I was thinking that I'd better have put my money on the right horse, or the consequences would be too drastic to imagine.

I sat back on my heels. The shoulder wound was the only injury Jack had. It had stopped bleeding. It looked awful. I didn't have any experience treating bullet wounds, but it seemed that the bullet had plowed through the top of Jack's shoulder; and since the bleeding had stopped, I knew it hadn't severed a major blood line.

So infection had to be the biggest danger. I'd have to clean the wound. Unless . . .

'Is there any chance of me taking you to the hospital?' I asked.

He shot me a look that said the question had been as futile as I'd feared. 'I'll get back to my place,' Jack said. He began trying to push himself up from the floor with his uninjured arm.

'Oh, sure.' I was scared of treating the wound, so my voice came out harsh.

'Obviously, this is too much of a risk for you,' he said, in an I'm-trying-to-be-patient voice.

Quelling my impulse to haul him to his feet, twist his good arm behind his back, and propel him into the nearest wall, I inhaled a calming breath. I let it out evenly, with control.

'You don't get to tell me what risks I'm prepared to assume,' I said.

'I can go back to Little Rock, but you live here.'

'I appreciate your pointing that out to me. Give me your hand.' I was going through my own set of shakes. Stepping outside in my nightgown had chilled me to the bone in all kinds of ways.

Jack reached out with his good hand, and I planted my feet, gripped the hand firmly, and pulled up. His face twisted as he rose to his feet. Standing, he was taller than me, his physical presence dominating. I decided I preferred him on the floor. No. I felt more comfortable with him on the floor.

'You're freezing!' he said, and stretched out his good arm as if he would gather me to him. My white bathrobe fell off him and crumpled in a dirty heap. The remains of his shirt hung in rags around his shoulders.

'We're going into the bathroom to work on your wound,' I told him, trying to sound confident. 'Can you walk?'

He could, and was sitting on the toilet seat in a few seconds. I got out all my first-aid equipment. I had some sterile water, and some bandages containing powdered antibiotic, and a tube of antibiotic ointment. I had a lot of gauze and some tape. The Lily Bard MASH unit for wounded detectives.

The sterile water was even in a squirt bottle.

I worked the rest of the shirt off Jack, tried not to be distracted by his resulting bareness, and draped him with my oldest towels. I swept his half-dry hair over onto his sound shoulder. I assumed nurses and doctors learned how to detach themselves from touching people so intimately; I had not. This felt very personal to me.

'I'm going to clean the wound,' I said.

'Yeah.'

I lifted the plastic squeeze bottle. 'So, did you recognize the men after you?' I asked. I squirted sterile water onto the bloody furrow. Jack turned whiter, and dark stubble stood out sharply on his lean cheeks. 'Answer me, Jack Leeds,' I said sharply.

'Not all of them.' His voice more of a gasp.

'Of course there was Darcy.' I squirted again, this time from the back. I thought of tiny fragments of shirt, or microscopic bits of the vest, that might be embedded in this tear in Jack's flesh. I felt dreadfully responsible.

'Uh-huh.' His eyes closed. I kept going with the lavage.

'Who was another one, Jack?'

'The kid, the one with the pimples, works on the loading dock at the lumber and home supply place.'

I patted the area dry with the cleanest whitest washcloth I had. I examined it. It looked clean, but how did I know? I wasn't used to cleaning on a microscopic scale. I squirted.

'And the guy with the big belly, the one who looks like a good heart-attack risk, I've seen him.'

'That was Cleve Ragland, works down at the mattress factory,' I murmured. 'Cleve's been arrested for drunken driving at least twice, got a kid in jail for attempted rape.'

Squirt, wipe.

'The other guy,' Jack gasped, 'isn't he a cop?'

'Uh-huh, Tom David Meicklejohn – in plain clothes. He kept to the back like it was possible for me to mistake him,' I said, hoping the plowed track of the wound was clean enough. At least Jack's eyes were open again, though he wasn't looking at my face.

'And then there was Jim, works in the gun department, works out with Darcy. Another coworker.' I patted again.

It looked dry. It looked clean. I leaned even closer to inspect it, and nodded in satisfaction. I hoped I hadn't hurt Jack too much. He had a very strange expression on his face.

'Lean forward,' I told him, I spread the antiseptic ointment on the wound. I put an antiseptic pad on the shoulder, with a strip of surgical tape to hold it in place.

'Lean back.' I padded the wound with sterile gauze in case he bled again, and unrolled surgical tape to secure the gauze. Jack's face relaxed while I did this, and I felt proud of myself. I turned and began to search the bathroom cabinet for a pain reliever. While my back was to him, Jack's finger traced the curve of my hip.

I stood still, not believing it.

'Are you crazy?' I said. 'You just got shot!'

'Lily, all that got me through that bandaging was your breast wobbling about three inches from my face.'

I couldn't think of anything to say.

'Did I hear you step out in front of them in your nightgown?' he asked.

I nodded.

'No wonder they were all quiet. Not a one will be able to sleep tonight.'

'You'd left a handprint on one of the posts.'

'You did a damn fine job of distracting.'

'I hated doing that. Don't talk like it was easy.'

'I hope I know better.'

'We need to get your wet clothes off so you can come get in bed.'

'I thought you'd never say it.'

I noticed that he wasn't any longer mentioning going home. And he'd never suggested we call the police, though in view of Tom David's presence, that had probably been wise. I shook out a pill, handed him a glass of water. He swallowed it and leaned back, his eyes closed.

I pulled off Jack's boots and socks, wiping off his wet cold feet with a hot washcloth and drying them vigorously with a towel. But I left him to remove his own jeans. I went outside one more time, to clean the bloody handprint from the post. That had been niggling at me.

It was still raining. Any other traces Jack had left would surely be obliterated.

I'd turned down the bed, and by the time I came in the room, Jack had managed to climb in and cover up. On my side. His chest was bare and it occurred to me he was most likely bare all the way down.

I'd given him one of the pain pills Carrie had left me a few months before when my ribs had been bruised. It had knocked Jack Leeds clean out, as I'd expected.

I yanked the blue nightgown off and stuffed it in the trash can. I pulled a pink one out of my dresser drawer. It was almost as pretty; I buy good nightgowns. I put the bloodstained bathrobe into my washer and set it to wash on cold; as an after-thought, I threw in Jack's damp jeans, socks, and underwear, which he'd left in a heap on the bathroom floor. Hot water would have been better for his stuff, but I couldn't stay awake for two loads. While the clothes churned through the shortest cycle, I straightened up the bathroom and set out a toothbrush, still in its wrapper. I rechecked all the locks. Then I put the washed clothes in the dryer.

When all the lights were out, I slid into bed on the wrong side. The night was silent except for the friendly sound of the tumbling dryer and the detective breathing heavily beside me, and I slept.

I opened my eyes about five-thirty, later than I usually get up. To see my clock, I had to raise myself to peer over the dark mound that was Jack. I thought I'd heard him go into the bathroom, heard the water running, but he seemed to be asleep again. I could barely discern the outline of his features. The bedclothes had fallen down, and I could see his exposed shoulder because of the white of the bandage. I covered him back up, very carefully, not wanting to wake him. His loose hair had fallen over his face. Gently, as delicately as I could manage, I brushed it back.

The rain was drumming on the roof again, loud enough to penetrate the comforting drone of the central heating. I made my own trip to the bathroom, rinsed out my mouth. I snuggled back down into bed, turned away from my sleeping companion. I sank into a half-doze, random thoughts floating through my head.

It was Friday. Not a good day to start back to Body Time, considering my interrupted night. Nor a good day to resume karate. But I had to work today . . . Deedra, the peculiar Mookie Preston, the Winthrops, another afternoon appointment . . . I waited expectantly, but I couldn't summon the surge of purpose I needed to feel at the onset of the working day.

What I felt instead was a surge of hormones. Jack Leeds had woken me the night before, beating on my door. Now he was waking me in an altogether different way. Jack was stroking my back and hips. I sighed, hardly knowing if it was one of exasperation or sheer desire. But I certainly didn't feel apathetic any longer.

I knew he could tell I was awake. When I didn't speak, he scooted closer, fitting his body to mine. His hand circled around, cupped a breast, resumed the rhythmical stroking. I had to bite my lip to keep silent.

'What happened to "after this job is over"?' I asked finally, and my voice was more like a gasp.

'Waking up in a warm bed with a beautiful woman on a rainy day in winter' – and while he was speaking his hand never stopped – 'has overcome my business instincts.' His voice was breathy and low. His mouth began to deliver little sucking kisses to my neck, and I shivered. He began to ease up the pink nightgown. It was now or never. What did I want? My body was about to take over from my brain.

I turned toward him, putting up a hand to press against his chest and hold him at a little distance – I think – but at that moment his fingers slid between my legs and instead I wrapped my arm around his neck and pulled him close for a kiss. It was so dark and private in my room, like a quiet cave. After a while, his mouth descended to cover my nipple through the nightgown. I reached down to touch him. He was swollen and ready. It was his turn to do a little moaning.

'Do you have . . . ?' he asked.

I reached across him to grope in the night-table drawer for protection.

Jack began to whisper to me, telling me about what we were going to do and how it was going to feel. His hands never stopped.

'Now,' I said.

'Wait a little.'

I waited as long as I could. I was shaking. 'Now.'

And then he was in me. I arched against him, found his rhythm. My pleasure was instant, and I cried out his name.

'Again,' he said in my ear, and kept on going. I tried to keep pace, once again matched him. I began urging him on, gripping him with my inner muscles, digging my nails into his hips. At last he made an incoherent sound and climaxed, and I did, too.

He collapsed on top of me and I put both my arms around him for the first time. I ran my hands over his back and bottom, feeling skin and muscles, planes and curves. He nuzzled my neck gently for a minute, withdrew from me, and rolled onto his back. The white gauze was spotted with red.

'Your shoulder!' I raised up on an elbow to look. My bedroom was getting a little lighter; the dark and secret cave had opened to the world.

'I don't care,' he said, shaking his head from side to side on the pillow. 'Someone could come in here and shoot me again, and right this moment I wouldn't care. I tried to stay away from you, tried not to think about you . . . if they hadn't been so close, I wouldn't have come here, but I can't be sorry. Jesus God, Lily, that was absolutely – wonderful. No other woman . . . God, that was sensational.'

I was shattered myself. Even more than by the physical sensations Jack had given me, I was a little frightened by the urge I had to touch him, hold him, bathe myself in him. In self-defense, I thought of all the women he'd had.

'Who are you thinking about?' He opened his eyes and stared at me. 'Oh, Karen.' I was frightened that he knew so much about me that he would read my face that way. His own eyes lost their glow, flattened, when he said the name Karen.

Jack Leeds had become a household reference right about the time Lily Bard had, in the same state, Tennessee; and in the same city, Memphis. While my name became linked with that of the crime committed against me ('Lily Bard, victim of a brutal rape and mutilation'), Jack's was always followed by the trailer, 'alleged lover of Karen Kingsland'.

Karen Kingsland, from her newspaper photos a sweet-faced brunette, had been sleeping with Jack for four months when catastrophe wiped out three lives. She was twenty-six years old, earning her master's degree in education from the University of Memphis. She was also the wife of another cop.

One Thursday morning, Walter Kingsland, Karen's husband, got an anonymous letter at work. A uniformed officer for ten years, he was about to go on patrol. Opening the letter, laughing about receiving it, in front of many of his friends, Walter read that Karen and Jack were having sex, and having it often. The letter, which Walter dropped to the floor as he left, was quite detailed. A friend of Jack's called Jack instantly, but he was not as quick as Walter. No one called Karen.

Walter drove home like a maniac, arriving just as Karen was leaving for class. He barricaded himself and his wife in the bedroom of their east Memphis home. Jack came in through the front door moments later, hoping to end the situation quickly and privately somehow. He had not been thinking well. He stood at the door of the bedroom and listened to Walter plead with his wife to say Jack had raped her, or that it was all a malicious lie on the part of some enemy.

By that time, the modest Kingsland home was surrounded by cops. The phone rang and rang, and finally Jack picked it up in the living room and described the situation to his coworkers and superiors. There was not going to be any private or amicable solution, and it would be fortunate if all three involved made it through alive. Jack wanted to offer himself as hostage in exchange for Karen. His superiors, on the advice of the hostage negotiation team, turned him down. Then Jack revealed to them what Walter did not know yet, what Karen had only told Jack the day before: Karen Kingsland was pregnant.

At that point, it would have been hard to find anyone in the Memphis Police Department who wasn't, at the very least, disgusted with Jack Leeds.

From the living room, Jack could hear Karen scream in pain.

He yelled through the door that Walter should exchange his wife for Jack, since torturing a woman was nothing a real man would do.

This time Walter agreed to swap his wife for his wife's lover.

Without consulting anyone, Jack agreed.

Walter yelled that he'd bring Karen to the back door. Jack

should be standing on the sundeck, weaponless. Walter would push Karen out and Jack would come in.

Detective Jack Leeds went outside, took off his jacket, his shoes and socks, his shirt, so Walter Kingsland could tell Jack wasn't carrying a concealed weapon. And sure enough, out of the bedroom came Walter and Karen. From inside the kitchen, Walter yelled to Jack to turn around, so Walter could make sure there wasn't a gun stuck in the back of Jack's slacks.

Then Walter appeared, framed in the open back door holding Karen by one of her arms, his gun to her head. Now there was tape over her mouth, and her eyes were crazed. She was missing the little finger of her right hand, and blood was pouring out of the wound.

'Come closer,' Kingsland said. 'Then I'll let her go.'

Jack had stepped closer, his eyes on his lover.

Walter Kingsland shot Karen through the head and shoved her out on top of Jack.

And this part, media hounds, was on videotape. Jack's yell of horror, Walter Kingsland's screaming, 'You want her so bad, you got her!' Walter's taking aim at Jack, now covered with Karen's blood and brains, trying to rise: a dozen bullets cutting Walter down, bullets fired unwillingly by men that knew him, men that knew Walter Kingsland for high-strung, hot-tempered, possessive; but also as brave, good-natured, and resourceful.

Jack had been a plainclothes detective, often working undercover. He had a stellar work record. He had a rotten personal life. He drank, he smoked, he'd already been divorced twice. He was envied, but not liked; decorated, but not altogether trusted. And after that day in the

Kingslands' backyard, he was no longer a Memphis cop. Like me, he sank to the bottom to avoid the light of the public eye.

This was the chronicle of the man I was in bed with.

'I guess we'll have to talk about that sometime,' he said with a sigh, and his face looked immeasurably older than it had been. 'And what happened to you.' His finger traced the worst scar, the one circling my right breast.

I lay close to him, put my arm over his chest, 'No,' I said. 'We don't have to.'

'The funny thing is,' he said quietly, 'Karen wrote that letter herself.'

'Oh, no.'

'She did.' After all this time, there was still pained wonder in his voice. 'It was from her typewriter. She wanted Walter to know. I'll never understand why. Maybe she wanted more attention from him. Maybe she wanted him to initiate a divorce. Maybe she wanted us to fight over her. I thought I knew her, thought I loved her. But I won't ever know why she did that.'

I thought of things I could say, even things I wanted to say, but none of them could repair the damage I'd recalled to his mind. Nothing could ever make up for what Karen Kingsland had done to Jack, what he had done to himself. Nothing could ever get back Jack's job, his reputation. And I knew nothing would ever erase the memory of Karen's head exploding in front of his eyes.

And nothing could ever erase what had happened to me a couple of months afterward: the abduction, the rape, the cutting, the man I'd shot. I felt the urge to make some good memories.

I swung my leg over him, straddled him, bent to kiss him,

smoothed his long black hair against the white lace-trimmed pillowcase. I was not ashamed of my scars with Jack Leeds. He had a full set of his own. I told him, close to his ear, that I was about to take him inside me again. I told him how it would feel. I could hear him draw his breath, and soon I could feel his excitement. My own heart was pounding.

It was even better this time.

'Why housecleaning?' He asked later.

'I knew how to do it, and I could do it by myself.' That was the short answer, and true enough, as far as it went.

'Why detective? What kind are you, anyway?'

'Private. Based in Little Rock. I knew how to do it, and I could do it by myself.' He smiled at me, a small smile, but there. 'After a two-year apprenticeship with another detective, that is. There was another ex-cop from Memphis working there. I knew him a little.'

So Jack must be working for the Winthrops.

'I have to get dressed. I have an appointment,' I said, trying not to sound sad or regretful. So my departure wouldn't seem too abrupt – cold, as Marshall would have said – I gave Jack a kiss before I swung out of bed. Somehow, the farther away from him I moved, the more I became conscious of my scars. I saw his eyes on them, seeing them for the first time in one frame, so to speak. I stood still, letting him look. But it was very hard, and my fists clenched.

'I'd kill them all for you if I could,' he said.

'At least I killed one,' I said. Our eyes met. He nodded.

I took a wonderful hot shower and shaved my legs and washed my hair and put on my makeup, restraining an urge to laugh out loud.

And I thought: Nothing. I will ask for *nothing*.

Jack had found his surviving clothes in the dryer and pulled them on. I eyed him thoughtfully, and rummaged in my drawers for one of those promotional T-shirts that are all one size. I'd gotten it when I'd donated blood. It had swallowed me, but it fit him, rather snugly; but it covered the bandage and his goose bumps. He winced as he maneuvered his left arm into its sleeve. I had the old jacket the hospital had pulled from its rummage closet, the one I'd worn home the day after the explosion. It fit, too.

He'd perked some coffee while I was showering, and he'd made an effort to pull the bedding straight.

'Normally I do better, but with my shoulder . . .' He apologized as I came into the bedroom to get my socks and sneakers.

'It's all right,' I said briefly, and sat on the little chair in the corner to pull my socks on. I'd put on two T-shirts, which works better for me in cold weather than a sweat-shirt – long sleeves are just a nuisance with housework. The edge of the pink tee peeked from under the sky blue of my outer shirt; happy colors. I'd picked pink socks, too. And my favorite pink and white high-tops. I was the brightest maid in Shakespeare. To hell with the cold and rain.

'Aren't you going to ask me? About what I was doing last night?' he said. He was sitting on the end of the bed, looking braced for an attack.

I finished tying one bow, put my right foot on the floor, lifted my left. 'I guess not,' I said. 'I'm reckoning it has something to do with guns, the Winthrop clan, and maybe Del Packard's murder. But I don't know. Better not tell me, unless you need someplace to run to when the bad guys are chasing you.'

I'd meant that lightly, but Jack thought I was telling him he should explain his business to me since he'd taken shelter in my home; that he owed me, since he'd 'used' me. I could see his face harden, see the distance opening.

'I mean that literally,' I told him. 'Better not tell me, unless they're after you.'

'What will you do, Lily,' he asked, putting his arms around me as I stood, 'what will you do, when they come after me?'

I smiled. 'I'll fight,' I said.

Chapter Seven

Getting Jack to his apartment, though it was just a few yards away, was quite a challenge. At least it was his day off, and his shoulder would have a chance to rest before he had to show up at Winthrop Sporting Goods. It would have looked better if he could have worked out at Body Time this morning, but it was beyond even someone as determined as Jack Leeds. He was hurting.

I gave him my last hoarded pain pill to take when he got home. He stowed it in his pocket. Then, when nothing was passing on Track Street, he ducked out my kitchen door and into my car. I backed out and drove out of my driveway and into the Garden Apartments driveway, going all the way to the rear parking area. When I was closest to the door, so close it would be hard to see from the rear windows of the top apartments, Jack jumped out and went inside. I pulled into Marcus Jefferson's former space and followed him in, to provide myself with a reason for entering the apartment parking lot. Even to me, this seemed a bit overly careful, but Jack had just given me a look to reinforce his admonishment that 'these people' were very dangerous.

So I climbed the stairs to work in Deedra's apartment, which was absolutely normal and gave me a bona fide reason to enter the building at this hour. I carried my caddy of cleaning materials up the stairs, expecting Jack would already be in his apartment and trying to get his clothes off to bathe, without upsetting his wound. I'd offered to help, but he wanted my day to run absolutely normally.

Far from being empty, the landing was full of men and suspicion. Darcy and the bullish Cleve Ragland were waiting in front of Jack's door. They were having a face-off with Jack, who was standing with his keys in his hand.

'. . . don't have to tell anyone where I spend the night,' Jack was saying, and there was a cold edge to his voice that meant business.

He hadn't wanted us to be publicly associated. For that matter, neither had I. I should unlock Deedra's apartment and trot back downstairs to get my mop leaving Jack to stonewall his way through this. That was what he'd want me to do.

'Hey again, Lily,' Darcy said, surprise evident in his voice. He looked bright-eyed and bushy-tailed, but Cleve was showing signs of wear and tear. He hadn't shaved, and maybe had slept in his clothes.

'You keep long hours, Darcy,' I replied, depositing my caddy at Deedra's door and joining the little group. Jack glared at me.

'We just come by here to see if Jared was all right,' Darcy said, and his flat blue eyes swung back to Jack. 'We rung him last night after the robbery and got no answer.'

'And I was telling you,' Jack said just as coldly, 'that what I do on my time off is my business.'

I approached Jack from his left, put my arm around him, blocking the wounded side in case they tried clapping him on the shoulder.

'Our business,' I corrected him, looking steadily at Darcy.

'Whoo-ee,' Darcy said, sticking his hands in his own jean

pockets as if he didn't know what to do with them. His heavy coat bulged up in semicircles around his tucked hands.

Cleve glanced from me to Jack and back again, and said, 'Reckon ole Jared got lucky.'

Immediately the tension eased. Jack slowly looped his arm around me. His fingers bit into my shoulder.

'Well, you were being a gentleman,' Darcy said approvingly.

'Now you got your question answered, can I get in my apartment?' Jack said, making an effort to sound amiable. But I could hear the anger pulsing in his voice.

'Sure, man. We're going this very minute,' said Darcy, a broad grin on his face that I wanted to wipe right off. I promised myself I would if I got half a chance.

Jack stepped between Darcy and Cleve, put his key in the lock, and turned it as they started down the stairs. He automatically stood back to let me enter first, then shut the door behind us. Jack relocked it and went over to the window to see if his 'friends' really left.

Then he swung around to face me, his anger open now and misdirected at me.

'We talked about this,' he began. 'No one was going to connect us.'

'Okay, I'm gone,' I said shortly, and started for the door.

'Talk to me,' he demanded.

I sighed. 'How else could you have gotten out of that?' I asked.

'Well, I . . . could have told them I'd driven to Little Rock to see my girlfriend.'

'And when they said, "Then why was your car parked here all night?"'

Frustrated, Jack brought his fist down on a little desk by the window. 'Dammit, I won't have it!'

I shrugged. No point in all this now. If he was going to act like a jerk, I'd go downstairs and get my mop. I had to work.

When I was on the top stair, he caught me. His good hand clamped down on my shoulder like iron. I stopped dead. I turned very slowly and said to him in my sincerest voice, 'How about saying, "Thanks, Lily, for bailing me out, even though you had to stand there and be leered at for the second time in twelve hours"?'

Jack turned whiter around the mouth than he had been, and his hand dropped from my shoulder.

'And don't you ever, ever restrain me again,' I told him, my eyes staring directly into his.

I turned, and with a sick feeling in the pit of my stomach, I went down the stairs. When I came up with the mop, I stood on the landing for a second, listening. His apartment was silent. I went into Deedra's to work.

So much drama, so early in the morning, left me exhausted. I scarcely registered the unusual order in Deedra's apartment; it was as if she was trying to show she'd changed her social habits by keeping her apartment neater. As I put away her clean underwear, I noted the absence of the pile of naughty pictures of herself she had kept underneath her bras. I expected to feel good about Deedra's changed lifestyle, but instead, I could barely manage to finish my cleaning.

As I dumped the last waste can into a plastic bag, I admitted to myself that even more than tired, I felt sad. It would have been a pleasant treat to have had a morning to think of Jack in the relaxed warmth of good sex, in the glow of – what could I call it? Happiness. But, thanks to his pride – as I saw it – we'd ended on a sour note.

There was a pile of pierced earrings on Deedra's dresser, and I decided to just sit there and pair them up. For a minute or two that was simple and satisfying; after all, they match or they don't. But my restless mind began wandering again.

A pretend robbery during a mysterious meeting at Winthrop Sporting Goods, in the middle of a most inclement night. The blue flyers that had caused so much trouble. The long, heavy black bags that the Winthrop house had been burgled to get – where were they now? The three unsolved murders in tiny Shakespeare. The out-of-place Mookie Preston. The bombing. I couldn't make sense of all the pieces at one time, but the shape of it was wrong. This was no group of fanatics with a coherent manifesto at work; it all seemed very sloppy. For the first time, I considered what Carrie had said about the timing of the bombing. If the goal had been to kill lots of black people, the explosion had come too late. If the goal had been to 'merely' terrorize the black community, the explosion had come too early. The deaths in the church had enraged the African-American people of Shakespeare. Whoever had planted the bomb did not represent white supremacy, but white stupidity.

As I locked Deedra's apartment – scorning to even cross the landing and listen at Jack's door – and descended the stairs to drive to Mookie Preston's modest rental, I thought about the unexpected, normally concealed aspects of the people around me, the part I was seeing the past few days. It was like seeing their skeleton beneath their outer flesh.

Bluff, hearty good ole boy Darcy Orchard, for example: I'd worked out with Darcy for years, and seen only the good-natured sportsman. But last night I'd seen him tracking a man, at the head of a pack of hunters. Beneath his yard-dog exterior, Darcy was a wolf.

I'd always known that about Tom David Meicklejohn. He was naturally cruel and sly, naturally an able and remorseless hunter. He was reliable in what he undertook, whether good or bad. But Darcy had kept this facet of his character buried, and something or someone had unearthed it and used it.

For the first time, I allowed myself to imagine what would have happened if the pack had caught Jack.

And I found myself almost sure they would have killed him.

I began work at Mookie's house in a grim mood. Of course her place couldn't be as dirty as it had been the first time I'd cleaned it, but every week she did a grand job of retrashing it. I scrubbed the bathroom in silence, trying to ignore the little questions and comments she tossed to me as she passed by the open door.

Mookie showed me her cuts from the bombing. They'd been caused by flying splinters, and they were healing well. She inquired after my leg. Would the woman never shut up and settle down to her work?

Once I got the bathroom decent again, I moved into the bedroom. This old house had big rooms and high ceilings, and Mookie's low modern bed and chest of drawers looked out of place. The bare wooden floors made a bit of an echo, footsteps clacking unnaturally loud. Maybe she liked the noise, maybe it kept her company.

'You know,' Mookie said, making one of her abrupt

appearances, 'they haven't got a clue who planted that bomb.' She'd been reading the papers. I hadn't.

'Is that right?' I asked. I really didn't want to talk.

'The device that started the explosion was a wristwatch, like the one you've got on,' Mookie said. She was very angry, very intense. I'd had enough angry and intense already today. 'All the chemicals in the bomb were things you could order from any chemical supply house. All you'd have to do is not order everything from one place, so they won't get suspicious.'

'I wouldn't know,' I said pointedly.

'It's in books you can check out of the library here!' she said, her hands flying up in a gesture of complete exasperation, 'It's in books you can buy at the bookstore in Montrose!'

'So it's probably almost as easy to make a bomb as it is to buy a rifle,' I said, my voice calm and even.

The rifle was not under her bed any longer.

'A rifle's legal.'

'Sure.' I was careful not to turn and look her in the eyes. I didn't want any kind of confrontation. That, too, I'd had enough of already today.

After I changed the sheets and dusted the bedroom, I looked around for an empty bag to dump the contents of the plastic garbage pail, which was full of soiled tissues, balls of hair, and gum wrappers. There, next to a Reebok shoe box, was a dark red plastic bag, and it bore the distinctive logo of Winthrop Sporting Goods.

I tried to persuade myself that there was nothing odd about this. People did mostly buy their sports shoes at Winthrop's, because the store carried a great selection and would special-order what they didn't have in stock.

But I'd seen another red plastic bag the week before. And I remembered seeing yet another crammed into the kitchen garbage. Mookie was going to Winthrop's very frequently.

Slowly I dumped the garbage pail into the bag and went to the bathroom to empty another one. Mookie barely glanced at me as I cleared the one by her desk. Her coarse reddish hair was braided today, and she was wearing wind-suit pants and a turtle-neck. She was tapping computer keys with great energy. The same charts were taped to the wall behind her. There was a pile of library books on the desk, studded with slips of paper marking pages she wanted to refer to.

'How does a genealogist work?' I asked.

For once, she'd been engrossed in what she was doing, and she took a minute to focus on my question.

'Mostly by computer these days,' she answered. 'Which is great for me. I do work for a company that advertises in small specialty magazines, or regional mags, like *Southern Living*. We trace your ancestry for you if you give us some basic information. The Mormons, oddly enough, have the best records; I think they believe they can baptize their ancestors and get them into heaven that way, or something. Then there are country records, and so on.

'Did you want your folks traced?' she asked me now, a hint of amusement in the set of her mouth.

'I know who my family is,' I said, and spoke the truth, for my mother's idea of a great Christmas present was a family tree ready-framed for my wall. For all I knew, she'd hired Mookie Preston's company to do the research.

'Then you're lucky. Most Americans can only name as far back as their great-grandparents. They're shaky after that.'

I tried to think of myself as lucky.

I failed.

I wanted to sit in the battered armchair in front of her desk and ask her what I really needed to know. Why was she here? What trouble was she getting into? Would I come to work next week and find her dead, for sticking her nose into a hornet's nest and getting stung?

Mookie laughed uneasily. 'You're looking at me funny, Lily.'

Bits of information slid around in my head and rearranged into a pattern. Lanette had come looking for Mookie secretly one night. Mookie had moved to town right after Darnell Glass had been killed. Mookie had an Illinois license plate. Lanette had returned to Shakespeare after living in Chicago for a time. I studied the round line of Mookie's cheeks and the strong column of her neck, and then I knew why she seemed familiar.

I gave Mookie a brisk nod and went back to work on the kitchen. Mookie was Darnell's half-sister. But there seemed no point in talking to Mookie about it: Strictly speaking, it wasn't my business, and Mookie knew better than anyone who she was and what she had to mourn. I wondered whose idea it had been to keep silent. Had Mookie wanted to do some kind of undercover work on the murder of her brother, or had Lanette been unwilling to admit to the town that she'd had a liaison with a white man?

I wondered if Lanette had left for Chicago pregnant.

I wondered if the father was still alive, still here in Shakespeare. I wondered if he and Mookie had talked.

The rifle, black and brown and deadly, had spooked me. I hadn't seen loose firearms in anyone's house since I began cleaning. I'd polished my share of gun cabinets, but I'd never found one unsecured and its contents easily available;

which didn't mean the guns hadn't been there, in night tables and closets, just that they hadn't been quite so . . . accessible. I felt I hadn't been meant to see the rifle, that Mookie's carelessness had been a mistake. I had no idea what Arkansas gun laws were, since I'd never wanted to carry a gun myself. Maybe the rifle was locked in Mookie's car trunk.

I remembered the targets. If they were typical of Mookie's marksmanship, she was a good shot.

I thought of the pack of men who'd been after Jack. Darcy knew Mookie's name and address. I thought of him thinking the same thoughts about Mookie that I'd been thinking.

I gathered up my things and told Mookie I was leaving. She was coming outside to check her mailbox at the same time, and after she'd paid me we walked down the driveway together. I thought hard about what to say, if to speak at all.

Almost too late, I made up my mind. 'You should go,' I said. Her back was to me. I already had one foot in the car.

She twisted halfway around, paused for a moment. 'Would you?' She asked.

I considered it. 'No,' I said finally.

'There, then.' She collected her mail and passed me again on her way back into that half-empty echoing house. She acted as though I wasn't there.

When I got home that night, all the sleeplessness of the night before and the emotional strain of the day hit me in the face. It would have done me good to go to karate, blow off some tension. But I was so miserable I couldn't bring myself to dress for it. Waves of black depression rolled over me as I sat at my bare kitchen table. I thought I'd left death behind me when I'd found this little town, picked it off the map because it was called Shakespeare and my name was Bard – as good a reason as any to settle somewhere, I'd figured at the time. I'd tried so many places after I'd gotten out of the hospital; from my parents' home to Jackson, Mississippi, to Waverly, Tennessee . . . waitressed, cleaned, washed hair in a salon, anything I could leave behind me when I walked out the door at the end of the workday.

Then I'd found Shakespeare, and Shakespeare needed a maid.

When Pardon Albee had died, it had been a small thing, an individual thing. But this that was happening now, this craziness . . . it was generated by a pack mentality, something particularly terrifying and enraging to me. I'd experienced men in packs.

I thought of Jack Leeds, who would never be part of any pack. He'd get over being mad at me . . . or he wouldn't. It was out of my hands. I would not go to him, no matter how many grieved girlfriends and widows passed through my mind. Sometimes I hated chemistry, which could play such tricks with your good sense, your promises to yourself.

When the knock came at the front door, I glanced at the clock on the wall. I'd been sitting and staring for an hour. My injured hip hurt when I rose, having been in the same position for so long.

I looked through the peephole. Bobo was on my doorstep, and he looked anxious. I let him in. He was wearing a brown coat over his gi.

'Hey, how are you?' he asked. 'I missed you at karate. Marshall did, too.' He added that hastily, as though I would accuse him of hogging all the missing that was going around.

182

If it had been anyone but Bobo, I wouldn't have opened the door. I'd known him since he was just beginning to shave; he'd sometimes been arrogant, sometimes too big for his britches, but he had always been sweet. I wondered how this boy had gotten to be my friend.

'Have you been crying, Lily?' he asked now.

I reached up to touch my cheek. Yes, I had been.

'It doesn't matter,' I said, wanting him to not notice, to drop it.

'Yes, it does,' he said. 'You're always beating yourself up, Lily. It does matter.' Amazingly, Bobo pulled a clean handkerchief from his coat pocket, and wiped my cheeks with gentle fingers.

This was not the way conversations with Bobo usually went. Usually he told me how his classes were going, or we talked about a new throw Marshall had taught us, or the boy Amber Jean was dating.

'Bobo,' I began uneasily, puzzled. I was trying to think how to proceed when Bobo acted instead, decisively. He gathered me up and kissed me hard, with an unnerving degree of expertise. For a few shocked seconds I stood quietly accepting this intimacy, feeling the warmth of his mouth against mine, the hard pressure of his body, before my internal alarm system went off. I slid my hands up and pressed gently against his chest. He instantly released me. I looked into his face, and saw a man who desired me.

'I'm so sorry, Bobo,' I said. 'I hope I'm always your friend.' It was a dreary thing to say, but I meant it.

Not that pushing him away was effortless: It was all too easy to envision welcoming Bobo – young, vigorous, strong, handsome, endearing – into my bed. I'd been hoping to wipe out bad memories with good ones; Bobo and I could certainly give each other a few. Even now I felt the pull of temptation, as I saw his face close around the pain.

'I – have someone else,' I told him. And I hated the fact that what I said was true.

'Marshall?' he breathed.

'No. It's not important who it is, Bobo.' I made another effort. 'You have no idea how tempted and flattered I am.' The unevenness of my voice gave witness to that. I saw the pride return to his face as he heard the truth in what I was saying.

'I've cared about you for a long time,' he said.

'Thank you.' I never meant anything as much. 'That makes me proud.'

Amazingly, after he'd opened the door to leave, he turned and lifted my hand and kissed it.

I watched his Jeep pull away.

'Touching scene,' Jack Leeds said acerbically.

He stepped out of the shadows in the carport and walked across the little patch of lawn to my front door. He stood inches away, his arms crossed over his chest, a sneer on his face.

I could truly almost feel my heart sinking. I thought of closing the door and locking it in his face. I wasn't up to another scene.

'Did you give him the time of his life, Lily? Golden boy, no past to slow him down?'

I felt something snap in me. I'd been pushed beyond some limit. He could read it in my eyes, and I saw him start to uncross his arms in sudden alarm, but I struck him as hard as I could in the solar plexus. He made a sound and began to double over. I folded my arm, aimed the point of my elbow at the base of his skull. I pulled it at the very last

184

instant, because it was a killing blow. But I had pulled the blow too soon, because he could launch himself at me. He knocked me back inside my front door onto the carpet. He kicked the door shut behind him.

This was the second time Jack had had me pinned. I wasn't going to have it. I struck his hurt shoulder, and over he went, and then I was on top. I had his jacket gripped with one hand while my other twisted his knit shirt, tightening the neck band, my knuckles digging into his throat while he made a gagging noise.

'Oh yes, Jack, this is love, all right,' I said in a trembling voice that I hardly recognized. I rolled off him and sat with my back to him, my hands over my face, waiting for him to hit me or leave.

After a long time I risked a look at him. He was still lying on his back, his eyes fixed on me. He was visibly shaken, and I was glad to see it. He beckoned me with an inward curl of his fingers. I shook my head violently.

After another long time I heard him move. He sat behind me, his legs spread, and pulled me back against him. His arms crossed in front of me, holding me to him, but gently. Gradually I calmed, stopped shaking.

'We're okay, Lily,' he said. 'We're okay.'

'Can this poor sense of timing be why you have such a – checkered career – as a lover?' I asked.

'I – am – sorry,' he said between clenched teeth.

'That helps.'

'Really sorry.'

'Good.'

'Can I—?'

'What? What do you want to do, Jack?'

He told me.

I told him he could try.

Later, in the quiet of my bed, he began to talk about something else. And all the pieces began to fall into place.

'Howell Winthrop, Jr., hired me,' he said. We were lying facing each other. 'He told me a week ago not to trust you.'

I could feel my eyes open wide as I absorbed all this.

'You saw the men last night. You have to have figured it out.'

'I guess Darcy is involved. All the others?'

'Yes, and a few more. Not the whole town, not even a sizable proportion of the white males. Just a few mental misfits who think their dicks are on the line. They think their manhood is tied up in keeping blacks, and women for that matter, in their place.'

'So they meet at Winthrop's Sporting Goods.'

'The group evolved that way. Most of them are passing through there to buy things pretty often anyway, so it just happened. Ninety-eight percent of the people that patronize Winthrop's are just regular nice people, but the two percent . . . Howell didn't know anything about it until he noticed that guns were being bought through the store accounts that didn't show up in the store. And it wasn't even Howell that noticed it.'

'Oh no.' I thought for a moment. 'It was Del.'

'Yeah, Del Packard. He went to Howell. Howell told him not to tell anyone else. But he must have.'

'Poor Del. Who killed him?'

'I don't know yet. I don't know if Del knew more than he told Howell, or if they were just scared of him telling it to the police – maybe they even asked Del to join them and he refused – but one of them took Del out.'

'Surely not all the Winthrop employees are in on it?' So many people worked at Winthrop's, at least twenty men and four or five women who did office work. Added to the staff of the Winthrop-owned lumber and home supply business right next door . . . and there was Winthrop Oil . . .

'No, not by a long shot. Only three or four men at the Sporting Goods place, that I've been able to make sure of. And a couple, maybe three men from the place next door. Plus a few guys who just joined in, like Tom David and the one you told me was Cleve Ragland. The day they came to steal back the bags at the Winthrops' house, they were in Cleve Ragland's car.'

Since Jack was in a tell-all mood, I decided I would ask as many questions as I could.

'What was in the black bags?'

'Guns. And rifles. For the past four years Jim Box has been the man who ordered for the store. Someone got the bright idea for Jim to order a little more than he thought Winthrop's could sell. Then they were going to stage a robbery and list those arms as stolen, which is why that excuse popped into their minds so quickly last night, I guess. They'd figured if they set up a robbery, no one could blame the store – Howell – if the guns were used for illegal stuff. Instead of walking out with one weapon at a time, they began stockpiling what they wanted in the storeroom at the back of the store in two black bags, waiting for the right moment to stage the break-in. They should've gone on and moved their pile after Del died, but we're not talking big brains here.'

'Then you and Howell took the bags.'

'Yeah, everyone in on it was gone to lunch, so we loaded

them into Howell's car and drove out to his house.' He kissed me. 'The day I saw you there. You had the strangest expression on your face.'

'I couldn't figure you two out. I was thinking you and Howell were maybe – thataway.'

Jack laughed out loud. 'Beanie's safe.'

'Why did you put them in Howell's house?'

'We wanted to see who'd come after them. We knew by then who on Howell's payroll was involved, but not the names of the rest of the group. I also figured lying concealed in Howell's house would be safer than hiding at the store every night, waiting for the staged burglary to take place. So Howell told Darcy about this strange cache of arms he'd found in the store, how he thought he'd keep them at his house until he decided whether he should call the police or not.'

'Wasn't that just a little more dangerous for Howell and his family?' I asked, trying to keep my voice even.

'Well, I knew the day they were going to try. And Howell has this conviction they won't hurt him or his family. He has this weird sense of – like he owes them, because they work for him. He doesn't even seem to want to turn them in when he finds out who it is . . . and he wants to know exactly. It's strange. He doesn't want anyone falsely accused, and I can respect that. But it's like there's something he's not telling me.'

I should have listened to that sentence harder, mulled over it like I mulled over so many things. But I was still trying to understand Jack and Howell's plan of action. So far, frankly, it didn't seem that much better than the thieves'. 'So you hid out in Beanie's closet. To wait and see who came to call.'

'Yeah. And you came in, I knew who you were the minute you hit me, but I didn't know your name.'

'You hadn't heard the men talk?'

'I'd heard people mention Lily, but I didn't know that was you. You didn't look like any maid I'd ever seen, or any karate expert, either. Or any weight lifter.'

'What did I look like?' I asked, very close to his face.

'Like the most exciting woman I'd ever seen.'

Every now and then, Jack said exactly the right thing.

He whispered, 'I wanted to touch you. I just wanted to lay my hands on you.' He demonstrated. 'When Howell heard about the bomb he called me and told me to go down to the hospital to verify how many hurt and dead there were. He knew it would seem strange if he did it. He's sure one of his employees set the bomb, and he wanted to know if one of them had been brought in hurt. He thought maybe they'd hang around to see the explosion, get caught in it. So I went down to the hospital. It was eerie. I just walked in, and strolled through the halls looking. No one stopped me, or asked me what my business was there. The idea was a good one, but it didn't pan out. No one associated with the group was brought in injured. But I saw you on the gurney.'

'You were at the hospital! I thought it was a dream.'

'It was me. I wanted to stay, but I knew that would look strange.'

'You asked me if there was anyone you could call for me.'

'I wanted someone to come take care of you. And I wanted to know if there was anyone ahead of me. Everyone had told me you were with Marshall. I felt he was pretty formidable competition. If you'd asked me to call him . . .'

'What would you have done?'

'I would have called him. But I would have tried to find some way to pry you loose when you were feeling better.'

We didn't talk for a while.

I got up to get a drink, came back.

'Why do you think Howell doesn't trust me?' I asked. That stung me. I had kept faith with the Winthrop family over and above the demands of my paycheck.

'I don't know. When I was asking him who had keys to the house, as a matter of routine, he said, "The maid," and he said you'd worked for him for four years and he was sure you were absolutely reliable. But then, about a week ago, he called me into his office first thing in the morning to tell me to avoid you, that he thought you were in on something.'

He kissed me to show me how little he'd listened.

'I can't think of what I've done to earn Howell's mistrust.' I stowed that away to think of later. 'What's their goal in stockpiling all these weapons?'

'From what I've pieced together, their goal is to start a white supremacist militia group here, using Cleve Ragland's hunting camp as a training base. They want to be a big-time organization rather than a few bastards who grouse and murder children in bombings.'

'Have you heard anything about Darnell Glass?' I asked.

Jack lay back, pushed his hair back with his fingers. 'It's strange,' he said finally. 'It's like there were two things going on. After meeting most of the men who are involved in this, at least I think I've met most of them, what I've been impressed with most is their stupidity. Keeping the arms they were stealing at the store: dumb. Trying to steal them back from Howell's house: dumb. Spray-painting Deedra's car, and that was the boy who works at the loading dock at the Home Supply store – I actually saw him do it – there again, dumb. I think Deedra snubbed him when she went in the store to get a new curtain rod, so he got her back. Then the bomb. The day after the bomb went off, when they'd heard Claude Friedrich and you were hurt and Sheriff Schuster was killed – they were all hangdog as hell. I think it bothered them about the little girl, too. You know why that all happened? The bomb didn't go off at the right time. That I did overhear, directly, Jim and Darcy venting their guilt. They were trying to shift the blame to the victims – you shouldn't have been there in the first place. Sheriff Schuster shouldn't have gotten out faster. The little girl should have been home doing her homework. Crap like that.'

'They killed those people out of incompetence.' I closed my eyes. I remembered the scene inside the church.

'There are groups that like to kill as many black people as they can, Lily, and don't care what age they get. These guys, no . . . they hadn't ever built a bomb before and they got it wrong.'

'How'd they get it in the church before the meeting?'

'The church is unlocked during the day. Jim just chanced it, best as I can piece it out.'

I felt sick.

'But Darnell, they haven't said anything about him?'

'No, but your name has come up a bunch of times.'

'Wait.' The most important question of all hadn't even occurred to me until now. Jack was new at the store. Why would they trust him to keep silent? 'How can you overhear all this?'

'Lily, I put a bug in the employee lounge.'

'Is that legal?'

'Well . . .'

'Hmmm.'

'It's not exactly true to say they haven't talked about Darnell's murder,' Jack said, perhaps to distract me from wondering about how much illegality he'd put up with. 'They all feel like he got what was coming to him. Don't ask me to explain their thinking, because that's impossible. And then they mention you, because I gather that was a real brawl. Did you have to pitch in?' He turned me to face him and looked me in the eyes. His own eyes were serious. I ran my finger down his cheek, down his scar, traced his neck to his collarbone.

'Don't think I haven't had regrets that the whole thing happened, that I happened to be there, even. I'm no activist. I want to be left alone. But I was there, and he was outnumbered, and those boys would've beat the shit out of him.'

Jack absorbed that, accepted it. 'But you see, from their point of view,' he said, very quietly, 'you defended Darnell, and you were there at Howell's when they came to reclaim the rifles, and you were in the church when it blew up. That's too many coincidences for them, no matter that you were minding your own business in every instance.'

'Do they think I'm you? Do they think I'm some kind of detective?'

'They think you like black people too much and they do think you might have something to do with their not being able to get the guns back. Then I spend the night with you on the very night they're trying to find out who was spying on them. So they wonder about you, a lot. At the same time, it seems like they have a weird kind of respect for you.'

'How did they come to chase you last night?'

'I was hidden in a sort of niche I'd made. If you think the customer part of the store is overwhelming, you should see the back of the store. Someone could live back there for a week and no one would ever know. Anyway, I knew they were going to be meeting after hours in the storeroom, and it's not bugged. I wanted to know what they were planning.'

'How'd they know you were there?'

'You're going to laugh,' he said gloomily, and I had a feeling I really wasn't. 'The boy, Paulie, who works at the Home Supply store, brought his dog with him. He's real proud of that dog, talks about it all the time. It cost some ungodly amount. A bluetick hound, I think. The dog sniffed me, started barking. It seemed smarter to run for it than to wait until they came to investigate.'

I was right. I wasn't laughing. 'They would have killed you.'

'I know it.' He lay staring at my ceiling, thinking about that real hard. 'I don't think all of them were in on Darnell's murder, but they would have killed me last night because they were all together and they were scared.'

'Do you think they're suspicious now?'

'Maybe. I got a phone call today from Jim. He said he'd heard from Darcy that I was courting Lily Bard. He suggested I'd be better off with some more traditional girl.'

'Courting, huh? That what this is?'

'Damn if I know. But I like it, whatever we call it.'

'And I'm a girl,' I said thoughtfully. 'A nontraditional girl.'

'Screw tradition, in that case,' Jack murmured.

'So what are you going to do next?'

'I'm going to keep on like I have been, as long as I can. Collecting the tape every night, listening to it, copying it, phoning Howell with any information I can glean. Waiting for him to decide what he's going to do; after all, he's my boss.' Jack put his arms around me. 'Lily, I get stubborn and mad and do the wrong thing sometimes. If I was really a great detective, I'd tell you I can't see you until this is over. Maybe I'm putting you in even more danger than you're already in. But maybe somehow, since they still believe my cover, I'm giving you a little credence with them. If a bad boy like me is interested in you, you can't be a snitch, they figure – I hope. But I just don't know.'

He sat up, swung his legs over the side of the bed. I was treated to a view of his bare back and bottom. I enjoyed it very much. I traced his spine with my finger, and he arched his back. 'You can tell,' he said, not looking at me, 'that I have a real problem with impulsiveness.'

'You're kidding,' I said, deadpan.

'Let's not joke about this, OK. I came to your house when I was wounded, brought you under more suspicion, maybe. Put you in danger. I made love to you on impulse. I can't regret that. I'd stay in bed with you for a year if I could. But I was impulsive starting that affair with Karen, and she died.' He turned a little to meet my eyes. 'I can't let my thoughtlessness put you in danger, like it did her.'

'I don't guess you'll be able to stop it. And I'm not Karen Kingsland.' There was a certain edge in my voice.

'Lily, listen to me! I know you're strong, I know you think of yourself as a tough woman, but this is not just one opponent who fights fair. This is a pack, and they would kill you . . . and maybe not straightaway.'

I stared at him. Somehow I had lost pleasure in the view.

'You're saying – stop me if I get this wrong, Jack – you're saying that I only think of myself as tough, I'm really not . . . that I can only win if my opponents fight fair . . . that Darcy and Jim and Tom David would rape me if they had the chance. Gosh, why would that occur to me?'

'I know you're getting mad,' he said, turning around and looking down at me. 'And I probably deserve it, but I just can't let anything happen to you. You just can't be involved in this in any way, any longer.'

'You'll just stop by when you have a minute to fuck? Insult my other guests?'

His sculpted lips tightened. He was beginning to get mad, too.

'No. I shouldn't have said anything about Bobo being here. I had no right. And I told you I was sorry. Hey, I never said anything about the cop sending you flowers, and they were still sitting on your kitchen table with the card stuck in them.'

'Which, of course, you had a perfect right to read.'

'Lily, I'm a *detective*. Of course I read it.'

I gripped my head with my hands. I shook it to clear it.

'Go,' I said. 'I can't deal with you right now.'

'We're doing this again,' he said helplessly.

'No, *you* are.' I meant it. 'You screw my brains out after telling me we shouldn't be publicly involved. Okay, I admit, I screwed you right back, and I publicly involved us – to save your ass. You spill your guts to me – on impulse – tell me my employer doesn't trust me, tell me I may or may not be in serious danger, and then tell me not to involve myself in the resolution of this mess.'

'Put that way, I admit, it doesn't sound like I'm doing the right thing by you.'

'Gosh, no kidding.'

'Why do we get so – so – crossways? I'm trying to do the right thing! I don't want you to get hurt!'

'I know,' I said. I sighed. 'You need to go on now. Come back and talk to me – somewhere public – when you decide what your current policy is.'

He stood. His face was full of conflict. He held out his hand.

'Kiss me,' he said. 'I can't leave like this. This is something real we have.'

Almost unwillingly, I held out my hand, and he pulled me up to kneel on the bed. He bent over and kissed me hard on the mouth. I felt the heat begin to slide through me again. I pulled back.

'Yeah. It's real,' he said, and dressed. He dropped a kiss on my head before he went out the door.

Chapter Eight

Carrie wasn't at the clinic that morning. It was the first time in a long time she hadn't been there on a Saturday. I hadn't realized how much I'd counted on seeing her until I pulled into the lot behind the clinic and found it empty.

She'd left me a note taped to the patients' bathroom door, since she knew I cleaned that first.

Lily – I'm following your suggestion. Today the entire off-duty police department is moving Claude downstairs to the O'Hagens' old apartment. Becca Whitley's putting in a ramp at the back door! Knew you would want to know.

I was a little disconcerted by Carrie's taking charge of Claude. I'd been to see him in the hospital a couple more times, and I realized now that both times he'd talked about Carrie. Maybe the reason I hadn't worried about the problems of Claude's homecoming was that I'd absorbed the clues that someone else was doing it for me? Well, well, well. Carrie and Claude. It sounded nice.

I got the clinic cleaned, though I felt lonely without Carrie. As I started work at my next client's, I brooded about what Jack had told me. It gnawed at me that Howell didn't trust me. I am very reliable, I keep my mouth shut, and I'm honest. My reputation as a cleaning woman depends on those qualities.

I struggled to recall all the contacts I'd had with Howell recently, trying to pick out one that would explain his sudden lack of faith in me.

By the time I was through for the day, I'd decided to make a call.

After checking the phone book and the map, I drove again into the black area of Shakespeare which surrounded Golgotha Church. I felt a wave of nausea when I passed the damaged structure, now bathed in bright winter sunshine. The cold wind rippled a large sheet of plastic over the hole in the roof, and temporary front doors had been hung. A junked pile of splintered pews lay outside in the grass. A whiff of burning still lingered in the air. Men were at work inside and out. A white man was among them, and after a careful look I recognized the Catholic priest from Montrose. Then I saw another white face: Brian Gruber, the mattress factory executive. And redheaded Al from Winthrop's Sporting Goods. I felt a little better after that.

My business lay a block or two away, in one of the few brick homes in the area. Tidy and tiny, it sat within a four-foot chain-link fence, with a 'Beware of the Dog' notice. The shutters and eaves were painted golden yellow to contrast with the brown bricks. I scanned the yard, didn't see the dog to beware of. I lifted the gate latch, and a big tan short-eared dog of unfortunate parentage tore around the house. He woofed and he growled, and he ran from side to side right within the fence.

A small black woman came to the front door, she was trim and tidy like the house, and she had picked rose red to wear today, her day off. At her appearance, the dog instantly silenced, waiting to see what the woman's attitude would be.

'What you want?' she called. She was neither welcoming nor repelling.

'If you're Callie Gandy, I need to talk to you. I'm Lily Bard.'

'I know who you are. What do we have to talk about?'

'This.' I held up the shabby brown velvet ring box.

'What you doing with Mrs Winthrop's ring?'

Bingo. Just as I had suspected, this had never been Marie Hofstettler's ring.

'Miss Gandy, I really want to talk.'

'Miss Bard, I'm not aiming to be rude, but you are only trouble and I don't need any more of that than I have.'

I had already learned what I needed to know.

'All right. Good-bye.'

She didn't answer. She and the tan dog watched me with poker-faced stillness while I returned to my car and buckled up. She closed her door then, and I drove home with even more to think about.

That afternoon I went to the grocery, cleaned my own house, and made some banana nut bread for Claude. He liked it for breakfast. It seemed very sweet, very personal to know that about a friend. That was what I'd missed most, without ever knowing it, in my wandering years and my first years in Shakespeare: the little details, the intimacy, of friendship.

I retrieved one of my homemade individual entrées from the freezer. Claude liked lasagna, I remembered. Feeling like a small-town paradigm of neighborliness, I walked over to the apartments.

The move was complete, apparently, and some of

Claude's cops were still there drinking a beer by way of thank-you. Claude was on his old couch, his bad leg propped up on an ottoman. The door was open, so I just stepped in, self-conscious at having an audience.

'Lily, are you a sight for sore eyes!' Claude boomed, and I noticed he looked better than he had since his injury. 'Come on in and have a brew.'

I glanced around at the men lounging in the living room. I nodded at Dedford Jinks, whom I hadn't seen since the Winthrop break-in, and Todd Picard. He seemed a little more relaxed in my presence than he had been in weeks past. Tom David was sitting on the floor, his long legs crossed at the ankle, a Michelob bottle in his hand. His bright mean eyes scanned me, and his mouth curved in a nasty smile.

Judas, I thought, drinking Claude's beer when you knew he was going to be in that church. Could you have kept that child from dying?

My face must have become very unpleasant, because Tom David looked startled then defensive. His smile faltered, then increased in wattage.

'Hoo hoo, it's Miss Bard, tore herself away from her new love long enough to pay you a visit, Claude!'

Claude just smiled, perhaps because Carrie came out of the kitchen at that moment. Carrie was wearing leggings and a University of Arkansas sweatshirt, and she looked – for once – carefree. Her glasses were propped on top of her head, and her eyes were round and brown and warm.

Tom David was taken aback when he realized no one was going to pick up on his cue. Dedford Jinks, the detective, ran a hand over his own thinning hair and gave Tom David a look of sheer irritation.

I smiled at Carrie, bobbed my head to Dedford and a patrolman I didn't know, a tall black man with a bandage on his arm. I looked at him carefully. I'd helped him up in the church. He recognized me, too. We exchanged nods.

I told Claude, 'I figured you wouldn't be baking anytime soon, so I brought you some bread.'

'Would that by any chance be banana nut? I can smell it from here.'

I nodded. 'Some lasagna, too,' I muttered. I wished everyone would look somewhere else.

'Lily, you are sure sweet,' Claude declared. 'Without Carrie helping me move and you cooking for me, I'd have to rely on pizza delivery.'

'Oh, of course, no one else in town will bring you meals,' Carrie said sarcastically. And she was right to take Claude's words with a grain of salt. He'd be inundated with food within days, if not hours.

'Where should I put this?' I asked Carrie, tacitly acknowledging her place in the apartment.

She looked a little surprised, then pleased.

'Come help me unpack the kitchen, if you have a minute,' she invited. She could tell I was uncomfortable. I followed her from the room gladly, giving Claude a gentle pat on the shoulder as I passed him.

Carrie and I were a little old for girlish confidences, but I felt obliged to say something. 'This what it looks like?' I asked, keeping my voice low.

She shrugged, trying to look noncommittal, but a little smile curved her lips.

'Good,' I said. 'Now, where you think he wants these spices?'

'I'm trying to put everything where he had it in the

apartment upstairs,' Carrie said. 'I don't want him to feel like a stranger in his own kitchen. I tried to remember. I even drew a diagram. But it got a little hectic up there with the men coming in and out.'

'Spices were here, I believe,' I said, opening the cabinet right by the stove. I was hoping Carrie wouldn't take this wrong, and she didn't, being above all a sensible woman.

Luckily, Becca Whitley (I assumed) had given the apartment a thorough cleaning after the O'Hagens moved out. All we had to do was put things in what we considered a logical place. After Carrie and I had worked a while, we took a break and had a Coke. Leaning against the counters in companionable weariness, we exchanged smiles.

'They carried everything down without a problem, but I guess the unpacking is woman's work,' Carrie said wryly. She lowered her voice. 'What's this Tom David was trying to start trouble with?' We could still hear men's voices in the living room, but we didn't know who'd gone and who'd come in.

'I'm . . .' To my horror, I could feel myself turning red, and I had to look off into the distance.

'Are you all right?' Carrie asked. She got her doctor look on.

'Yes.' I took a breath. 'I'm seeing the new man at Winthrop's Sporting Goods.' For an awful minute I could not remember Jack's cover name. 'Jared Fletcher.'

'The one who lives here in the apartments? The one with the lips and the hair?'

I nodded, grinning at this description.

'How'd you meet him?'

'I went in to buy some weight-lifting gloves,' I said, sifting through the weeks past to find something believable.

'That's romantic,' Carrie said.

I looked at her sharply to see if she was teasing me, but she was dead serious.

'Didn't I see him at the hospital the night of the bombing?' she said doubtfully.

Now, that was before I'd officially met Jack. But Carrie didn't know that, didn't know when I'd bought my new gloves. This was so complicated. I hated telling lies, especially to one of my few friends.

'Yes,' I said.

'He came to see about you?'

I nodded, figuring that was a little better than trying to sort partial truth from fiction.

'Oh, wow,' Carrie said, all dewy-eyed.

As if on cue, I heard a familiar voice from the living room.

'Hey, I hear you deserted us upstairs. There must be a secret benefit to living down here!' Jack said heartily.

Claude's response was less audible, but I heard the word 'beer' clearly.

'I just may do that,' Jack answered. 'I've been working all day and I could use some liquid refreshment. Speaking of which, I picked up this bottle for your housewarming.'

'Thank you, neighbor,' Claude said, more audibly. He must have turned his head toward a moving Jack. 'You'll have to come share it with me when I open it.'

Jack appeared in the kitchen doorway, wearing his red sweatshirt with the Winthrop logo and his leather jacket. He betrayed his surprise at finding me there only by a widening of his eyes.

'Lily,' he said, and kissed me on the cheek. His hand

groped for mine, squeezed it hard for a moment, released it. 'The chief says you have some loose beer in here.'

I pointed at the refrigerator. Carrie beamed at Jack and extended a hand.

'I'm so glad to meet you. I'm Carrie Thrush.'

'The good doctor Thrush. I've heard great things about you,' Jack said. 'I'm Jared Fletcher. New man in town.' He was smiling genuinely. He set a bottle of bourbon on the counter, Claude's homecoming gift, and opened the refrigerator to extract a beer.

'You'll have to bring Lily down for supper some night. Maybe she and I can collaborate on cooking and you and Claude can evaluate the result,' Carrie said cheerfully.

'Tom David told on us, Jared,' I said, trying to speak lightly. But I haven't done that in a long time, and it came out sounding very unnatural. Carrie swung a look in my direction, then back to Jack.

'That would be great, Carrie,' Jack said smoothly. He looked at me to tell me he'd gotten my message: the little cabal was having conversations about us.

'Lily brought Claude some bread and some lasagna,' Carrie said, pushing my praiseworthy aspects.

'Did you, baby?' Jack looked at me, and if there was a flash of heat in his eyes, there was none in his voice.

Baby? I was trying to imagine double-dating with Carrie and Claude. I was trying to imagine everything being straightforward, Jack really working at Winthrop's Sporting Goods, having no other agenda than making a living. I would just be a maid, and he would just sell workout equipment . . . We'd date, go out on real dates, during which no one would get shot. We'd never hit each other, or even want to.

'Claude took care of me when I got hurt last spring,' I said, suddenly feeling very tired. I didn't owe Jack an explanation, but I needed to say something.

'You got hurt . . .' Jack began, his eyes narrowing.

'Old story. Go out there and have your beer, *sugar*,' I said dismissively, and gave him what I hoped was a loverlike shove to the uninjured shoulder. He righted himself after a tense second and stalked into the living room.

'Did I catch some undercurrent there?' Carrie asked.

'Yeah, well, nothing's easy,' I muttered.

'Not with you, anyway,' she said, but her voice was gentle.

'Actually, in this case, it's him,' I told her grimly.

'Hmmm. You think this is going to work out?'

'Who knows?' I said, exasperated. 'Let's get this kitchen done.'

'It hardly seems right for you to work so hard, Lily. You spend all week cleaning and arranging other people's things. Why don't you go sit out there and have some down time?'

With Claude and Jack and Tom David? 'Not on your life,' I told her, and finished placing pots and pans in the cabinet.

We worked on the bedroom next, sliding all the drawers back into their correct position, rearranging the clothes in the closet. I polished all the furniture after I found the cleaning supplies, and I quickly stowed away the bathroom things while Carrie set Claude's desk to rights in the second bedroom.

Then I was through, and I knew it was time for me to leave. Carrie would have to be helping Claude do personal things, I supposed; he would be tired.

He was, in fact, asleep on the couch. All the men had left except Jack, who had opened a box of books and was shelving them in the low bookcase. He'd gathered up all the beer bottles and put them in a plastic garbage bag. He half-turned as he heard my steps, smiled at me, and pushed a dictionary into place. It all seemed so pleasant and normal. I didn't know what attitude to take. He'd severed our connection until this episode was over. But we were alone in the room except for the sleeping policeman.

I knelt by him, and he turned and kissed me, his hand going to the back of my neck. It was a kiss that started out to be short and ended up to be long.

'Damn,' he breathed, moving back from me.

'Gotta go,' I said very quietly, not wanting to disturb the sleeper.

'Yeah, me, too,' he whispered, standing and stretching. 'I need to listen to today's tape.' He patted his jacket pocket.

'Jack,' I said in his ear, 'if Howell won't call the law, you have to. You'll get in awful trouble.' It was an idea that had consumed any extra minute I'd had during the day. I darted a glance at 'the law', sound asleep on the couch. 'Promise me,' I whispered. I looked straight into his hazel eyes.

'Are you scared?' he breathed.

I nodded. 'For you,' I told him.

He stared at me. 'I'll talk to Howell tomorrow,' he said.

I smiled at him, rubbed my knuckles against his cheek in a caress. ' 'Bye,' I whispered, and tiptoed out Claude's door.

I pulled on my coat in the hall, zipping the front and pulling my hood up. It was really cold, biting cold; the temperature would be well below freezing tonight. I wouldn't be able to walk even if I needed to. But after extracting Jack's promise I felt very relaxed. It might not take me too long to sleep.

Just to make sure, I walked the four streets around the

arboretum twice, very briskly, and then took the trails through the trees. When I emerged onto Track Street, it was full dark. My feet were feeling numb and my hands were chilled despite my gloves.

I was halfway across the street, angling to my house, when a Jeep rounded the corner at a high speed and screeched to a halt a foot away from my right leg.

'Where've you been, Lily?' Bobo was hatless and frantic, his brown coat unbuttoned. There was no trace of the ardent young man who had kissed me the night before.

'Helping Claude move downstairs. Walking.'

'I've been looking for you everywhere. Get inside your house and don't go out tonight.'

His face, almost on a level with mine because of the height of the Jeep, was white and strained. No eighteen-year-old should look like that. Bobo was scared and angry and desperate.

'What's going to happen?'

'You've been too many places, Lily. Some people don't understand.' He wanted to say more. His teeth bared from his inner tension. He was on the verge of screaming.

'Tell me,' I said, as calmly as I could manage. I snatched off a glove and laid my hand over his. But instead of soothing him, my touch seemed to spark even more inner storms. He yanked away from me as if I'd poked him with a cattle prod. From between clenched teeth, he said, *'Stay in!'* He roared off as fast as he'd come, as recklessly.

My own anxiety level jumped off the scale. What could have happened so suddenly? I looked up at the facade of the apartment building. Claude's new windows were dark. Deedra's, above him, were also out. But Jack's lights were on, at least some of them. His living room window was faintly illuminated.

I stood in the middle of the street in the freezing cold and tried to make my brain work.

Without deciding it consciously, I began to run – not toward my house but toward the apartments. Once I was inside the hall, hurrying past Claude's door, I tried to walk quietly. I went up the stairs like a snake, swift and silent. I tried Jack's door. It was unlocked and open an inch. A ball of fear settled in my stomach.

I slipped inside. No one in the living room, lit only by the dim light reaching it from the kitchen. Jack's leather jacket was tossed on the couch. Further down the hall, the overhead light in the spare bedroom glared through its open door. I listened, closing my eyes to listen more intently. I felt the hair stand up on my neck. Silence.

I'd only been in here once, so I picked my way through Jack's sparse furniture very carefully.

No one in the kitchen, either.

I was biting my lip to keep from making a sound when I stood in the doorway of the guest bedroom. There was a card table holding a tape player, a pad of paper, and a pencil. There was a Dr Pepper can on the table. The folding chair that had been in front of the table was lying on its side. I touched my fingers to the Dr Pepper can. It was still cold. A red light indicated the tape player was on, but the tape compartment was open and empty. I ran back to the living room and fumbled through the pockets of the leather jacket. They were empty, too.

'They've got Jack,' I said to no one.

★

I covered my eyes to think more intently. Claude was downstairs unable to get around on his own. At least some portion of his police force was corrupt. Sheriff Schuster was dead and I didn't know any of his people. Maybe the sheriff's department, too, contained one or two men who at least sympathized with the Take Back Your Own group.

What if I couldn't save Jack by myself? Whom could I call?

Carrie was a noncombatant. Raphael had a wife and family, and without putting it to myself clearly in words, I knew a black man's involvement would escalate whatever was happening into a war.

If I went in and was captured, too, who would help?

Then I thought of someone.

I remembered the number and punched it in on Jack's phone.

'Mookie,' I said when she answered. 'I need you to come. Bring the rifle.'

'Where?'

'Winthrop's. They've got – my man.' I was beyond trying to explain who Jack was. 'He's a detective. He's been taping them.'

'Where'll I meet you?' She sounded cool.

'Let's go in over the back fence. I live right behind the Home Supply store.'

'I know. I'm coming.' She put her phone down.

This was the woman I'd cautioned about leaving town yesterday, and now I was urging her to put herself into danger on my say-so. But I didn't have time to worry about irony. I ran down the stairs, leaving Jack's door wide open. It wouldn't hurt for someone else to become alarmed. I ran to my place, let myself in. I pulled off my coat, found a heavy

209

dark sweat-shirt, and yanked it down over my T-shirts. I found Jack's forgotten watch cap. I pulled it over my light hair. No gloves, I needed my hands. I untied my high-tops and pulled on dark boots, laced them tight. I would have darkened my face if I could have thought of something to do it with. I came out of my front door as Mookie pulled in. She leaped out of the car with the rifle in one hand.

'What's your weapon?' she asked.

I raised my hands.

'Cool,' she said, and we began to run for the tracks without further conversation. From the high point of the railroad, we surveyed the back lot of the Sporting Goods store. There were lights on in the store. The back lot was always lit, but there were pools of darkness, too.

'Let's go,' my companion said. She seemed quite happy and relaxed. She required not one word of explanation, which was refreshing, since I wasn't sure I could manage anything coherent. We jogged down the embankment. I was about to take a run at the fence and accept the barbed wire at the top, but Mookie pulled wire cutters from a pocket in her dark jumpsuit. This was no fashion model garment, but a padded, heavy, dark workman's jumpsuit with many pockets. Mookie had a knit cap pulled over her hair, too. She went to work with the wire cutters, while I looked around us for any signs of detection.

Nothing moved but us.

Finally the opening was large enough and we scrambled through it, Mookie first. Again, nothing happened. We moved into a pool of darkness and crouched there behind a gleaming new four-wheeler. Mookie pointed at our next goal, a boat. We had to cross through some light, but made the boat safely. We waited.

In this run-and-wait fashion we worked our way from the rear of the lot to the back of the store. There was a customer door at ground level and a loading dock with a set of four steps going up to it. From the dock there was an employee door leading inside to the huge storeroom. The customer door was dark. I was willing to bet it was heavily locked.

They'd left someone on guard at the loading bay door. It was the pimply boy from the Home Supply store, and he was shifting from foot to foot in the cold, which I no longer felt. He had a rifle, too. Mookie whispered, 'Can you take him out silently?'

I nodded. I'd never attacked anyone like this, someone who hadn't attacked me first, but before that thought could lodge firmly in my consciousness and weaken me, I focused on his rifle. If he had it, I had to assume he was willing to use it.

The boy turned to peer through the window in the employee door, and sneezed. Under cover of that noise, I leaped silently up the steps, came up behind him, snaked my arms around him to grip the rifle, and pulled it up against his throat. He struggled against me but I was determined to silence him.

He weakened. He grew limp. Mookie helped me lower him to the concrete platform. She pulled a scarf from one of her pockets and tied it around his mouth and bound his hands behind him with another. She took his rifle and held it out to me. I shook my head. She placed it down against the base of the loading dock, out of sight. She evidently thought he was alive and worth binding, so I didn't ask. I didn't want to know now if I'd killed him.

I wondered if they'd come to check on him. I stood sideways to the little head-high window reinforced with diamond-patterned wire, and looked through into the lighted storeroom. I could just see movement past a wall of boxes and racks, but I couldn't tell what was happening.

'Cover inside,' I whispered to Mookie. 'Go left when we go in.'

She nodded. I took a deep breath, turned the knob, praying that it would not make a noise. To me, the twist of the metal was loud as cymbals, but no one appeared at the gap in boxes to investigate. I pulled the door open and Mookie went in low, rifle at the ready. No one shot her. No one shouted. I went in after a second, dropped to a squat right inside the door, letting it ease shut against me.

Mookie was crouched behind a chest-deep pile of stenciled boxes. An array of huge metal shelves, all labeled and aligned, loomed ahead of us. To our right, across the aisle left open for passage to the back door, was a rack of camouflage jumpsuits in the colder, grayer, green and black of winter camo. There were more rows of shelves in front of the rack.

I could hear voices now, the raucous laughter of men high on their testosterone. In the middle of the laughter there was a cut-off yelp. Jack.

I was ready to kill now. I worked my hands, getting the stiffness and cold out of them. Mookie eyed me with some doubt.

'Which man is yours?' she asked almost inaudibly.

'The one who yelled,' I told her. Her eyes widened. 'He's got long black hair.' She would need to know which one was Jack.

'We'll work our way up there, see what happens,' she breathed.

That was as good a plan as any. We ducked around the

boxes and concealed ourselves behind the next row of shelves. We could see through the gaps in the stacked goods. Darcy was there, Jim was there, and Cleve Ragland, Tom David Meicklejohn. About who I'd expected. There was at least one person I couldn't see; I noticed the men turn to their right a few times, addressing a remark to whoever sat there.

They were torturing Jack.

As we worked our way to the front of the storage area, I saw more and more. I saw too much. Jack was tied to a chair, a wooden one on rollers. His arms were tied to the chair arms. He had the beginning of a black eye, and a cut on one cheek, maybe from when they'd grabbed him in his apartment. They'd taken off his shirt. They'd pulled the bandage off his bullet wound. Darcy had a hunting knife, and Cleve had devised his own little implement by heating an arrowhead with a lighter and putting it on Jack's skin. Jim Box looked nauseated. Tom David was watching, and though he did not look sick, he did not look happy, either. His eyes flickered toward whoever was seated out of sight, and back to Jack.

Darcy turned away from cutting Jack right under the nipple. The knife glistened with blood. I would kill him first, I thought, so consumed by the thought that I could not reason, could not plan what I should do. I had forgotten Mookie's existence until she nudged me. She pointed a slim finger to a man sitting on his haunches in the shadow of a shelving unit, a man I hadn't seen before, and I thought I would vomit. I recognized the pale floppy hair instantly. Bobo. Darcy said something to him.

Bobo raised his face to look at Darcy, and I saw tears on his face.

'I gotta ask you, boy, where you went just a while ago,' Darcy said genially. He raised the knife so the light caught the part of the blade that was not red. Bobo stood up. His shoulders squared.

'I'm hoping you didn't betray your family by telling anyone what we'd caught here,' Darcy said, waiting for Bobo to answer.

When the silence dragged on, everyone turned to look at Bobo, even Jim Box. Jack was taking advantage of the respite by closing his eyes. I saw his hands working under the tight cord around his wrists. He was biting his lower lip. There were a dozen cuts and burns on his chest, and they'd reopened the bullet wound. Streaks of blood clotted his chest hair.

'Did you go tell that blond bitch?' Darcy asked, quietly. 'You tell that gal her little bedmate was in trouble here?'

Bobo didn't speak. He stared at Darcy, his blue eyes narrowed with turmoil. Something hardened in his face as I watched.

'I hope she does come looking,' Cleve said suddenly. 'We get to reenact her worst nightmare.'

Darcy looked at Cleve in some surprise. Then he realized what Cleve meant. He laughed, his head thrown back, the overhead light scouring his face of any sign of humanity.

Jack's eyes were open now, all right. He was looking at Cleve with a brand new nightmare for Cleve in his eyes. Cleve looked down, flinched. Then he seemed to recall that he was in charge.

'We can give her a real good time right here,' he told Jack. 'You can watch, Bobo. Learn how it's done.'

Tom David's eyes were slitted in distaste. He was looking at his coconspirators as if he'd just learned something about them that he didn't like. Bobo's face said he couldn't believe what he'd heard. He was waiting for some other explanation of the words to occur to him.

'This is going to be a pleasure,' Mookie said in my ear. She pulled a knife from one of her pockets, handed it to me.

'I cover you, you cut him free,' she said. 'We get out the best way we can.'

I nodded.

'Or maybe I'll kill them all,' she said, to herself.

'They killed Darnell?'

'Yeah, I do believe. My mother got some calls after Darnell's death, anonymous, nasty, really explicit about Darnell's injuries. They came from this store. She has caller ID,' Mookie whispered. 'Dumb shitasses didn't even think about a black woman having caller ID. Get ready.'

She stepped out then, her rifle up at her shoulder.

'Okay, assholes,' she said. 'Down on the floor.'

They all froze, Darcy in the act of bending over to put the knife to Jack's chest again; Cleve had the arrow in one hand, the lighter in the other. Beyond them, Tom David was still leaning against the wall, his arms crossed on his chest. Jim Box was beside him. Bobo, who'd been close to the door into the store, turned and stepped through it, and the clunk as the heavy door closed behind him made Cleve jump.

In that flicker of time, Darcy threw the knife at Mookie and dived to his right. Mookie fired and ducked to her right. Her bullet hit Jim Box, who'd been beyond Darcy; I glimpsed a red flower blossoming on his chest. And the knife missed her, but got me. I felt the sudden cold where my shirt sliced open, felt the pressure, but I was running for Jack. Cleve charged me, his thick chest and heavy chin

215

making him look like an angry bull. I stepped aside as he came to me, and I extended my arm. It caught him in the throat. His head stayed still, but his feet kept on going. When the rest of his body didn't follow, they flew up in the air, and down he went. His head thudded against the concrete floor. And I heard the clunk of the door again. Someone else had fled into the store.

I knelt by the chair, cutting at the cords binding Jack. I was awkward about it, but Mookie's knife was sharp. I heard a rush of feet, light and quick, and then the *paw!* of the rifle. Mookie passing by, doing God knows what damage. I thought I heard the door again.

I could pay attention to nothing else while I was using the knife, and when I'd sawed through the second set of bonds and I could look up, everything had changed.

I saw no one, at least no one moving.

Cleve was down for good. I felt a flash of satisfaction. Jim Box had vanished, but there were drops of blood on the floor where he'd been standing. I saw there was a chair in the shadows, across from Jack's. It was empty.

Jack whispered, 'Help me up.'

I jumped to my feet, held out my hands. To my horror, I could not meet Jack's eyes; that seemed worse, much worse, than what I'd done to Cleve Ragland. Jack made an awful sound of pain as he pulled himself up on me. There was a discarded brown coat, Bobo's, lying on a nearby shelf. I grabbed it. I had in mind fleeing through the rear door, trying to make it through the back lot and hole in the fence to my house, calling – someone. Fleetingly, I thought of the FBI men, who might still be at the motel where they'd been camped since the bombing.

'Put this on,' I said urgently, holding out the coat to Jack.

I was thinking of the bitter cold, Jack's wounds, shock, God knows what.

I kept lookout while Jack tried to manage, but in the end I had to help him. I was so intent on maneuvering Jack's left arm into the sleeve that I did not know anyone was behind me until Jack's face gave me a second's warning. Just as Jack began to move, something slammed against my shoulder. I shrieked involuntarily, knocked to my right, off my feet. I slammed my head into the shelves and fell to the floor hard enough to knock the breath from my lungs. I couldn't move. I stared up at the bright lights of the storeroom, high above me. I could see tall dark Jim Box, his shirt soaked with blood. He gripped an oar, holding it like a baseball bat, and he was swinging it back. He was going to hit me in the head, and there wasn't a damn thing I could do about it.

Jack went mad. He launched himself at Jim, wrenched the oar from him, and slammed it into Jim's head. Jim went over like a felled tree, without a sound. Jack stood over him, his blood-spattered chest heaving, wanting Jim to move, wanting to strike again.

But Jim didn't move.

With a rush the air came back into my lungs. I moaned, not only from pain but from black despair. We were both hurt now, weak. How many more were in the building? Where was Mookie? Had they killed her?

Jack stood over me with the oar. Gradually some of the madness seeped from his face and he crouched beside me.

'Can you get up?' he whispered. I saw the finger marks on his throat for the first time. They'd choked him, enough to almost cost him his voice. I wanted to tell him no, I couldn't move, but found myself nodding instead. That was a mistake. Pain rocketed through my head. I had to lie still a moment, before I rolled over on my stomach, pushed up to my knees. My arm, sliced by Darcy's knife, was bleeding. I touched my hair, which felt – funny. There was blood on my hand when I took it down. I'd hit a shelf with my head when I'd gone sideways, I remembered slowly. Maybe I had a concussion. As if to confirm that suspicion, I vomited. When the spasm was over, I felt like I would welcome dying. But Jack needed me to get up.

I gripped the nearest upright, a corner bar for the shelves, and tried to gain my feet while Jack stayed alert for another attack. Finally I was standing, though I could feel myself swaying from side to side; or maybe I was still and the warehouse was swaying? Earthquake?

'You're really hurt,' Jack rasped, and I could hear a little fear even in his strained voice.

I felt weak and shaken. I was letting him down.

'Go,' I said.

'Right,' he whispered, the sarcasm diminished by his voice level.

'You can move. I'm not sure I can,' I faltered. I hated the wavering of my voice. 'They won't kill me. How many more are there?'

'Two in the store, and the old man.'

What old man?

'Bobo won't hurt me,' I reassured Jack, thinking he was counting Bobo as one of the adversaries.

'No, I don't think he will. I think he didn't know any of this. I hope to God he's calling the police.'

That was funny. Speaking of old men, it sure looked to me as if Howell Sr., uncrowned king of Shakespeare, was standing right over there by the door.

'Look,' I said to Jack, amazed.

Jack turned, and old Mr Winthrop raised a hand. To my bewilderment, it held a gun. I opened my mouth to yell something, I don't know what, when two strong arms wrapped around the old man and lifted him from the floor.

'No, Grandfather,' Bobo said. The expression on the wizened old rat terrier's face had to be seen to be believed. Howell Sr. struggled and wriggled in his grandson's grasp, but it was a futile effort. If I'd had any inclination toward humor, it would have been funny. Bobo walked through the storeroom and out onto the loading dock carrying the old man, who called him names I'd never heard an elderly person use.

Bobo's face was tragic. He didn't look at me, at Jack. He was alone with the bitterest betrayal of his short life.

I didn't care where he was taking his grandfather, because the measure of that betrayal was unfolding itself to me. Howell Sr. had used his own son's business as a cover for his little hate group. Howell Sr. was the reason his son, Jack's employer, had kept secrets from Jack. Howell must have suspected his father's involvement from the first. So he hadn't contacted police, or ATF agents, or the FBI. He'd hired Jack.

And here we were, thanks to old man Winthrop, bleeding and maybe dying in a damn storeroom.

'Where's Mookie?' I asked Jack. 'The woman with the rifle.'

'She went in the store after Darcy,' Jack whispered. The jacket hung open over his bare bloody chest. He'd laid down the oar in favor of Mookie's knife, the knife I'd used to slash his bonds.

'Tom David,' I said.

Jack was puzzled for a minute. Then his face cleared. 'I don't know. He may be in the store, too.'

'Naw, I'm here,' said a taut voice from a few feet away. 'I'm out of the fight.'

I staggered over in the direction of the voice despite Jack's telling me not to. I didn't seem to have much control over my actions. Tom David was lying on the floor to the right of the door. The left leg of his jeans was soaked with red. Now I knew where Mookie's second shot had gone. The policeman's face was absolutely white. His eyes shone brilliant blue.

'I am sorry,' he said.

I stared down at him.

'You can call the police, it'll be safe. I'm the only one.'

I nodded, and nearly threw up again.

'I don't hold with what they did to Jared, and I wouldn't have hurt you,' he said wearily, and closed his eyes.

'Did you kill Darnell?' I asked.

He opened his eyes at that. 'I was there.'

'Who did it?'

'Darcy and Jim. The old man. Paulie who works over there,' and he moved his head infinitesimally in the direction of the Home Supply store. 'Len. Bay Hodding, Bob's dad. He ain't here tonight. Wedding anniversary.' And Tom David grinned a horrible grin. Those blue eyes were now not so bright. 'Who cares, anyway? Nigger. Now, Del Packard . . . that was Darcy. I regret it.' And his face relaxed. Looking down at the pool of blood beneath my feet, I thought Tom David Meicklejohn had closed his mean eyes forever.

But the policeman's final testimony had taken valuable

time, and in that time things once again had happened without my awareness or participation.

I was alone.

The bright storeroom, with its long stretches of shelves and dark shadows, was empty except for the silent bodies of the fallen and dead. I felt like an actor onstage after the play is over.

Then, from the store, I heard a scream.

I shuffled toward the door. The clear pane set at eye level had gone dark. The store lights had been shut off. As my hand closed around the knob, I realized that when I opened it, I would be silhouetted against the storeroom lights. I switched them off. Then I opened the door and propelled myself through it, and seconds later heard the distinctive *clunk!* of its falling shut.

There was a whoosh of sound over my head, a heavy impact. Then silence. I reached up cautiously. A hunting arrow protruded from the wooden doorframe. My skin crawled. Darcy was an avid bow-hunter. He and Jim had discussed it morning after morning this fall.

I had to get away from the door. He'd be coming. I pulled myself forward on my elbows, trying to hug the floor as closely as possible. It was all too easy, and I cursed myself for a fool in thinking my venturing into this trap could help anyone.

I tried to summon up the floor plan, see it in my head. I felt hopeless when I thought of how familiar it was to Darcy.

'I got your yellow friend,' he called to me. 'She's de-ad. Got an arrow in her he-ad.' He was singing. He was having a good time.

I didn't believe it. Mookie had screamed; at least, I was

almost certain it had been her. You can't scream if an arrow goes through your head. But I knew my reasoning, like my sense of balance and my judgment, was very shaky just now. If only I knew where Jack was, I thought, I'd just curl up somewhere and go to sleep. That sounded good. I laid my head on the rough indoor-outdoor carpet and began to drift.

'I'm com-ing,' Darcy crooned. Darcy, who had beaten a young man to death for being black. Darcy, who had crushed his friend's throat.

He sounded so close I knew I shouldn't move. I didn't feel sleepy anymore. I felt close to death. I thought of the hightech bows I'd seen dangling from the ceiling on my trips to the store, the ones that looked so lethal they would've scared Robin Hood . . . Wow, was I drifting . . .

A foot fell on the carpet an inch from my face. His next step would be on me. Act or *die*.

Galvanized, I shrieked and scrambled up, grabbing what I could, hoping for an arm. I locked my arms and legs around Darcy Orchard like a lover, holding him as tightly as I'd ever held Jack or Marshall, squeezing till tears ran from my eyes. I was riding his back.

He was so big and strong, and not wounded. He didn't go down even with my full weight wrapped around him. I'd scared the shit out of him, and it took him seconds to recover, but only seconds. He heaved and bucked, and I heard the clatter of something falling, and I thought it might be the bow. But he had an arrow in his hand, and he began stabbing backward with it, though not with the full force or range of his arm since I embraced him. He jabbed my thigh the first time, and he could tell where to go after that, and he scored my ribs a dozen times. Scars on scars, I thought through the terrible pain. I wanted to let go. But it seemed I couldn't, couldn't get the message to my fingers to relax. Death grip, I thought. Death grip.

The lights came on. The glare seemed to shoot a lance through my eyes, made me so sick I nearly fainted, but I was shocked into alertness by something so awful I could only believe it because it was this night, this bloody night. Behind one of the counters that held a display of knives, I glimpsed Mookie fixed to the wall by an arrow through her chest. Her head sagged to one side and her eyes were open.

Then past Darcy's shoulder I saw someone running toward us, toward Darcy and me locked in our little dance. It was Jack, with a rifle in his hands. We were too close, he couldn't shoot, I thought. As if we had one mind Jack reversed the rifle and clubbed Darcy in the head with the stock. Darcy howled and lurched, wanting to go for Jack, but I would not let go, would not would not would not . . .

Blackness.

'Wake up, honey. I have to check you.'

No.

'Open your eyes, Lily. It's me, Carrie.'

No.

'Lily!'

I slitted my eyes.

'That's better.'

Blinding light.

'Don't moan. It's just – necessary.'

Back to sleep. Nice period of darkness and silence.

Then, 'Wake up, Lily!'

*

The next day was agony. My head ached, a condition that bore no more relationship to a normal headache than a stomachache bore to appendicitis. My ribs were notched and gouged and the skin above them a bloody mess stitched together like a crazy quilt. The wound in my thigh, though not serious, added its own note to my symphony of pain, as did the slice in my arm.

I was in a private room, courtesy of Howell Winthrop, Jr., Carrie told me when I demanded to go home. When I realized someone else was paying for it, I decided to rest while I could. He was paying for Jack's room next door, too. Jack came in during that horrible morning, when even the medication that made me mentally dull could not smother the hurt.

When I saw him in the doorway, tears began oozing from the corners of my eyes, running down the side of my face to soak my pillow.

'I didn't mean to have that effect on you,' he said. His voice was husky, but stronger.

I raised a hand, and he shuffled slowly to the bed and wrapped his own around it. His hand felt warm and hard and steady.

'You should sit,' I said, and my own voice sounded distant and thick.

'Got you drugged, huh?'

'Yes.' Nodding hurt more than speaking. 'How'd they get you, Jack?'

'They found the bug,' he said simply. 'Jim spilled a Coke in the lounge, and in the process of mopping up the mess, he found it. Jim called old Mr Winthrop. He advised them to watch from concealment and see who came to extract the tape; and that was me. They had to consult with each other for a while. They decided they could find out who hired me if they put me through the wringer. Cleve and Jim thought all along it was Howell, but the others voted for something federal. They thought Mookie was federal, too. They thought about going to get her, bring her along to join the party. Said she'd been in the store too much to be natural. Lucky for me they didn't. Why did you think of calling her? Who the hell is she?'

I tried to explain Mookie to him without revealing any of her secrets. I am not sure I managed, but Jack knew I worked for her, that she had a personal stake in uncovering our fledgling white supremacy group, and that I had known she could shoot. Jack held my hand for some time, rubbing it gently as he thought, and then suddenly he said, 'When he knocked you down, when you hit the shelf and the floor – and I swear to God, Lily, you bounced – I thought he'd killed you.'

'You went crazy,' I observed.

He smiled a little. 'Yes, I did. When you could stand, and you could walk – sort of – I knew you'd be okay. Probably. And after a look at Tom David, I knew he wasn't a threat to you . . .'

'So you left.'

'Hunting.' He was not apologetic. He'd had to pursue the man who had degraded him. I, of all people, could understand that.

'Who's dead?' Carrie had refused to talk about it.

'Tom David. Jim Box.'

'That's all?'

'I wanted Darcy to die, but I didn't hit him that final time that would have settled it. His jaw is broken, though. The cops were there by then, for one thing.' Jack sank into the chair, and thoughtfully punched the button to lower my bed so I could see him more easily.

'How come?'

'Bobo called them, when he went into the store after all the shooting started. And he was trying to find his grandfather. The old man had armed himself, and Bobo managed to track him down just in time.'

I remembered Bobo's face as he'd lifted his grandfather and carried him off. A few more tears oozed down my face. I wanted to know what would happen to old Mr Winthrop, but it could wait. Roasting in hell came to mind as fitting. 'Mookie's alive?' I had belatedly realized her name was not on the dead list.

Jack closed his eyes. 'She's just hanging on. She wants to talk to you.'

'Oh, no.' I felt so washed out, and washed up, I couldn't stand the thought of one more confession. 'She's really not going to make it?'

'The arrow went right through. You saw.'

'I was hoping I made it up.' I looked away, at the curtained window.

Jack kept holding my hand, waiting for me to make up my mind.

'So Cleve didn't die?' I was stalling.

'He has a fractured skull. Much worse than your concussion.'

'Not possible. Okay, get a nurse or two to load me in a chair.'

After a lip-biting interval, I was being pushed into Mookie's room. There were blinking machines, and a constant low hum, and Mookie was hooked into more tubes than I had ever imagined a human being could be. Her color was ashen, and her lips had lost color. Lanette was in the corner of the room, her hands over her face, rocking back and forth in a straight chair. Her firstborn child was dying, and she had already lost her second.

The nurse went to stand out of earshot, and I raised my hand, with great effort, to touch Mookie Preston, that odd and lonely and brave woman.

'Mookie, I'm here – Lily,' I said.

'Lily. You lived,' she said very slowly, and her eyes never opened.

'Thanks to you.' If I had gone in there by myself, I would have died horribly and slowly. By asking her to go with me, I had set her death in motion.

'Don't be sorry,' she said. Her voice was slow, and soft, but the words were distinct. 'I got to kill some of them, the ones that killed my brother.'

I sighed softly. I had been thinking, while in my haze of pain and drugs. 'Did you kill someone else?' I whispered.

'Yes.' She dragged out the word painfully.

'Len Elgin?'

'Yes.'

'He was involved in Darnell's death.'

'Yes. I talked to him before I shot him. He was my . . . father.'

I should not remind Mookie of Len Elgin. I should say something else to Mookie Preston, something good. She was on her way to meet her Maker, and I could not send her out thinking of the deaths she had caused.

She spoke again. Her eyes opened and fastened on mine. 'Don't tell.'

I understood after a moment, even through the drugs. 'Don't tell about Len,' I said, to be sure.

'Don't tell,' she repeated.

This was my punishment for leading this woman to her death. I would know the truth, but could not reveal it. No matter what happened to Len Elgin's extramarital lover, Erica Moore, and her husband Booth. No matter what suspicions attached to Mary Lee Elgin.

'I won't tell,' I said, accepting it. I was so doped up it seemed logical and appropriate.

'Mama,' she said.

'Lanette,' I called, and she leaped up from her chair and came to the bed. I motioned to the nurse who was waiting in the doorway, and she came to take me back to my room.

I think Mookie died before I got there.

After three days, I went home. The doctor herself drove me.

This homecoming-from-the-hospital routine – the stale house, the life untouched while I was gone – was getting old. I didn't want to get hurt anymore. I didn't want pain. I needed to work, to have order, to have emotional quiet.

What I had was pain and phone calls from Jack.

He'd had to talk to many many people: local, state, federal. Most of that I had been spared because of my concussion, the second I'd had in a month, but I'd had my share of interviews. Some questions I just hadn't been able to answer. Like: Why had I called Mookie Preston? The answer, because I thought she could help me kill the men who had Jack, just wasn't palatable. So I had lied, just a little. I said that I'd called Mookie when I discovered Jack was gone – I figured they could find that out somehow from the phone company – and that she'd agreed to accompany me to Winthrop Sporting Goods because I was so distraught. Yes, I knew what Jack was doing, so I suspected where he'd been taken and who had taken him.

I never said that Mookie had brought the rifle or the knife, and I think they all assumed both weapons came from the store stock. When it was found the bullets that had killed Tom David (and ultimately Jim) had come from the same weapon that had killed Len Elgin months ago, the official line of reasoning seemed to be that someone from the store's little cadre of bad boys had been responsible for shooting Len. A motivation for this assassination was never uncovered, but it was assumed that somehow he had thwarted one of their plans or uncovered evidence that implicated one of them in the death of Darnell.

So Len Elgin came out looking better in death than he'd been in life, and I never opened my mouth. The police knew, from all of us, that Mookie had shot men in the store; but since they all supposed she'd found and loaded the weapon when she got there, Mookie, too, emerged from the inquiry looking posthumously brave and resourceful – as, indeed, she had been.

The Winthrops pulled up the drawbridge and weathered the siege. Howell Winthrop, Sr., was arrested and promptly made bail, and he was denying all involvement in the bombing and in the deaths of Darnell Glass, Len Elgin, and Del Packard. He was admitting he'd been present during Jack's torture, but alleging he'd thought Jack was a renegade white supremacist. No one believed him, but that was what he was saying. Bobo transferred to a college in Florida (Marshall told me), and Amber Jean and Howell Three just left school and went on a vacation with Beanie in an unspecified location.

Howell called me one afternoon before I left the hospital,

and we had a brief, horribly uncomfortable conversation. He assured me that he would pay for every ache and pain I endured for the next few years, and I assured him just as earnestly that this hospitalization and the ensuing pharmacy bills were the only ones I would appreciate him paying.

'Your mother can have her ring back,' I said.

'She'll never want it,' he answered.

'She told me it was Marie Hofstettler's bequest to me.' I wanted to be sure Howell knew I had not taken the ring as some kind of bribe, which is what he had assumed when he saw the brown velvet box – which he knew to be his mother's – in my hand. 'Why did your parents want me to come to their house?'

'I can't talk about that,' he said stiffly. 'But Bobo told me I had to tell you he knew nothing.'

I am sure we were both glad to hang up. I thought about that strange evening on Partridge Road, the big white house, the tiny old people. I hoped Arnita Winthrop had not known about her husband then, had really been the gracious woman she had seemed. Maybe she had reasoned I deserved something tangible for being Marie's friend; maybe that was why she'd given me an old ring of her own, passed it off as a posthumous gift. Maybe her husband had had a curiosity to see me, had asked her to think of a way to get me to the house so he could look me over. The running figure that night had been Jack, he'd finally told me. Jack had been asked to watch the comings and goings at the Partridge Road house whenever he could. He'd been at Marie's funeral to get a good look at the older Winthrops, since there was no casual way for him to meet them.

Jack made the papers, state and national. He was something of a hero for a while. It was good for his business. He got all kinds of inquiries, and as soon as he could manage physically, he left for Little Rock. I had a feeling it was a relief to get a little distance between himself and the place and time of his ordeal. He'd been overpowered, bound, and tortured; he had managed to regain some measure of maleness, of wholeness, back by conquering Jim and Darcy. But I knew the bad nights he'd have, the self-doubts. Who could know better?

As the days passed, I began to have the dreary conviction he would write me off as part of that time. Sometimes I was anguished and sometimes I was angry, but I could not return to my former detachment.

I had been back at work for three weeks, back to working out at Body Time for one week, when I came home to find Jack's car in the driveway. He had flowers – a bigger arrangement than Claude had sent me, of course – and a present festooned with a huge pink net bow.

I felt a rush of joy at the sight of him. Suddenly I didn't know what to say to him, after weeks of imagining this moment. I pointed to the flowers. 'For me?'

'Jeez,' he said, shaking his head and smiling. 'If you are still the Lily Bard who sucker-punched me right here in this doorway, these are indeed for you.'

'Want me to do it again? Just to verify my identity?'

'No, thank you, ma'am.'

I unlocked the door and he followed me in. I took the flowers from him and headed down the hall with them.

'Where you taking those?' he asked, with some interest.

'My bedroom.'

'So . . . are you planning on letting me join you in admiring them?'

'I expect so, depending on your good behavior this

231

evening. I'm assuming you brought a doctor's note, to prove that you're up to such vigorous . . . activity.'

'We are so playful this evening, Miss Bard. We are so relaxed and – normal-date-like.'

'It's a stretch,' I said. 'But I'm up to it.'

Acknowledgments

My thanks to Larry Price and Pat Downs, who described being blown up; and to members of my karate class, who kindly enacted fight sequences and offered various lethal suggestions. Dr John Alexander has also been polite about answering some very peculiar questions.